Of Atlantis

by

Lanaia Lee

royal publishing
the future of digital publishing

Copyright © 2008 by Lanaia Lee

ISBN: Softcover   978-0-6152-0768-1

All rights reserved. No part of this book may be reproduced or transmitted in any form or by any means, electronic or mechanical, including photocopying, recording, or by any information storage and retrieval system, without permission in writing from the copyright owner.

This is a work of fiction. Names, characters, places and incidents either are the product of the author's imagination or are used fictitiously, and any resemblance to any actual persons, living or dead, events, or places, is entirely coincidental.

First Printing

This book was printed in the United States of America.

To order additional copies of this book, contact:

Roval Publishing & Digital Services
P.O. Box 822441
N. Richland Hills, TX 76182-2441

1-888 485-8830

www.rovalpublishing.net

Illustration: Charles Davis of Northfield, MA.
www.davisimages.com

Editor: Charlene Larose of Pepperell, MA.

Dedication

I dedicate this first book to my dear friend and adoptive sister, Cheryl Pillsbury, founder of AG Press, and author in her own right. Without her dedication and faith in my stories, this book would not have been possible.

Tribute to Travis Burns

Travis was a young, hard worker for Roval Publishing. During work on production of this book, he lost his life in a tragic car accident.

He worked hard and long to present a wonderful book, but was unable to finish it. So his friends at Roval Publishing completed what he had started. I dedicate this book in his honor. His presence will be missed, but his dedication and laughter will always be remembered and engraved in my heart.

A Continent Once Alive

I get up each morning and fling the shutters open to see another beautiful day.
Looking out on this beautiful city by the sea.
Everyone seeming so happy, as they work, as they play.
No idea in the near future, we would pay a tremendous fee.

The day has started, much like any other.
But soon the earth starts to violently move.
No where to run, no where to hide, there is no cover.
I must pray to the Supreme Being, for my fears to be soothed.

Soon the sky seems to become completely black.
It is raining, but not water, it seems to be ash.
It's hard to breath, it seems like the Gods themselves have attacked.
It is even thundering, sounding like the God themselves clash.

People are running amuck, with really no where to go.
Why oh why, Supreme Being, God of all, why have you abandoned us?
You have always provided us with everything, being a friend, not a foe.
I have to find a safe place, this is a dire must.

Where does on go, when the earth violently shakes?
The sky has opened raining ash, it is evident we will die.
Soon looking out, I see an ominous cloud, spreading fast, looking like an ash lake.
I beseech you mighty Supreme Being, I have to know why.

My beautiful city, would soon be buried for a very long time.
Most of us would die, history would never forget this day.
Knowing there is no escape, I accept the fact with the Supreme Being I must dine.
Our beautiful city now destroyed, once alive and known as being a continent
of Atlantis, on this awful day did die.

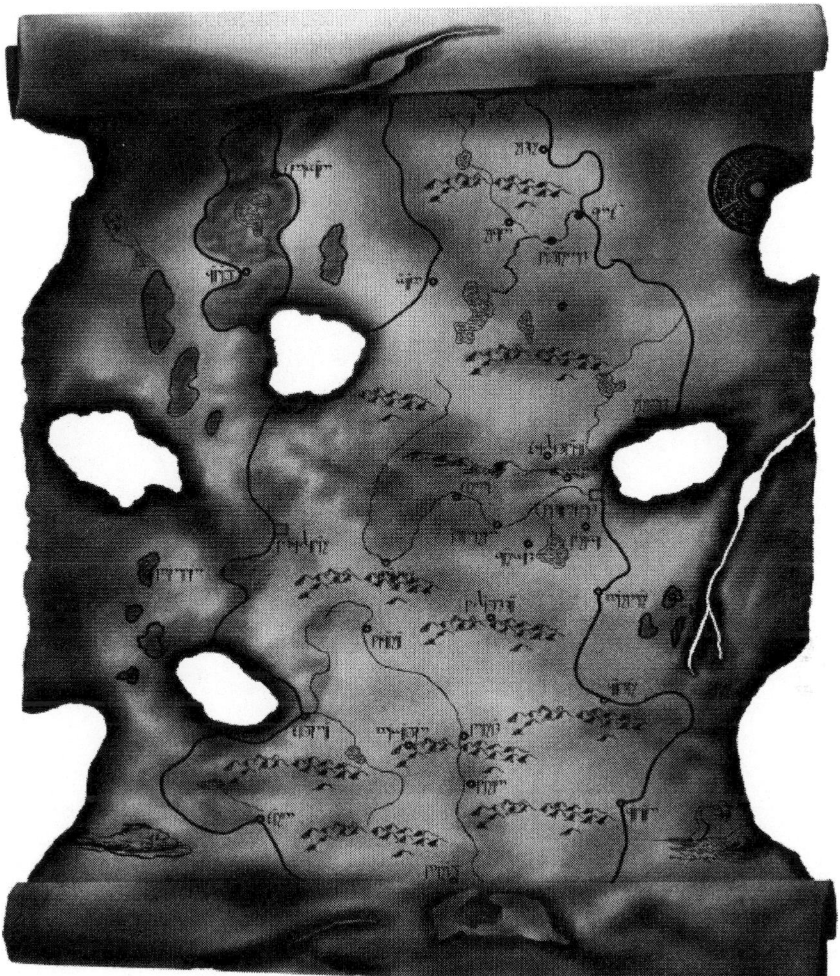

Of Atlantis

Prologue

Archimedes, heir to the throne of Atlantis, played alone in the courtyard of his home, the palace. His father the King, always seemed gone to fight bloody battles with his enemies. On this day, Archimedes' father, King Lionus, left for another battle, and a young child worried if his father, whom he so loved, would return to him or fall in battle, like so many others did when they met their death.

Across the courtyard, near his mother's beloved roses, he saw his nanny in deep conversation with two members of the palace guard that were appointed as the child's body guards. Archimedes could always tell his body guards were very uncomfortable around him, because he was no ordinary child. At only four, he could feel the discomfort that his body guards displayed, when they were in his presence.

The last time King Lionus had gone into battle, he had come to say goodbye to his son, totally dressed in his amour that he wore into battle. At that time, just like now, Archimedes was in the court yard playing, when he saw his father and ran straight to him with open arms.

When he got to his father, his father reacted like he always did. Lionus told the poor child, "Keep your distance! Be a man like me and say goodbye the way I would. That is the way I taught you, so that is what I expect!"

Archimedes tried his best to hide his tears from his father, because he knew if his father saw, his father would think he was weak. The child knew even his own father feared him because he was different and could not help this.

King Lionus said to the child, "I came to say goodbye because I will be gone this time for a couple of months. You are a prince and I expect you to conduct yourself in this way during my absence. It is very important you act like a man, especially for the sake of your mother. She worries enough, and I don't want you to give her any reason to do so."

Archimedes looked at his father after secretly wiping the tears from his eyes and then said, "I totally understand what you ask of me sir. But I do wonder will you return? I just don't want you to die. I just love you so father."

King Lionus bent down on one knee to face his son, "Archimedes, you don't have to worry. Don't I always return? I am Atlantis, and killing me is no easy task. You know I have been wounded several times, but I have always returned. It is my destiny to rule this country, so I shall return. My subjects, your mother, and you, I know need me, so I always return. Just be a man for your mother and help Lord Uric with your studies. It is important to me that you behave and be a good boy."

Archimedes answered his father, "I will do my very best to be a man for mother sir, but I will miss you father. I love you father!"

For a moment the child softens the heart of the King, and the King starts to reach out for his son. But then the fear of his son takes over so King Lionus, says, "Goodbye son," then he turns and walks away.

Archimedes watched his father walk away from him, until he could no longer be seen. On the other side of the wall around the perimeter of the courtyard, Archimedes could hear the laughter of other children as they played. The child started to think about what the other children might be playing such as hide and seek, or maybe even tag.

Having heard their laughter made Archimedes sad, because the other children always shied away from him thinking he was so different. This made Archimedes a very sad and lonely child. He always wanted to play with the others, but they too were afraid of him. As he listened to the other children it made him wish he didn't have powers. His powers made him feel like he wasn't as good as the others, and how the poor child longed just to be normal.

Archimedes mother gave him a small puppy and hoped this would provide much needed companionship for her very lonely son. Archimedes always tried to be very careful how he played with the dog because of his extraordinary powers. One day while they were playing, the dog jumped up on the child and scared him. He was still too young to control his powers. He pushed the dog aside. Then, right before the boy's eyes, the dog just disappeared.

The child had not meant to hurt his only friend, the puppy he so loved, but Archimedes was still too young to know how to control his very special gift.

The child honestly believed his special gift was some sort of demonic curse and this made the young prince very sad.

Archimedes loved all kinds of animals and even insects. He looked at them as his only friends. He walked over to the roses his mother so loved and listened to the birds as they sang. He listened to the bees from the rose bushes as they buzzed, going about their business of doing their most important work.

One bee found its way to Archimedes and stung him, hurting the child. Archimedes did not know that after a bee stings someone it dies. So, the small child said, "Where are you? You hurt me. If I find you, I will kill you."

His nanny standing close overheard this and admonished him, "Archimedes, you should be ashamed. A child of your age shouldn't say such things!" His nanny kept a safe distance from the boy because she, just like every one else, was afraid of what the young child was capable of. His nurse continued, "You should come inside now. It is almost time for your nap!"

Archimedes replied stubbornly, "I don't want to go inside. I want to play some more!" But his nanny was very persistent and just kept fussing at the child.

Archimedes was very frustrated with her. He could feel the rage boiling within his very being. He had the feeling of wanting to hurt her, but he knew this is wrong, so he took a deep breath and went inside with his nanny.

He followed his nanny to his bedroom, where his nanny cautiously tucked him in his bed for a nap. Archimedes watched his nanny until he saw that she was gone. Then he jumped out of bed, and very quietly made his way to his mother's chambers. When he arrived there, he slowly opened the door and peeked inside.

His mother, Queen Cheris, was brushing her hair when she spied her small son. She smiled at him and with open arms she cried out, "Archimedes, come to me." The child ran and they embraced. Archimedes really loved his mother, as he considered her his only true friend. He never picked up on feelings of fear from his mother. He loved her so.

As Cheris held her son, she noticed the child seemed to be hot. She mentioned Archimedes this and then from a pitcher, she poured her son a cool glass of water which he greedily drank.

Cheris then said, "I know you didn't have lessons today as your teacher was sick. What did you do all day?"

Archimedes answered, "I played in the gardens all day by myself. Mother, can I have another puppy to play with? I promise to be careful so I don't hurt this one. I just want someone to play with. I hear the others playing outside the wall and I feel so bad. I have no one to play with. Everybody is afraid of me."

Cheris looked down as she answered her son, "Let's see what we can do about getting you another puppy. I know you are lonesome my son, but when you are older, I promise you will understand everything."

The thought of a new puppy made the young child very excited. He replied, "Mother I promise to be very careful so I won't kill this puppy. I didn't mean to hurt the other puppy. I don't want to hurt or kill anything. I want someone to play with me," He looked up at his mother with tears in his eyes.

It broke Cheris' heart to see her son in such a state. She said, "Son, when your father returns, we will go to our castle in the hills, where you can run and play and yes, maybe even with a new puppy."

Archimedes answered, "Mother you do think father will return don't you?" Cheris answered, "Of course my son. Your father is a very good warrior and he has Lord Uric by his side to advise him. Your father will be fine."

The child says, "Last time father went away I heard him and Lord Uric talking when father returned. They said hundreds died. I don't want father to die. I love father even though he doesn't like me!"

This angered Cheris, to hear her son talk this way. She grabbed her son and shook him. As she did, she said, "Archimedes don't say such things. Your father loves you. You are his heir. One day you will fill his shoes as King. Never think anything different. Your father loves you and he is very proud of you."

"Mother you are hurting me," Archimedes said with tears steaming down his cheeks. Cheris apologized to her son as she hugged him to show him how much she loved him. As she held him in her arms she said, "Son, I promise you this when you are old enough and the time is right, I will tell you everything about your special gift."

The small child said, "I want to know now. I promise I will understand!"

Cheris replied, "You tell me you would understand, but my son, you are still too young. When the time is right, I promise to tell you everything." Archimedes felt safe and warm in his mother's arms. he fell asleep in his mother's arms and soon he began to dream. Cheris noticed he was talking in his sleep as well. "I see them. I see them all. I see father, Lord Uric, and Percius."

That was a name Cheris hasn't heard in years. Archimedes then woke up and asked curiously, "Who is Percius, mother?"

Cheris turned away. She didn't want her son to see her tears.

Chapter One

Uric stood before the boy, as ever he watched Archimedes with intent, almost savoring every detail of the child.

"Your father will be back soon." The words made Archimedes feel uncomfortable. "The victorious hero returns!" Uric almost spat. "He fears you boy, you know that don't you!"
"My father loves me!"
The boy felt tears well up and fought for control,
"No Archimedes. He cannot love what he fears. It is not his nature, though he does well to hide it. One day though, that fear will overtake all other emotions and he will seek to have you slain." Uric rested one long hand on the child's shoulder. "But I do not fear you boy. I feel the power in your soul. It is a gift, used wisely it is a gift that can gain the world!"
"I do not want the world!" The boy's emerald eyes seemed to cloud. An inky black liquid appeared to drift across his gaze.
"Yes boy," a smile spread across Uric's face. "Let the power come fore."
And at once the child was drawn back, his eyes clear and green. He turned and fled, the echoes of Uric's laughter chasing him down the long marble corridors. "You will know young Prince! You will know when the time has come. Seek me out! Only I can help!" Uric shouted after the scampering child. "You will know." He whispered to himself. Uric turned to face the large ornate mirror. He studyied the powerful frame; the olive skin and dark thick hair. His face was cruel and angular, his hair pulled back into an almost painful topknot. Stepping closer he examined his skin, dismayed to see the lines of age already appearing. "I will have your knowledge boy; I will wear the mantle of power." With a sudden turn his black robes danced into the air, and as always he gracefully went his way.

One by one they entered the great hall. The Kings of Atlantis appeared proud in their heritage and stature. Lionus stood, his huge frame at home at the head of the long golden table. "My Lords, I beg you sit." As one they sat, each eyeing with suspicion their fellow rulers. At once servants ran forward and in swift motion large goblets of sweet red wine were laid before each King. "I, Lionus of Aisla have called you here today. No longer do we need to fear the barbarian hordes. My armies have slain them and wiped them from history." His words echoed and boomed around the walls. "Peace is ours for the taking!" Lionus clenched a mighty fist. "Is there any here who would declare this not so?" His eyes scanned their faces, reading what he could from each expression.

Atlantis was split between five Kingdoms. Aisla had long been under Lionus' family's rule. It was the largest Kingdom of Atlantis. His armies outnumbered any single foe. But single foes he did not fear.
"Lionus, a peace under whose rule? Your rule? As Great King?" Conavar spat. His body was trim, built for speed and agility, with blond hair and deep blue eyes. Many felt the King of Ames a kind and considerate man. What few knew was the anger that swelled within. The thirst existed to take revenge upon Lionus for slaying his Father some ten years past.
"Under no one rule, young Conavar, we live in peace, trade in peace, settle arguments as men should! We do it with wisdom, not the blade."
"Wisdom from your friend the wizard?" Conavar retorted pointing at the lone figure of Uric standing behind Lionus by the large window overlooking the harbor. A small smile crossed Uric's face as he bowed in recognition.
"Tis true Lionus. Is this the wizards idea?" Romen stood, King of Servia. "Long have we been friends, longer still we have had no quarrel." He gestured towards Uric. "But him I do not trust."
"My advisor has no say in this. Long have I been at war. For what? To see my wife grow older? To miss all that will shape my son into the man he will be?" At once his face seemed weary. Robbed of the presence he normally radiated, Lionus sat back upon the golden throne that headed the table. "Long are the days that I am away, longer still the nights. For what? To clear our lands of the ungodly. Yes, to fight noble foes? Such is folly. I am tired my Lords, so very tired."

Debate continued, boundaries were set and treaties drawn. Lionus finally called a halt to the gathering and each leader departed. Uric stood beside his King.

"Sire, much burden do you put upon yourself. With petty squabbles this rabble would bring ruin to the land." Lionus looked at his advisor hard.

"You think this be folly my friend? If so speak freely, long have you stood by my side. My father learned to put judgment on your word, as have I."

"I think my Lord that there are those that will see your desires are weakness, they believe that we are a race of warriors rather than teachers. The strong seek will to dominate. I say tread carefully. The disbanding of our forces is not wise."

"Uric, the treaty has been set. To break before beginning will only bring war. Conavar will have his spies watching all we do."

"True my lord, yet Conavar is not a subtle man. His actions are easy to read and easy to deflect. Send report of pirates attacking our eastern shores or send the armies to settle in the eastern garrisons as protection for our people. The treaty gives scope for such action."

"This reeks of treachery Uric. I cannot commit myself to such actions. How can I ask that of others but deny it to myself. I should be setting the example."

"My Lord, this is true. But if the decision was not your own then you have little to worry over. Treanious can easily assume command of the army, sending the forces north. It is then his decision and if questioned by our supposed allies, you can then claim investigation." Lionus thought long and hard. Treanious was the General of the armies, second in command to Lionus on the battlefield.

"It shall be so. See that this is arranged."

"My Lord," Uric bowed in servitude. Lionus realized that Uric's position had not moved and he frowned.

"You have more to discuss?"

"My Lord, events have some to my attention that need your consideration. It concerns one of your allies. It saddens me to report such events." Uric waved his hand at the two guards that stood at the great chambers entrance. "You may leave us; we are not to be disturbed." With this dismissal the guards bowed and departed. The heavy clunk of the doors echoed around the chamber. "There are those that sat at this table that would conspire against you. They would use what you hold dear to challenge your promise of peace. I have, as you know, many sources, many friends in different palaces." Uric bent in close to a whisper. "I have heard that there are those that would take your wife, your son. That they would use your grief against others."
Lionus hand gripped the long sword that swung in the golden scabbard around his waist. His eyes met with Uric.

"Tell me what you know. Spare no detail. Who is this? Conavar, Beretta?" Lionus hissed. "Speak now man!"

"My lord my news is grievous. The name my spies have uncovered is a sore wound, deep and painful. It is King Romen."

Lionus stood shocked, his hands falling from the hilt of his sword.

"Roman is my staunchest ally. Long has he stood by my side when others fled. I cannot, and will not, believe this."

"Your denial is understood my lord, I only ask why would my sources lie? They have nothing gain and no recourse." Uric again whispered to the King. "He sits close, watching, learning. Under the cover of friendship he knows all that he needs. His words at your gathering tell of declaring peace and the disclosure of all arms. He failed to mention the fleet of warships under construction, the new barracks that hold fifty thousand gathered on the Northern borders under cover of the Isleian Mountains."

"You have proof of this, man!" demanded the King.

"Of his barracks, of course. Of the construction of the fleet, yes. I have the word of my most trusted comrades on the plans to see those you hold dear, murdered."

"And of the others? This nest of tormented vipers!"

"I know little else, save that such a bold move would indicate at least one confidant. We must be wary."

"Put my best man at his side. Percius." said Lionus. Uric face showed discomfort.

"I would rather see the man Janus as he is wise in the way of the assassin."

"No Uric, in this you are wrong. I know that Percius is no friend of yours. But he is the best man I know with blade or bow. He is diligent and gallant. I will hear no argument. Now send Treanious to me. We have plans to make. I need our land protected until such time as my enemies make themselves known." Uric bowed to the King's words, then at once he purposely pushed through the large doors.

In his chambers Uric drank deeply from the pitcher of wine. The warrior Janus stood before him, his cruel face masked in concentration.

"My Lord Uric, is it not grave news that Percius now looks over Archimedes. Our influence will weaken with the boy."

"Not at all Janus. It is a problem easily resolved. What was important is that Lionus now moves his armies in direct confrontation with Romen, a matter that I shall see brought to Romen's attention. From there, the other King's will bring their own warriors into domain. I have already arranged for the pirate attacks to draw attention away from any ill conceived thoughts. Soon this land shall be at war, and with each drop of blood spilled, my power will grow, and Archimedes will be mine!"

"And Percius," Janus spat.

"Yes, I know you hate the man. He is everything you are not, yes? Kill him Janus. Let the hero die bravely protecting the boy. But you must not be seen!"

"I am worthy with the blade my Lord but…"

"I said kill him you fool, not fight him. A man may be talented with the sword but arrows in the night are not easily deflected. Now go, I will tell you when this needs to be done."

"My Lord," Janus bowed and left.

Uric walked towards his balcony, taking in a deep lungful of air. As he stared downwards, he saw the boy Archimedes, alone. The boy stood watching the birds.

"You shall be mine, boy, and all you are."

Chapter Two

Archimedes was as late as ever. He dashed along the winding corridors knowing his tutor would be displeased. He liked the old man, almost loved him. He was one of the few men that had never feared the boy. Percius, brave Percius, thought Archimedes, catching the eye of his personal guard as he leapt through the doors leading to his classroom.

It was a year after the Great War had begun. Percius had taken to escorting the prince, keeping him under his watchful eye. At first distant, the Atlantean hero soon warmed to the quiet, studious boy. He took time to talk, even play with the child. Archimedes had never known such comradeship. On the Kings orders, they had journeyed south, seeking refuge in Samothrace, the summer palace with the Queen. Percius had longed to join his comrades in battle but was never one to question an order, certainly not a King's order.

Percius first came to renown when Isenia, niece to the King, had been kidnapped by nomads who sought bounty on her head. He had single-handedly fought three nomads, killing two and crippling the third.
Then after receiving a nasty strike by a crossbow bolt to the shoulder, he had ridden after the kidnappers, leapt upon their chariot, took the young girl in his arms and leapt to safety. The two remaining kidnappers thought better of returning to confront the wounded swordsman.

Percius soon found that favor of the King bought favor of his court. His name was suddenly added to each rich gathering; his opinion was sought on all matters that were once considered beyond his comprehension. Percius, though was a man of simple tastes; his manner belied the fierce intelligence that lay behind his piercing gaze. His body tensed as he saw Uric approach with the man's lackey, Janus, just behind the King's advisor. Percius bowed slightly in greeting.

"My Lord Uric, how can I be of assistance?" Percius had never taken to Uric. He was one of the first to court his friendship after the Isenia affair. Percius soon recognized the man for what he was.

"To begin with Percius, you can explain why Janus here was sent from your service in protecting the young heir? I was distressed that you deem him unworthy of a position!" he snapped.

"My Lord, the King has given me the position of protecting the Prince. In the palace I need no other men to confuse the situation. On any excursion I will use the man that I know and trust. With these men I have fought many battles. I trust them with my life and my charge." Percius looked into Janus' eyes, and saw the malice and hatred there. "Janus' reputation is somewhat different to that I would expect in protection."

"You miserable swine!!" Janus hissed. His hand swiftly clutched his sword. As the blade begun to pull free, Uric spun on the man.

"Janus, sheath the weapon now. Drawing a weapon in anger, in the palace of the King, is treason. Do you wish to hang from the Gabala?" Janus bit back a reply and angrily pushed the blade back into its scabbard. The Gabala was an ancient Atlantean custom, where those that broke the Kings laws were hanged till death. "And you Percius should not listen to rumors. Janus has done nothing else if not serve the King well." Percius knew better than to question Uric, though agree he did not.

"As you say my Lord, though this position has been set before me and under my jurisdiction. I will not have a man I have never worked with before under this command."

Uric felt his anger rising but sought to qualm it. He was now too close to risk any open confrontation. "Of course though, I disagree and I will petition the King on his return." Percius resisted the urge to smile.

"My Lord, the Queen speaks in his absence. I am sure she will welcome any suggestion that details her sons' protection." Uric smiled beneath his contempt. The Queen distrusted him and would never argue against Percius.

"I am sure such a small matter is not worth worrying the Queen. It shall be as you say. Now I need to see Archimedes as his Father wishes me to teach him certain arts." Percius stepped to one side as Archimedes entered the teaching halls. As Janus made to follow, Percius stepped before the man. "I am afraid that you will have to wait outside. None are allowed in the Prince's presence without my command."

Janus tensed. As Uric disappeared behind the closed doors, the smaller man looked up at Percius.

"Mighty Percius!" he exclaimed, "How courageous you are with the King's ear." Percius felt the hot breath of the man against his skin. "When you lose favor, and be sure you will, watch for me!"

"Watch for Janus? I believe that would be a welcome surprise. I hear that most of your enemies have been slain from behind!" Percius leaned over the smaller man, glaring into Janus' eyes. "Know this Janus, I know not what game you and your master play here, however, my eye is upon you. As the eyes of the Queen as well. When I know what deceit you harbor, there will be no hiding place." Janus fell back under his heavy gaze. "Tell that to your master, I fear him not."

Queen Cheris sat upon the balcony gazing out to the sea. The city was protected by heavily manned walls. The only entry to the city that was accessible without heavy losses, would be the ocean. In respect of this, Lionus had placed ten long ships across the bay. His worries over his wife and child, necessitated such action. Cheris took a long drink from the watered wine, the golden goblet shimmered in the mid-day sun. Cheris turned to her hand maiden and said, "Hermione, you may leave. I think I shall take a sleep for the sun seems to drain my energy." The hand-maiden bowed and backed the required distance before turning and leaving the room. Cheris stood alone and stared across the sea as she remembered the flight from the Capitol to the summer palace.

"My place is beside you Lionus!" she had raged, "What will our enemies think if I am to leave like some criminal in the night!"

Lionus tried to calm her and replied, "Cheris my love, please listen to reason. Assassins could lurk around any corner. Our borders have been open too long and the entrance to the city has been open as well. I have no way of knowing what spies could be here! In Samothrace, the city has been purged for only those of true blood occupy. I know that you would be safe, as well as the boy." he added as almost an after thought. "Beretta and Conavar have already declared their borders closed. Romen has an army awaiting journey south to pillage our lands. I would ask that you allow me clear thought to organize our force."

"Ask or command, Lionus?" Cheris demanded.

"I ask as a husband." Seeing the look of consternation on her face, he grew angry. "But I command as your King!" he shouted. "Woman, you will be little more than a concern if you stay here. I will not allow that! Is it not enough that Percius is to protect you both? Uric is also to accompany you until I command his presence!"

"Uric?" Cheris was startled. "Why that snake of a man? What good can come of his accompaniment?"

"Cheris, do not speak of my friend in such manner. Uric will organize Samothrace's defenses before I journey south. There I will meet with all my Generals before taking our armies north." As Cheris rose to speak, the King cut her off. "As your manner dictates how I can approach this, I have little choice. You shall do as I command, my wife. I will not allow the manner of your brethren to override my command!" Cheris was born of a highbred family, unused to accepting orders and more inclined to giving them. "Now see the servants pack whatever you desire. This conversation is over!"

He turned and stormed from the room. Cheris was tearful only in the shame of conflict caused between herself and the King. Their departure was cold and brief. Lionus seemed more occupied with Uric and Percius than herself and their son. The boy appeared frightened and bewildered by the departure. He hugged his mother close for the arduous journey.

Within three months they entered Samothrace. Three times the party had been attacked by the wandering Nomad tribes. Their losses had been few but the attacks had highlighted the position Cheris felt she was now in. Alone and afraid. Percius had been a welcome companion. The man was both courteous and gallant. He took time to play with the child, and once the boy was at ease, answered Archimedes' numerous questions. More than once, Cheris felt Uric's gaze upon her, and at times, the lustful measure of his companion Janus' leers. Only in Percius' company did this ill feeling abate. She longed for the King's return, the safety of his embrace. Yet her fears hinted that she would never feel as safe again.

A soft knock at her door roused the Queen from her thoughts. On her command the door was opened and her heart lifted some as Percius entered.

"My Lady." He bowed in welcome.

"Come Percius, I have on more than one occasion told you such formality is unnecessary in private." She smiled and Percius drank in the beauty of her face.

"I apologize…Cheris." He said awkwardly. He smile grew broader at the swordsman's discomfort. A matter of vanity she knew, but his reaction did not displease her.

"How can I be of service Percius?"

"I come from Archimedes' room. The boy is asleep. Both Simon and Gregor stand watch. He is learning fast. His teacher believes that his acumen is that of a boy twice his age. He will make the King very proud." He noted the downward glance and the smile falter. "Have I caused offence my Lady?" He continued cursing inwardly at the formal address.

"Percius, you have very rarely if ever caused offence." Her smiled returned if only briefly. "The King has not often been proud of his son. I often wonder whether we were sent here in exile rather than for protection."

"My Queen, long have I been in service for the King. On many battlefields I have stood by his side. By many fires I have spoken long with him." In shocked realization he understood that he longed to take this woman in his arms. "My King has only ever spoken with affection for his son, and with devotion for his wife. I stood in his council regarding this journey, I would state if not the case but only your safety was in question."

"Verily?" The Queens eyes stared directly into his, searching for the truth.

"On my word."

"Then a Queen must take the word of her most favored champion." The smile had now returned a fact that made Percius more uncomfortable than ever.

"Now I must retire and check the sentry posts." He bowed and turned rather quickly feeling the heat raise his blood. As he departed he heard the soft laughter of the Queen behind him. He longed to turn and re-enter but knew such actions were not to be undertaken. A quick nod to the attending guard and Percius began his duties.

Samothrace was a large settlement. Centralized around the large palace were several barracks and large homes that belonged to the Kingdom's wealthiest citizens. Surrounding this was a thick wall standing the height of at least ten men. Archery posts had been built every twenty paces, with enough room to house ten archers. The only entrance was through a thick wooden door that was heavily guarded and held barred at all times.

Percius though was concerned only with the palace guard. Uric was given command of city protection but the palace was Percius' domain. As Percius walked the corridors he was joined by two of his senior officer.

"Report." snapped Percius in a tone expected.

"Nothing of significance sir. We have no missives from the wall or from the warships to indicate any infiltration."

"Thank you Thomas." Percius stated as they briskly matched on. "All I ask is vigilance. The King's advisors are sure some sort of attempt is to be made. Here we can contain and eliminate. If we cannot protect the Queen and Prince here, we have little chance elsewhere." Percius glanced through the large stone windows noting three nobles waking through the gardens. "Gerard." He nodded to his second officer.

"Sir, we have thirteen families currently in Samothrace, three more are expected next week and then further migration. News of the conflict has spread. We have sent word that passes will be needed to enter the city and that garrison commanders can issue these."

"Damn it! I was hoping that we could avoid any traffic. Too many people brings confusion and confusion is the enemy's ally." At once Percius stopped. His two officers watched his face strain with concentration. "The gardens. Are they not off limits?" He questioned Thomas.

"Yes my Lord, on order of Lord Uric." Percius looked out upon the gardens, the three men he had seen had disappeared. He noted the direction they were taking, direct to the palace gates.

"Thomas, get down to the garden entrance, question the guard and then bring as many men as you can to the palace entrance. Seek out the princes' chamber." As Thomas broke into a run Percius and Gerard turned and ran in the opposite direction. "Gerard, take whoever is available and get to the Queen. Do not alarm her. Tell her it is an exercise. Whatever happens, she is not to leave her quarters. Bind her if necessary!" Gerard broke away from Percius as they reached a winding staircase. Percius leapt down the stairs. As his feet hit the floor he drew his sword and ran onto the corridor where Archimedes' room was located. He saw the two guards lying in pools of blood outside the Prince's chamber. Cursing, he smashed through the door and as he rolled to his feet, he scanning the room. No one to be seen though signs of a struggle were evident. He rushed to the balcony and saw the three men running towards the beach where a small boat awaited. One of the men carried a bundle that Percius knew to be the boy. Percius vaulted from the balcony and gave pursuit. The boy was obviously struggling which gave the kidnappers cause for delay, Percius was quickly gaining ground. As his feet hit the sand the two men not carrying the boy turned to face him. The third man was struggling with the boy trying to force him into the boat.

With a scream, the man dropped Archimedes who ran past the two men to stand behind Percius. Archimedes gripped Percius' leg as the third man approached to stand with the others. All had drawn their swords.

"Give us the boy and you will live." The middle man spoke. The tone was guttural, and Percius recognized this accent as one from the Northern Kingdom. They were men sent by Conavar.

"Leave this place now." Percius commanded. "You trespass in a foreign land and the penalty is death. I grant passage for your leave." Percius knew that to fight three men whilst protecting the boy would be dangerous. He had to take the boy to safety.

"So be it." The man who had struggled with Archimedes exclaimed, "Now you die!" He ran forward sword aloft, as the other two advanced.

Percius pushed the boy away. "Run!!" he yelled and Archimedes ran towards the palace. The first kidnapper drove his sword down. Percius feinted to his left, ducked to his right and the sword cut through the air. Percius smashed his elbow into the man's head, leapt into the air and in a dazzling arc drove his sword down through the man's neck.

He turned to engage the remaining two men. At once he knew he was in trouble. The first man had been clumsy and arrogant. The two remaining assailants were neither. With thrust and parry they drove Percius back. A cut appeared on Percius' cheek, the blood trickled down his chin. He was weakening fast and knew that he would not last much longer in the searing heat. In desperation he drove forward, seeking a small opening to exploit. The lead attacker parried his blow and thrust forward. Percius leapt sideways and the blade skimmed his stomach. With all the strength he could muster, his sword swept up cutting the hands from the arms. The man screamed but he cry was short as Percius spun round and beheaded him. As Percius fell to the ground, the last kidnapper walked forward sword raised.

"Now you die whore son!" His arm raised and the sword came down only to to be met with the chime of metal upon metal. The kidnapper turned, startled.

Janus stood, sword in hand, watching the scene. "Well my friend. Let us see how you fare one against one?" He sneered. The man danced forward. His sword swept round at Janus' stomach. Janus stepped inward and caught the man's arm between his own body and arm. The man struggled to free his sword arm but to no avail. "Not very good it seems!" whispered Janus in his ear. Then with sickening force Janus drove his head into the man's face. Time and time again he thundered home blows with his head. The man fell, his face an unrecognizable mess. Janus slowly drew his sword across the bloodied neck and the sand turned red.

"So it seems the hero failed?" Janus said to Percius who shakily regained his feet.

"Why?" Percius was shocked at the events which had taken place.

"Why save you? Percius that is my duty." With those words he turned away passing the guards running towards their leader.

In his chamber Janus sat with Uric. "The fool nearly let them escape. But perhaps the outcome is more beneficial, though you should have let me kill the fool." Janus stated. "I have been given position in the guard; with the deaths of those that were closet to Archimedes I am in position of trust."

"Indeed Janus, now we can begin to manipulate the boy. And when Percius is taken care of who better to take his place than you, the man whom he shall grow to trust. After all, you saved the wretch's life. Events are unfolding as expected. This is most welcome."

"How did you manage to get them into the city Lord?" questioned Janus. "The gates have closed since we arrived."

"Janus, they were already here. My plans have been long in the making. Soon all will be as it should be."

Chapter Three

The sun settled over Samothrace, the fading light sprinkled across the ocean. To Percius' eyes the sea became alive like the glittering of a thousand diamonds. Slowly the languid waves rushed up onto the shore, reaching his resting point upon the giant rock that according to legend the God Youanis had cast down to slay the sea serpent that had fed upon his minions. His thoughts drifted to Archimedes. It was several years since the kidnapping attempt had been foiled. Percius had watched as the boy grew ever closer to Janus. The Prince's new bodyguard had grown in popularity with the men and Archimedes alike. And why not he mused, there was now much to like. Janus no longer sat at the knee of Uric and his demeanor had softened. Percius himself had spent a few days in the man's company finding him not without wit; grudgingly Percius found himself liking the man. It was this very morning when doubts had arisen once more. It was a look, Percius told himself this, just a look. But it had passed between Janus and Uric when reports has been read regarding the war.

The King's forces had a lack of success from routing the enemy from fortified positions in Aisla. The armies of Ames and Servia had formed alliance against Aisla. The armies were stretched thin. King Beretta of the Highlands was constantly raiding the eastern borders, and fear was that once Beretta had claimed victory over King Alain of Lentria he would set his sights on raiding further inland. Further to this, there were claims that barbarian pirates had begun pillaging the costal villages, for with the men away at war they were easy pickings. Rumor had spread that these pirates would risk attack on Samothrace soon, with little to fear as they had been unopposed. They would find pillaging Samothrace an ill move as several thousand soldiers were now garrisoned. But it was an enemy Lionus could have done without.

It was the look that bothered Percius. A passing of intimate knowledge; a mention of news that was expected, and thus gloated upon by both parties.

Percius looked to the skies.

"What is wrong with you man? Janus is a changed man. Uric has nothing to gain by our misfortune." But the doubts persisted. His thoughts were interrupted by a figure approaching. At once he was tense, his hand resting upon his blade. The dying sun spurned his vision until a soft voice he heard.

"Percius, you may relax. It is only me," the voice soft and sweet. Cheris deftly climbed upon the rock to sit beside the swordsman. Percius awkwardly tried to stand as protocol demanded but a hand gently clasped his arm. "Please, sit. Relax in my company. So few do."

"My L…" he stuttered remembering Cheris' request. "Cheris, you are far from the walls. Where is your guard? I shall have the the man flogged!" Anger rippled through his voice.

"My guard is where I told him to wait. He is in my chambers, and you shall do no such thing! Am I not free to walk our own lands?"

"Cheris, the King would be most unhappy if you were left unprotected and something happened. It was not so long ago that Archimedes…" Cheris placed a single finger on his lips.

"I know what happened with my son, Percius. And to the heroes that saved him!" She smiled at Percius' rising protest. "I will not be a prisoner. And where safer could I be than with Aisla's greatest hero." The smile was lightly mocking but the words were not. "Why is it you are here alone? You looked in deepest thought. Are you troubled?" Percius wanted to answer, to air his doubts. But the Queen disliked Uric as it was, he did not want to cause further enmity, and Janus was guard to the Prince. The Queen needed to trust him.

"I am longing to join my countrymen in battle my lady. I am a soldier before even a man. My place is in the battlefield. The reports we have heard only increase my longing." Percius lied. In shock he realized that there were few places he would rather be than here with Cheris now. He looked away, embarrassed and ashamed.

"Percius, none doubts your honor or your bravery. It may be soon that we are need of your sword arm here. I speak not of the pirates, but of Conavar and Romen. Soon they could be upon us."

"The King will not allow that my Lady. Together they are strong, yes. But not strong enough. They shall soon turn on each other like the snakes in nest that they are."

"So sure are you Percius?" She questioned.

"Of course, our armies are well trained, the men strong and proud." But there was that doubt again, nagging at his mind. Like the doubt he had over Janus and Uric. He frowned.

"Percius?" Cheris leant her head to one side peering into his eyes. Slowly Percius looked upon his Queen. The sun now shone her face with a new radiance. It was as if almost to breathe was too difficult. How he longed to touch the perfection of her face, to feel the warmth of her embrace. "Percius?" Her voice no more than a whisper.

"I..I..I….." Percius found no word that would come. She shifted slowly drawing her face to his one, looking deep into his eyes.

"Speak my Lord," she whispered, like the soft breeze through the air.

"My Lord!" came a shout and the spell was broken, the world moved on and Percius' dreamlike state shattered. He saw two foot guards approaching. Deftly he leapt from the rock and returned the quick salutes, noting both guards questioning looks upon the Queen.

"What is it then man!" Percius barked drawing their attention back to himself.

"News from the front. The King has won through! The army has driven the Amesian armies back. The Servian's deserted, and the alliance has been broken!" The guard spat in excitement. "Lord Uric thought it best to tell you at once."

"And he was quite correct Willis! This is wondrous news!" shouted Percius his smile mirrored back upon him by the two guards. "Has the rallying call come at last? Are we to march with the armies into Ames and end this war for once and all?" Percius at once craved to be away from Samothrace.

"No my Lord. The King has re-established the border." Willis hurried. "He is coming here!"

"Here? When the chance is ours to crush the enemy? Are you sure?"

"Lord Uric has the letters my Lord. I was told to instruct these points to you and request your presence in the war chamber."

"So be it." Percius glanced upon the Queen. "My Lady, the King returns. Such blessings we should be thankful for."

"Indeed Percius, for such blessings we should."

Percius turned towards the guards.

"Escort the Queen back to the palace at her wishes, I shall attend to Uric,"With a swift salute the swordsman began a swift jog back to the palace.

Cheris watched him disappear. Her heartbeat had slowed now. The close proximity of the young hero had moved her, and something had been shared between them. As he became a speck in the distance she jumped to the sand and ignored the helping hands offered.

"Gentlemen, I believe that a gentle stroll back to the keep is in order." Slowly they fell in behind the Queen, but with every step she took, her heart felt heavier.

Percius entered the war-chamber. Uric sat hunched over the letters that had been sent.

"They found you then my Lord?" The voice was almost a sneer. "I do wish you would appraise me of your whereabouts at all times. We can't have the hero disappearing now, can we?" A laugh that was devoid of humor escaped Uric's mouth.

"My Lord, I believe there are papers I need to see." Percius stated.

"So lofty now Percius? The papers are addressed to me and me alone. As commander of the garrison I thought it best to enlighten you. Do not forget your position!" Uric said sharply. "The King will be here in two months. His Highness intends to visit other garrisons before resting here for a month or so. He then intends to gather forces and smash through Ames and Servia. We are confident the others shall then fall into line."

"We my Lord? Do your gifts include being able to advise from such a distance?"

"My gifts, as you put it, are far beyond your ken. How is our Queen?" The sneer appeared once more.
"The Queen is as she ever is. Strong and hopeful to see the King again." Percius

dismissed the remark and looked towards the letters. "Why are we not pursing the divided forces as their morale will be low, supplies in need? We can rout the armies before they have any chance to regroup."

"You speak against the King's orders Percius? You think him unwise?" Percius was wary now, his every word would be relayed to the King he was sure.

"I only speak as commander of many disputes. I think aggression is called for rather than regrouping."

"Be careful Percius, it is not your place to question the King's orders. Perhaps your position here has given you a greater goal in life?" Percius bit back reply. Rather than argue any point he turned and left the chamber. As he stormed down the corridor he charged into Janus, knocking the smaller man to the floor. Anger flashed in his eyes and he lurched to his feet grabbing Percius by his tunic.

"Watch where you are going fool. Apologize!" he hissed.

"Get your hand off of me now," Percius retorted. The grip tightened and rather than letting go Janus pushed his face forward. Before any words escaped, Percius drove his head down into the nose of Janus. There was a sickening snap and blood began gushing from his nose. As Janus let go reaching for his nose Percius drove a knee upwards into his groin and with a quick jab sent Janus to the floor. Without a word he continued down the hallway. Janus pulled himself to his feet. Anger fueled his battered form. He reached for his sword and realized that it was in his chambers. Slowly he gained pace silently running at the walking figure of Percius. With a roar he leapt upon the man's back. At the last minute Percius turned and fell to his knees. As the sprawling Janus leapt above him, Percius reached for his tunic.
With all the might he could muster and using Janus' momentum against him Percius threw the man through the wooden doors into the gardens.

Archimedes sat watching the boys run around, each squealing with delight as the chosen boy sought to catch the others. He longed to join in but no doubt excuses would be made and he would soon be alone once more. At nine years old the boy was uncommonly tall, his piercing eyes and blond locks would have made him the envy of every mother. However the curse of rumors made him feared. At six, Uric had taught him techniques to quell his emotion and control the powers within. His touch no longer caused pain. As the last two years had passed his abilities had changed. Alone in his chambers he had calmed his mind, watching distant battles, even influencing the thoughts of those he watched upon. Though never his Father, Archimedes knew that his Father would sense his presence. Of course this was not true, but fear held sway. Suddenly a crashing sound stopped the boys in their tracks. Archimedes turned towards the sound of the commotion. He was stunned to see the crumpled figure of Janus lying in the flower beds. At first he felt fear, alarmed at the thoughts of the kidnapping attempt. He was then amazed to see the lean figure of Percius leap through the door and draw his sword. He slowly approached the stricken Janus.

The two soldiers who were guarding Archimedes ran forward but a sharp command from Percius stopped them in their tracks.

Janus struggled to raise his head, blood was pouring from both mouth and nose, an eye closed with the force of the impact. Percius took the tip of his sword and placed this beneath Janus's chin slowly lifting his head.

"Now listen to me. Listen well, for this is the last time I shall speak to you in such manner. Never lay your hands upon me again. Never. And the next time you raise a hand to me, I will end your life, you miserable cur." With the words Percius whipped the sword away and Janus fell head first to the floor. Percius looked up. Anger commanded he take the man's life. He then saw Archimedes looking upon him. It was then he saw the dire look of disappointment on his face. Percius staggered back as if hit by an arrow. Throwing his sword to the floor he fled back through the broken doorway.

Archimedes approached the battered and bloodied man and knelt before him. One of the guards exclaimed that he would find the surgeon. Archimedes turned upon him.

"Leave us; he shall be well soon enough."

To all that heard the voice sounded alien. But none doubted the authority. Archimedes leaned beside Janus and placed his hands upon the man's forehead. At once a terrible heat was fashioned, the pain almost unbearable for Archimedes. Still he held on, and those that saw watched the cuts and bruises begin to heal. The flesh knitting back together and fragments of the broken nose rebuilt itself.

Janus coughed, he moved gingerly, expecting pain but feeling none. Slowly he raised a hand to his face feeling the wetness of the blood but the healed skin and bone. He looked in awe at Archimedes.

"My Prince, how?" The words he could not find. And at once Archimedes collapsed.

Slowly Archimedes came round; his vision swam in and out of focus. He knew he was in his bed, in his chambers. He could feel the cold compress upon his head.

"Well now boy, welcome back." Janus said and the boy was able to focus on him. Archimedes saw the smiling face and with effort returned the smile. "That was some trick my Prince. Many a time I could have benefited from a healer that wasn't a charlatan." Janus frowned. "Why help me though? I thought Percius was your friend."

"Why?" Archimedes whispered. "Why did he hurt you?"

"I asked him to apologize, it seems that he questioned your Father's commands, my Lord Uric reprimanded Percius on his words and I happened to be in the wrong place at the wrong time. Lord Uric wanted him arrested but I have managed to overt that."

"Again, why?" The boy asked.

"I have no friends here, Percius has many. I need no more enemies."

Archimedes watched Janus carefully. As he sat up in bed he clasped a large clay mug filled with water. While he drank deeply, the boy's eyes fixed clearly on Janus. Janus shifted uneasily from one foot to the next.

"Am I not your friend?" Archimedes asked.

"I would like to think so my Prince. Indeed I would."

"Then friends we are."

Janus reached forward hugging the boy. "Such friendship creates our destiny." Janus smiled inwardly. So far everything Uric had described had come true.

"And are you sure Willis." Uric walked around the trembling guard. "Alone with the Queen acting suspiciously? You have further witnesses?" The guard nodded. "Oh dear. Say nothing of this to no one. Can I trust you Willis?" The guard nodded once more. "Good I have need of you. I need you to watch over the Queen. Report her whereabouts and company back to me each day." Uric grabbed the guards' throat. "I want every detail. And if you comply, you shall be well rewarded. Now get out!" The guard fell to the floor but scrambled in retrieval, as he rushed from the room.

Percius sat upon the rock. The sun was hidden beneath the dark clouds and the rain fell heavily. For two days he had bared shame at his actions. He stood feeling the wind lash his body, and then he saw her. Cheris walked slowly towards him. He leapt deftly down. He resisted not at all as her arms wrapped around his body. The rain fell, tracing patterns down his face. No one could see where the rain ended and the tears began.

Willis watched from afar, a small smile of triumph when he saw them embrace.

Atlantis

"There have been those that have called me a dealer in death. Strange for one that has lived so long, I have only ever struck downfour enemies in anger. Others have sought to harm those that I have cared for. And those I have sent to the netherworld with grief."

Chapter Four

Argentous was not a vain man. He knew his place in the world and accepted this without question. He had been lucky to have been high born and thus became a competent General. His abilities were never questioned, every command was obeyed. Some thought him cautious, others wise. That was until the second year of the war. A nomad tribe had attacked the city in which his wife and child had been sheltered. In despair he learned of their deaths and he was forever changed. He became enraged, now seeking the enemy at every quarter. His men loved him and died for him. At the thick of every battle he would be standing side by side. Victories were gained that were thought impossible. He forever drove his men forward and the fiercest of enemies retreated from his onslaught. Never a handsome man, the rigors of the war had scarred his face. The etching of battle stained his face, giving him a quality both admired and made him feared amongst both friend and foe. As his exploits grew in fame, he soon found his services enlisted by the King. Together they fought, and together they drove the armies of Romen and Conavar into retreat.

Samothrace held no desire for Argentous. He no longer wanted to sit and plan. He was a man of action, though he was deeply honored to serve with the King and obeyed every order at command.

For five days now they had tracked a nomad killing party. On route to Samothrace, they had found several villages burned, the occupants put to horrendous death. Lionus ordered that those responsible be found and punished. Argentous had at once volunteered for the task. Taking sixty of his most capable killers they had tracked the nomads to their settlement. Now as dead of night crept upon them, the men awaited Argentous' orders.

He called his three captains together, men of iron who had fought many battles with him.

"The nomads number no more than fifty. The King has given order that none are to survive. If we ride in then some will escape. This is not an option."

Argentous, to his distaste had ordered the men to don clothes of black cotton, foregoing the golden amour of Aisla. "Let us be upon them and let them know that our vengeance is both swift and fatal." The men nodded and silently retreated to their posts.

Like a creeping bank, the men of Aisla swept down amongst the sleeping nomads. Six sentries had been posted. All had been silently slain. Now havoc reigned amongst the settlers. The first scream echoed into the night and the Aislean's were upon them. Two nomads rose gathering their weapons and charged at the waiting General. Argentous unclasped his two curved swords and ran to meet the nomads. As a blade whistled over his head, he swiftly disemboweled the first nomad, parrying the blade of the second. With a vicious back slash he tore the man's head from the shoulders. He glanced around seeking more foes. But his men had savagely torn through the camp. As dying screams filtered away, Argentous heard a small sound to his left. He fell on one knee as his sword swept round stopping a hair's width away from the child's throat.

The girl was perhaps six. Her blond dirt matted hair hung over her face. Her eyes were huge and fearful and stared deep into the General's face. His body tensed as Argentous prepared to kill the girl swiftly.

"What is your name child?" The words came as a shock to Argentous. What do I care for her name? he thought. The child trembled.

"Dianu." The word was nothing more than a whisper. A single tear fell from her right eye, tracing a clean river down her grubby face. Argentous strained against his will, and with all the will he could muster he sheathed his sword.

"Child, come here. I will take you to safety." Gently he lifted the girl into his arms. She was soft and light. His heart ached in the memory of Petra, his daughter. She would have felt like this he thought. To his amazement the girl wiggled and cuddled into his chest. He groaned inwardly, as the grief he had suppressed almost rose out of control.

"Are you a hero? My mother told me there were heroes," she whispered into his body.

"Your mother?" He asked the question tormenting him. "Was she here?" Fearing for the answer.

"She is dead." The answer was blunt. "Corn took me to sell as a slave."

"You shall be no one's slave my dove."

"Then you are a hero."

"No child, I am no hero."

"My mother said that all heroes say that." And then she was asleep. The captain Forlain walked up to Argentous.

"It is done sir. They are all dead." Looking upon the slaughter Argentous could see the bodies of women and children.

"Good, the King will be pleased." He motioned to turn away.

"General?"

"Yes, Captain?"

"The girl, you want me to deal with her?" Argentous knew that Forlain meant to kill her.

"No Captain, she is coming with me." Then he turned and walked slowly to his waiting horse.

They rode hard and fast, and entered the camp around dawn. Argentous quickly dismounted and carried the girl to his tent. His whore Arian was waiting for him. She looked up from the bedding in surprise at the girl he was carrying. Without question Arian rose and took the girl from his arms, and placed her on the bed.

"Arian, see that she is given all that she wants when she wakes." Arian nodded. She had been with Argentous now for a year. He was kind and considerate, by no means a cruel lover like others before him. Yet he was cold and distant, and never showed emotion. Now she saw a different man before her.

"Of course." Arian looked upon the girl. As she turn to question Argentous, he was gone.

Lionus sat hunched over a candlelit table. He had studied the latest reports with interest throughout the night. He absently took a chuck of buttered bread and began to eat as he once more re-read the last message. Argentous entered his tent and bowed low. He noted the torn and stained canopy. He knew that this had been his King's home for many years, always not far from the war.

"Ari, I trust your mission was successful?" Lionus questioned.

"Indeed Sire. The nomads died to the man, no one escaped."

"Excellent we are ten hours from Samothrace. At least there we shall be able to rest and recuperate." As he saw the mild look of disgust Lionus laughed. "So I presume you stand by your argument that we should have harried Romen's men and followed them on invasion?"

"Highness, I think we have a chance to end this war once and for all."

"Indeed, then you will be interested to read this." He threw a scroll to Argentous. He quickly scanned the contents, then looked up amazed.
"Is the content safe?"

"It is. So it seems Conovar's desertion was a lie, a deceit to have our forces give chase, which let Beretta follow through and surround us."

"But Beretta's armies were further west. How could he have gotten so close so quick?"

"It seems he was never so far west. His army moved east some time ago."

"How long have you known this Sire?"

"Suspected? Some time ago… but I confirmed it this very night." Argentous looked at the table and recognized the seal of Uric. But Lionus was not offered that scroll.

"Sire with your leave I shall go now to rest. We have ridden all night."

"Of course Ari. But one thing before you leave. You know Percius, do you not?"

"We are not close friends Sire but we fought together many times."

"And your judgment?"

"We disagreed on certain elements of warfare but I would have him by my side over any man."

"And his honor?"

"Honor?" Argentous laughed. "That is why we disagreed. Percius sees everything in a certain shade. He has iron principles and is the most honorable of men."

"Very well. You may go now. Rest well, General."

Argentous departed, and thought why the King would question him about Percius. His thoughts were interrupted by the approaching Forlain.

"Yes Captain, how can I help?"

"The girl sir. It has been playing on my mind. Why did you spare her? We have killed countless others over the years." he queried.

"Captain, I have no real idea. At once I could not do it."

"I am sorry to ask sir. It is just that I was concerned."

"No need, get some rest." Argentous continued to his tent. He found Dianu lying in Arians arms. Softly he pulled the cover over both of them. He rolled up an old cloak and lay upon the floor, resting his head upon the cloak. Slowly he found sleep, and once more he dreamt of his golden haired daughter.

"The King is coming!" The shouts came up from the watch towers and soon Samothrace was alive with activity. The Queen had planned for a welcome parade and all inhabitants of Samothrace raced to their duties. In the past years the population had risen by thousands, all refugees fleeing homeless from the ravages of war. Many settlements had been erected for the newcomers. The former controls on migration were abolished on the Queen's demand after she once saw the hoards of starving children once camped outside the city walls.

As the King rode through the city gates, garlands and flowers rained down upon him. Even Argentous felt his heart swell with pride at the reception he received. Together Lionus and Argentous led the army through the winding city roads. The adoring crowds cheered them at every turn. Once through the city, they came upon a huge podium which had been erected before the palace gates. Upon the podium stood Cheris, resplendent in a shimmering white gown. Beside her stood the smiling Archimedes. Flanking them both were Uric and Percius. Lionus leapt from his horse and raced up the steps to embrace the Queen. The crowds roared louder as the King lifted her into the air. Lionus then put Cheris to ground. Next, in an unheard of display of emotion, Lionus lifted Archimedes to his shoulders and presented the boy to the masses.

"My son, your heir!!" he shouted and the cheers grew ever louder.

Archimedes thought his heart would burst with happiness. Never had he felt so loved, so welcome. His father was home, and he loved him!

The King softly put the boy down and turned to the smiling Uric. As he went to kneel, Lionus stopped him.

"Never will you kneel to us again. Even as you are so far apart, your council has been invaluable. So many lives have been saved on your account. Thank you my friend." Lionus grasped Uric's hand as his advisor whispered thanks. The words were not lost on either Percius or Argentous who stood behind the King. Lionus turned to Percius, and all that were close noted the change in the King's stance.
"It seems you are the hero once more." Lionus said. "Our people thank you for the protection of the heir." The words though friendly were spoken with cold indifference. Percius merely bowed in thanks and the King turned once more to the crowds.
"Tonight we shall feast. We shall talk of glories old and glories new. For soon our enemies shall tremble with fear as we revenge the wrong done upon us. We fight for peace and justice!!" he roared and the sentiment was echoed back upon him. Uric ushered the King from the podium speaking urgently in his ear. Argentous approached Percius and they gripped hands in the warriors' handshake.

"You have been sorely missed my friend." Argentous stated.

"There is no place I would have rather been than with you." Percius replied.

"Percius, there is little time now, but I must speak with you. Get to my quarters as soon as you can. I fear for you my friend." Argentous noted that the news was of little surprise. Percius simply nodded and left the podium unnoticed by some.

Janus stood upon the ramparts and saw the departing swordsmen. He quickly nodded to guardsmen awaiting his signal and they left in pursuit. Janus then turned his attention to the General. Argentous was a man neither Janus nor Uric knew. His reputation had been borne of the war. Reports stated him as ruthless and without mercy. Uric had said that they might find another pawn to use here. But Janus was worried; there was something about the man that struck him as noble, a trait that would not benefit their cause. He would watch the General carefully. Uric lead the King into the banquet hall. Argentous fell into the rear behind the Queen and Archimedes. As the doors were shut, Lionus turned upon them. "Ari, you must be tired. Leave for your quarters. I will call upon you later. Uric, take Archimedes to his chambers, I have need to speak with the Queen alone." Uric bowed and soon they were alone.

Cheris ran to the King and took his hands in her own. "Oh, Lionus how wonderful it is that you are home. I have never seen our son so happy!"

The King looked hard upon her face. The war had been unkind to Lionus. Scars crisscrossed his face. His skin was pallid and shallow, and his once golden locks grey and thinning. From almost deep within, a growl seemed to rise growing in power and ferocity.

"Whore!" he cried, backhanding Cheris and sending her sprawling to the floor. "I spend every hour fighting for a country I believe in, for ideals far beyond your comprehension and I hear that you are rutting like a common whore with Percius, the man I trusted to protect you!" Lionus stormed across to the stricken Queen lifting her to her feet. "If I could, I would take your eyes and hang you from the palace walls, but the people need moral. So you gain reprieve, bitch, but it will not always be the case!" He struck her again and she fell heavily.

"My Lord!" Cheris sobbed, "Please I beg you. What lies have been fed to you? How can you believe such things. I am as ever faithful to King and Country!" Heavy sobs racked her body. "Long have I awaited your return, Percius is my friend and your servant."

"Lies, woman!" he yelled. "So many lies! I have heard from those closest to you!"

"Uric the deceiver!" she spat.

"No, not just Uric, others, many others. You have been seen!" Lionus took several deep breaths. "You may be protected but he is not. He shall not see nightfall, and he will be buried in a pauper's grave with the other vermin." Lionus grabbed the Queen once more pulling her to her feet. "Now whore, go to your chambers and await me there! Now!" Cheris ran from the hall. Her sobs followed her every step. Uric slowly entered, carrying a large goblet of wine.

"Is it done Uric? Is he dead?"

"We have men looking for him now. It will be over soon."

"The man saved my son's life. Is this an evil deed?"
"Percius did his duty. He has now betrayed a King he was sworn to obey, used a Queen he was sworn to protect, and used a child as a pawn. You have no choice. Do you want him brought before you before his execution?"

"No! Do what needs to be done and give me word when it is over. Now leave me. Please." Lionus walked slowly to the grand table that split the hall. He poured a large goblet of wine and sat down heavily. He drank long and hard then cast the goblet to the floor, cradling his head into his hands.

Argentous entered his quarters and at once he knew he was not alone. His two swords slipped from their scabbards as he heard a dry chuckle.

"Put up the blades Ari, it is me." Percius stepped out from behind the large claret drapes bordering the large window. "Though trouble I had entering unnoticed for there were two men following me, I eluded them easily. However a guard was watching your quarters so I made entry through the window. You know what is happening here. I would beg you tell me."

Argentous eyed the swordsman closely.

"Listen to what I say Percius. I know little of what is true or false, only what I know of you, the man. It has been said that you and the Queen are lovers and that she has been seen fornicating with you. The King knows of this. I fear he has ordered your death."

"The snake Uric! Long has he wanted me out of the way, I will plead to the King for long has he trusted me!" Percius stood to leave.

"Sit down boy. The King has other sources than Uric. They have confirmed his suspicions. The man is not who he was. The war has taken its toll. I have argued your corner, but he hears only the gossip-mongers. Why Uric is probably with him now pouring poison in his ear."

"The Queen! What will happen to her if I am condemned to death?" Percius face grew red and angry. "I will see him dead before my own death!"

"Be quiet! Listen, the Queen is safe. Lionus knows her standing with the other nobles. He dare not harm her without true evidence, and she would never confess to actions untrue."

"What am I to do Argentous? Am I to face death for deeds unfounded? My name a blight on history?" Percius sat heavily.

"You must leave, and leave now. If they had men following you then they mean to take you."

"I will not kill my own men as they are comrades I have fought beside!" stated Percius.

"Then be clever. The alarm will soon go up if you are not found. I will condemn you, stating that any man taking flight is guilty. If I renounce you in front of the King, I can help you escape."

Percius looked at the older man.

"Argentous, why? We were never close friends. Indeed. I thought my beliefs angered you. You must find it humorous that with my principles I am in this position."

"Percius, long ago I lost something precious, I think I have found that once more. I understand, now more than ever, your ideals. I have done many grievous things and some I will never atone for. This is my way of balancing the scales. It may be only a little but it is beginning."

"And what of Uric?"

"He plays a game beyond my ken. But I shall watch him. Thus the careful Argentous of the past will return. And when the time comes I will bring him down."

"So be it." Percius once more took the hand of Argentous, "now I call you friend."

Chapter Five

Argentous watched carefully as Uric sat whispering into Lionus' ear. He watched as the color rose in the King's face, as he sensed the discomfort in Uric's demeanor. The court of the palace was alive with guards and servants. Each staff member hurried around each other but cast furtive glances towards the King and his advisor.

"Enough!" bellowed the King. Uric nearly fell back to the floor as the King jumped to his feet, which caused his throne to screech back on the marble floor. "I do not want excuses. Bring me Percius before break of dawn."

"Yes my Lord, he shall be found. Yet I state again, he must have allies within the palace to have avoided capture so far." Uric cast a blatant stare at the General. Argentous stormed forward.

"If you look to accuse me little man, be careful!" he raged. The hustle and bustle of the court seemed to some to a halt as Argentous squared up to Uric. "Your poisonous bile bothers me little Uric. But cast no aspersions my way lest you yearn for the feel of cold steel!"

Uric staggered back, almost seeking refuge behind the King.

"Argentous." The King stared deep within the eyes of the General. "We are brothers of the blade, and have fought many battles together. Yet I command you to stand down now. Lord Uric casts no doubt over those that are loyal." Argentous stood his ground, glaring at the smile that drifted across Uric's lips. "Stand down!!" screamed the King. This last outcry almost shook him from the red mist of anger. Argentous looked at the King.

"As you wish highness." Argentous said as he stepped back. Uric seemed almost disappointed at the outcome.

"Sire, I go now to find the traitor. No stone will be left unturned. If he is being harbored we shall see that those that defy your word will burn with him." Uric left as he once more cast a look of contempt at the General. With Uric's departure the King sagged, and almost fell back into his throne.

"Argentous, I will ask this of you once. You were seen talking to Percius after the procession. What did you speak of? Have you seen the cursed wretch?" Lionus looked up, his eyes red rimmed. At once he seemed to age another ten years. "What has become of our hero? If Percius and Cheris betray me then who can I trust?"

"Sire," Argentous offered as he bent before the King on one knee. "My heart falls to see you in such despair." The King waved him away and the General stood once more. "Percius questioned me on the many battles that have passed in his absence. He asked after men and friends that had died in battle. You know I have never deemed Percius a friend. We are much unalike. He has questioned too many of my decisions in battle for us to be anything but military comrades. I have not seen him since our discussion, nor do I expect to." The King raised his eyebrows.

"How so General?"

"Percius may be many things, but a fool, though, is not one of them. If we cannot find him by now I would suspect that he has already fled the palace and is beyond the city walls. He has many friends here. He is revered as a hero and champion." Argentous took a long slow breath. He could see the King's anger rising once more. "But I beg you Sire. Are you so sure of his guilt?"

"Guilt Argentous? He was condemned by his own eyes, and the eyes of his lover, the Queen. You think I have only Uric's word on this matter. I command many eyes my General, and I have watchers, watching those I have set to watch. I need no burden of proof!" Lionus' voice was slowly rising. Argentous knew that the game he played was dangerous but he needed to put doubt into the King's mind.

"Sire, Percius was always a sanctimonious man. His preaching was better situated to a children's campfire than the bloodied grounds of battle. Yet he was righteous and honorable. I cannot believe that a man with such principles could defy you and betray us in such a manner." Argentous watched as the King began to shake with fury. As he stood once more, Lionus shouted.

"Honor! Righteous! Your words fall on deaf ears General but your purpose does not. You seek to sway my course of action! Argentous, if I hear one more word in defiance of my command, you shall join the cursed wretch on the gallows. We have fought together, and nearly died together but you forget your place!" Argentous then fell to one knee before the King. He knew his life hung by a precarious thread.

"Sire forgive me. I sought only to council you if others have failed. I see now that this is not the case. I will stand beside you and defend your word against any man that defies you. If I find Percius I will bring him before your court. I will fight and kill any man that seeks to weaken our resolve." Lionus lurched forward drawing Argentous to his feet.

"Like Uric your words do not impress me General. Find the whore son and bring him here, alive if possible, dead if necessary." His words were a cold whisper. "Too long my commands have gone unheeded, my threats unheralded. My joyous homecoming has become another nightmare. I will have my vengeance. No longer will those that oppose me find me merciful."

Argentous stepped back with his head bowed.

"And I shall be with you my lord. I will champion your word and cause."

"Then bring me the traitor." Lionus turned his words echoing in Argentous' ears. "Do not present yourself to me until he is in chains."

Argentous walked away noting the scared looks of those that milled around him. He heard the King shout for more wine and saw the serving girls rush forward. As he left the court, Argentous stopped and noticed a guard on duty at the doors.

"General." saluted the young soldier.

"Thymus." Argentous returned the salute. "I need you to send for me the moment any sightings are reported of the traitor Percius. I want to be on hand the moment we have him."

"Yes sir!" came the snapped reply.

Argentous walked away. He knew that he would have to fashion several diversions to allow Percius a chance of escape. He had hoped to be able to disguise the swordsman in a search party of his own. He knew that this was impossible now as Uric would undoubtedly have spies watching him. As he approached his chambers he saw three guards standing outside.

"What do you want?" he snapped as all three looked sheepish. Argentous noted their armbands and knew them to be guards loyal to Uric.

"General, we have been ordered by Lord Uric to search your rooms!" the captain said, a smirk now on his face.

"Your Lord Uric does not command here!"

"But our King does!" replied the captain, handing Argentous a scroll signed by the King.

"This is preposterous!" he stormed. Then he countered, "Very well, but damage anything and I will see you pay!" The three guards entered before Argentous, while his hand gripped his sword. He knew that Percius and himself were more than a match for any three guards but he did not want to spill any innocent blood. As he entered, the three guards busied themselves looking through the adjoining chambers.

"General. Apologies but these were our orders. I will report there was nothing amiss. If it makes you feel any better all the quarters are being searched." The captain offered a poor salute.

"No it does not. A traitor lurks within these walls and you waste time searching my rooms!" The guards left and Argentous looked around. There was no hiding place. Percius had left, and Argentous had a horrid feeling he knew where he was.

"Percius you fool," he whispered.

Percius' arms began to burn. He could feel the muscles cramping, and cursing He could only wait until the guards above moved on. He knew this was insane, he knew that his life was forfeit. Yet he had to see her. With each passing moment he felt his grip weaken. He knew the drop to the courtyard below would not kill him, but it could easily break his leg and certainly give away his whereabouts. Finally the guards were gone, chuckling away to each other on the merits of the whorehouse in the sailor's quarter of the docks. Percius swung his legs back and forth. The motion soon got faster and with extreme effort he swung his body up and onto the safety of the ramparts. He landed gently face down, ever watchful for approaching guards. Silently he got to his feet. He set off on a loping run. As he scampered along the battlements, as expected, most of the guards were in the palace looking for him. The last place he might be expected to be seen was out in the open. He knew where he was going. He had traced these steps on many occasions. He knew how to get to the Queen's chamber, and it was a concern of his when he organized her security.

The Queen's chamber was situated in a high tower, adjacent to the centre of the palace. There was only one entrance, through the halls at the bottom. However, Percius knew that from the battlements a carefully placed hook and rope could snag the outcrop of the roof and allow secure climbing. He had hidden the hook and rope earlier in the month, and had planned to test the sentries on guard. However, it now had a more meaningful purpose. As the hook now swung in large circles, the wind picked up. The noise disguised the whirring sound of the rotating hook. With a burst of effort, the hook flew from his hands. Percius winced as contact was made with the roof. He felt the hook sliding down, ready to pull up any slack if he missed, as to avoid detection. He yanked hard on the rope which was now secure. Percius looped the rope through his belt and twisted a coil around his arm. Then he swung from the battlements. With deft skill he softened the impact and gently bounced off the tower walls. Slowly he made his ascent and looked down. There, he saw five guards circling the tower. He knew he had to pick up speed as one errant look and he would be done for.

Cheris paced around the room, cursing inwardly. She felt no fear. Insted she felt outrage. Yet the King had seemed so different. He had always been a hard man. In private he could be loving and caring. Certainly he never was one so quick to accuse. The war had taken its toll on many points.
"How can I make you see sense?" she whispered.
"I am afraid it is beyond that Cheris."
She turned stunned for sitting in the window was Percius, a half smile on his face.
"How did you get here? Do you know what they will do if they find you?" Cheris ran to Percius and took his hand. "This is my doing Percius, as the lies of Uric have tainted my King. I should have been more careful!"
"Cheris we have done nothing wrong," Percius answered with conviction.
"Truly? Has not your mind cast thoughts that are shameless and unworthy?"
"We cannot control our thoughts," he replied. "It is how we act that counts. Lionus has judged due to those that have his ear. There was little either of us could have done."
Cheris looked into his eyes, strong and afraid, powerful yet timid.

"Why is it that you risk your life to come here? You must flee," she pleaded.
"It arranged my Queen. I had to see you." He raised his hand to her face and saw the bruise as he turned her head to the flickering candle. "So he has struck you." Anger welled within Percius. "I will take the hands from his arms." he hissed.
"No Percius, you shall not. My husband is unwell. You will not harm the Father of my child." She turned and the flame cast a web of shadows across her face. Gently she stepped in closely and planted a single soft kiss upon Percius' lips.
"We are guilty in the mind, Percius. Who knows what events might have transpired if we were here another long year." A tear fell from her eye. "We are guilty." Percius turned away, the bile of bitter defeat hard to swallow.

"Come with me my Queen." He prayed for her answer, yet he knew it could not be so.
"And my son? Is he to be raised in hiding, in denial of his heritage? You know I cannot do this." He felt her hand take hold of his shoulder. "This is beyond us, my Percius."
"The world has gone mad," he stated, simply and without feeling. "I leave now my Queen. Where I go the path is not yet clear. I will never see you again. I came to feast on your beauty, to give my strength and courage to do what I must." Percius stood on the ledge of the window. "I love you Cheris." And then he was gone.

Cheris ran to the window. She saw that Percius was already shimmying down the rope. She also saw the guards in the courtyard below. Quickly she ran to her chamber door. She pushed against it as hard as she could. as it crashed open, she let out a piercing scream.

Percius saw the guards disappear and he smiled. He knew that Cheris had given him one last gift. Within twenty feet of the floor he let go of the rope and dropped gently to the floor. He knew what he had to return to Argentous' quarters as soon as possible. He also knew the General would be angry at his actions. He kept close to the walls under cover of shadow and carefully made his way across the yard.

Suddenly Percius heard a low sounding twang and pain instantly lanced through his right arm. Percius immediately groped for the area and saw the protruding crossbowbolt. He looked up at the grinning Janus who now walked across the yard His small crossbow was in his hand, set with another bolt ready for firing.

"Percius, how predictable," he laughed. "A fond farewell I gather," Janus pointed to the rope. "I hope she is worth dying for." Before Percius could move, Janus fired again. The bolt ripped into Percius' left thigh. Janus now cast the crossbow aside and drew his sword. "Time to die traitor." Janus swung at Percius who ducked as the wild blow struck the concrete walls. Percius drew back his left hand and thundered a blow to Janus's stomach which sent him reeling backwards. At once, Percius' sword was free of its scabbard and the two men began to circle each other.

Percius thigh was perilously weak and his right arm now useless, Janus planned to attack to the right, for he knew the weaker man would be ultimately defeated. Percius knew a duel could only have one outcome. He needed to win and win quickly.

"You never answered my question Percius. Is she worth dying for?" Janus sneered.
"I would die for her without question or pause," he stated simply. This reply seemed to enrage Janus who thrust forward. Percius parried the thrust, but then Janus drove his knee up into Percius' ravaged knee. He fell on to the other knee heavily as Janus rose, and brought his sword downwards. Percius ducked and rolled to one side. He sword then flicked out and sliced into the tendons of Janus' ankle. As Janus screamed in agony, Percius dragged himself to his feet and smashed the sword hilt against Janus' head. He fell heavily, unconscious. Percius took his blade to Janus' throat. As he was about to kill the man he turned. Four guards ran from the tower, swords in hand.

"Put it down sir for we don't want to kill you." The tallest of the four said. Percius knew him as Bison. It wasn't that long ago he had taught the man the fine arts of horsemanship.
"Bison, all is not as it seems."
"I have my orders Percius. You are wanted for treason. Put the sword down!" His eyes were cold. There was no reason there. Percius scanned the others, and saw no give in any.
"So be it," he whispered as he placed his sword into a defensive position.
"This is madness Percius, look at you. I know that you are good but you can barely stand. I suppose you would rather die here than on the gallows. Very well, careful lads, let's take him!" As one they began to approach.

"No one is dying here," Percius turned once again and saw Argentous appear from the shadows. "Put up your weapons. I will take the traitor into my custody." This caused some confusion but Bison was not for standing down.

"Begging your pardon General, but the King would be most pleased with whoever brings him Percius. I think we shall keep him to ourselves."
"As you wish." Argentous bowed. Within a breath, his two swords were unleashed. They flew through the air taking the fourth guard in the chest. Before they moved again, Argentous leapt into the air, and circled round taking the head from the second guard. Bison struck with a double overhand blow while Argentous' sword rose to meet the blade. The third guard thrust forward slicing across Argentous' chest. With a snarl he backhanded the guard sending him sprawling to the floor. He leapt up, his two feet thudding against Bison's chest. The man fell heavily. The fallen guard rushed at Argentous. He swatted the man's sword away. Then back cutting across his throat, the man died screaming silently. As he turned, Bison's blade glanced off Argentous' forehead. He managed to sway back just in time. He kicked out taking Bison at the knee. Then as he fell back, Argentous punched his sword through the man's chest. A sound came from behind him. He swept the sword up, throwing it through the air. The blade caught the man in the throat and he fell back dead. Argentous walked forward, pulling one sword from the body of the first guard. In horror he saw that the last man he had slain was the boy Thymus. The surprised expression was frozen on the boy's face on moment of death.

"Someone will pay for this. I swear." Argentous turned and walked towards Percius. He knelt before the slumbering swordsman, and judged the wounds. With vicious precision he pulled the bolts clear. Then he roughly bandaged the wounds with torn cloth. "You are lucky for the wounds, while deep, are not serious."

"I feel so lucky." whispered Percius.

Argentous heard the noise as did Percius. They spun together and saw Janus trying to string another bolt into his crossbow. Argentous walked purposely forward. As Janus watched the approaching General, he panicked and dropped the bolt. He fell back against the wall, petrified.
"Your life depends on this answer scum. Do you know the game Uric plays." Argentous spat.
"No!" Janus shook his head.
"Is that the truth!"
"Yes!"
"Then what use to me are you?" Argentous said. Janus eyes opened wide in realization as the General's sword drove into his body. "Many good men have died because of you and your master's meddling. It ends tonight." And Janus was dead.

Argentous sat watching Uric. He was hidden sufficiently within the ramparts, but was close enough to see the King raging.
"He was where?!!" screamed Lionus.
"We believe he went to the Queen's chambers." cowered Uric. "Get her moved to our joint quarters now. Janus dead and five others? Are you all incompetent!"
"Sire, he must have had help. I am sure he is within the Palace!"
No he is not, thought Argentous. Just a short time ago he had seen Percius safely hidden within a rich merchant's house in the plushest quarter of the City. Rectus was an old family friend and would treat Percius well. Then when he was recuperated he would leave the city at night, by sea.

But other thoughts spurred Argentous on. He had killed those that he called brothers of the blade, comrades he had fought beside. His life lacked the purpose it once had. He meant to rectify that tonight. Uric would die.

He had given his whore strict instructions that if anything was to happen to him, both she and the young child would be looked after.

For now, he would watch and wait.

"You bitch!" Before Cheris could move, Lionus' hand lashed out smashing against her cheek. She fell heavily to the bed as blood began to stain the cotton sheets. "He was here wasn't he? You still shame me! You still flout my rule and cast defiance in my presence!" Lionus grabbed Cherish and lifted her to her feet. "So my royal whore!"

He backhanded her this time and her body was slightly airborne. "When I am finished with you, no man will want you!"

"Father." The timid voice came from the door. Lionus looked round and saw Archimedes.
"Boy go back to your rooms. Now!!" He yelled.
"Archimedes, leave us." cried Cheris though tears and blood.
"Father, leave my Mother alone." The words were clear, no longer timid. Lionus lurched to his feet. Cheris sensed that Lionus was about to hit the boy. She automatically reached out while screaming at the King. He slapped her again and Cheris fell back to the floor.

"So, another one who defies my orders?" Lionus spat advancing towards the boy. "Get out now or suffer what the whore will!"

"No." The words were almost musical. Lionus, in a strange thought, wondered where he had heard that sound before. He turned almost dumbstruck and confused. He saw Cheris lying in a ball crying. The rage took over once more. Lionus ran across the chamber drawing his foot back and unleashing a terrible kick to her stomach.

"NO!"

Lionus turned and saw Archimedes walked slowly towards him, his eyes burning a bright gold, a terrible grimace on his face.
"You will hurt my mother no more!" he cried. Lionus stepped back in fear; he tried to run but could not. A strange and unsettling sensation ran through his body. He looked down and realized that his body had risen above the floor. His face contorted as a burning pain ran through his blood.

"You are fond of orders old man." Archimedes said, his voice suddenly unnaturally old. "Here is an order for you. Harm my Mother once more or try to harm me, and I shall come for you. I will send your soul burning into purgatory." Archimedes raised his arm and in a sudden movement the body of the King was thrown across the room, and crashed into the wooden door. "Go now, before I change my mind." Lionus, almost squealing with fear rushed to his feet while blood poured from several large cuts to his scalp. He clumsily unlatched the door and fled into the corridor.

"Mother." Cheris looked at Archimedes with fear. "You shall never have cause to fear me Mother." He raised his hand and golden light emitted from every pore. Cheris felt her body bathed in the light as slowly the wounds she suffered began to burn and itch. The light faded and she was healed. Then slowly the light faded from Archimedes' eyes. He looked bewildered as if waking from a dream.

"Mother?" The question was weak and shaky. He then burst into tears as Cheris wrapped him in her arms.

Argentous slowly crept into Uric's chambers. He was cut in several places after the fight with the guards. In such confined space such injuries were expected. The long curved knife was clamped in his hand. It would end here. He swore it to himself, on pain of death. Silently the General crept through the rooms. Until he saw Uric sitting at a table with his back towards him, scribbling over some notes. More lies and poison thought Argentous, though these will go undelivered. He maintained great stealth as he crept towards Uric, each muscle tensing, every minor sound almost deafening in the silence. Then he was upon him! Uric struggled for all of a heartbeat as Argentous plunged the blade deep into his back. Time and time again he stabbed, his right hand clamped over Uric's mouth. Soon the struggling stopped, the protests died, and Uric's body slumped to the floor.

Argentous was aghast. He was not an assassin. He had never killed anyone in cold blood beforeand certainly never from behind. Yet Uric had used many tools and now Argentous did not care. He dropped the dagger to the floor and slumped in a heap.

He was not a deceitful man. So much had been hidden in shadows, and he could no longer bear it.

"I will go to the King, declare my deeds and accept the punishment." He declared as he dragged himself to his feet. Slowly, he bent and retrieved the dagger. In another moment he had wiped it clean on the hooded cloak he wore.

"Such honor from an assassin that creeps into a chamber and stabs a defenseless man in the back? Argentous, I never took you for a hypocrite; a fool, yes, but never a hypocrite!"

The words stunned Argentous. He spun round, dagger at the ready. His mouth dropped open while the blade fell uselessly to the floor. Before him stood Uric, unmarked, his clothes torn by the striking blade but with no other visible wounds.

"How?" whispered the General. "I killed you, I saw the blood. I...." Words failed Argentous.

"Fool! Do you think one such as I can be killed by one such as you." Uric started walking towards the General. "I was born before recorded time. I have lived a thousand lives. You think steel can hurt me?" Argentous continued to back away. The shadows cast by the fire seemed to engulf the room and Uric became one with them. "You think that one such as you could stop me? Fool. You came here for death did you not? So be it." Argentous tried to scream. It died in his mouth. A bony finger stretched forward from Uric and touched Argentous in the chest. He inhaled as his chest tightened. "Argentous that experience you are feeling is your heart stopping." The General looked into Uric's eyes. Uric raised his palm open. "And this is it bursting." He clenched the fist; Argentous fell to his knees as blood poured from his mouth, nose and ears. He pitched forward and fell face down, dead. Uric stepped over the body and returned to the table that he sat upon when Argentous entered. As he sat to study the papers before him Argentous body began to shudder and smolder. Soon there was nothing left.

Chapter Six

The fire raged. Uric sat watching as the dance of the cracking tongues reached their crescendo. He looked at the diminishing pile of ashes that was all that remained of the General.

"Fool," he whispered. He drank heavily from the goblet in his hand. He noticed the shaking and he tried hard to control his body and failing. "You are growing weaker," he muttered to himself. "Your body finally betrays your true age." The faintest of smiles ghosted across his lips. "But soon that will change." He half stood and half stumbled to his feet as he reached desperately for his long couch. Uric fell heavy on to the cushioned bench. His breathing became heavy as his eyes began to lose focus. "Sleep. I must sleep. Strange, I never had the need before."

The feeling of despair settled over him. He was so close to his ultimate goal yet still so much could go wrong. The heat of the flames fell upon his body while darkness came as he swayed in and out of consciousness. He welcomed the oblivion that sleep held and was soon in her rapture. Yet the sleep was not that like one might rest. He dreamt, long and hard of memories that were unbidden for centuries, now flowed through his mind. He was young again; it was a time of despair, of deceit, and yes, of love.

Kal-az Umar ran to his father's side. The boy was but six and had already idolized his father since he could remember.

"Father, father. Have you heard? He is coming here! Kallis is coming here! He is to speak tonight at the dock!" Hasan-az Umar looked down upon the child and ruffled his hair.

"I know Kal, but you shall not be there!" He laughed at the boy's darkening expression. "You know these are dangerous times Kal. Your mother would not look kindly upon me if I were to grant you permission to attend. You shall be tucked away safely in your bed. The overlords from five tribes have condemned him. Yes, trouble is expected!"

"The overlords won't stop Kallis!" Kal shouted exuberantly. Hasan noticed several looks in their direction and he sternly turned to the boy.

"Be silent! Will you never learn, boy? These streets have ears. The overlord will be watching to see who supports Kallis. We need no trouble!"

Kal nodded solemnly, an expression which always drew the same result from his father. Hasan lifted him to his arms. Then he whispered into his ear.

"But I shall tell you all about it tomorrow, when we feast upon your mother's finest honey cakes!" Kal giggled as Hasan put him to the ground and hurried him along. Hasan was troubled though. The outlander Kallis had spoken at ten of the thirty settlements. Every time the common man had backed him. Hasan knew that soon change would come, and change was not always good.

The Rasonites had occupied Atlantis since any could remember. They were a simple yet peaceful nation. Each man knew his place and none questioned their lives. All was what it should have been. They spanned over thirty tribes, each boasting a population of around thirty-thousand. The Rasonites had learned to use the skills they were given. They had no religion, no royalty. Each tribe was governed by an overlord who was born to lead. The population worked the lush fields, hunted for game and fish, and lived under rule.

Then the stranger appeared. Washed up on a local shore, Kallis was introduced to the people. Though they spoke a foreign tongue, Kallis mastered this with ease. He stated that he was a survivor of boat wreckage from a far away land. His survival was a message from his God Zocor. He was a gift to these people. Kallis was a skillful orator. He quickly questioned those that surrounded him, as these were many, as none had seen an outlander before. With a power to captivate Kallis soon found enmity of the overlords. Rather than take council with them Kallis questioned the tribal population as to their lack of knowledge and wealth.

"The land here is rich and plentiful. Who gives right to govern that which is yours to claim?" he bellowed. And soon those that had never thought began to. Kallis was clever. He used those that were driven by lust and greed, and they spread the word efficiently as they sought a role of importance in the time to come.

Days became weeks and everywhere the outlander traveled, more and more tribesmen followed, leaving their tribal duties. The overlords became incensed and ordered other tribesmen to hunt them down and make them return. This tactic failed as many of the hunters joined Kallis' group while the others, severely outnumbered, returned in failure and were whipped for their disgrace.

And then things began to change. Kallis no longer spoke of the riches deserved by the people, only of the anger they had instilled in the God Zocor. As he stood before hundreds of men, his oratory power filled the masses with fear. As he condemned the overlords for their open defiance of Zocor's law, he swelled within the seed of malice. With greed, jealousy and fear he commanded the masses.

Certain overlords spoke against Kallis, though many kept quiet because they realized their perilous situation. As Kallis and his entourage were due in Zinbare, the last of the settlements, Hasan and his wife Fele had discussed the repercussions. Rumors were rife that certain overlords had ordered Kallis arrested, to be banished or executed. With the mood high with rebellion and anger, any such actions could bring about disaster. The overlord Kinbaire had always been kind to Hasan and his wife. He had never taken any action that affected their lives, and Hasan would hate to see the man hurt. Yet he hedged opinion. When in the company of those that followed Kallis' lead he spoke of his admiration and excitement for the coming years. In the company of the overlords' minions he spoke of the respect he had for Kinbaire. Soon he would be unable to sit upon the fence. The decision made could have serious repercussions upon his family.

The evening began well. There were parties in the streets and the people were in a buoyant mood. News that Kallis would be speaking in the town square spread. Hasan took his place in the ramparts for unlike others, he had a queer feeling, as if the merriment of the occasion was hiding a more menacing purpose.

From the moment he saw Kallis, his views changed. It was as if the man's aura lifted those that surrounded him. He was a beautiful man, tall and resplendent in a golden robe. His dark hair bordered a serene face and the bluest of eyes. He quickly called for silence and the words began to flow.

"My brothers, I come before you as a servant of the one God Zocor. He who is mightiest upon the throne of the sky. He watches us all, my brothers. His judgment is upon us."

Hasan felt as if he was as light as air. Kallis' words were gentle, yet it was as if he was whispering into his ear. He felt his body sway under the hypnotic voice. It was all he could do to raise his head and see that all others were as transfixed as himself.

"There are those that have led you from his path. There are also those that would make you servants of man. We serve only one, He watches, and his wrath grows!" Hasan felt the fear grow in his body as several cries could be heard as men fell to their knees, pleading forgiveness and direction. "But I have been sent, sent to cleanse you, to lead you on the path to fulfillment. I have also been sent to punish those that deny you your place in this world."

At once a path was cleared. Then, hooded men were dragged by several tribesmen, who threw them to the floor of the square. Hassan felt the atmosphere change. Before he knew it, he was shouting abuse at the prostrate figures while hatred burned within his body. "Now they shall know the price to be paid!" Kallis whispered. His hands reached to the air, the air grew thick so that it was almost impossible to breathe. Hasan watched as the overlords began to scream and blood ran from their terrified eyes. Kallis began to incant in a tongue Hasan had never heard before. At once the overlords burst into flames. Their screams echoed into the night and fused the delirious delight of the crowd.
"Now my children, a new order shall arise, one of devotion and might. The Rasonite time has come!" bellowed Kallis, and in abject devotion his followers bayed.

What followed few could understand but fewer still found objections. Kallis commissioned the building of several temples to Zocor. Everyone was to attend each day before dawn and each night before sunset. Next, Kallis set about creating his priests. Each man was picked because of his undying fealty to Kallis and each chosen had the cruel temperament needed to govern their flock. Soon two great cities were planned, binding the tribes and keeping them under a watchful eye. Yet the land was held in fear. Every fifth day Kallis demanded a blood sacrifice, the youngest child in a family drawn from runes. Hassan feared greatly for little Petra for she was only six and idolized Kal.

Time passed and every fifth day the children were taken to the temples of Zocor, led away by the high priests, and never seen again. For many months Hasan and his wife Laos, considered fleeing. Unlike their fellow Rasonites they could not bear the thought of losing their son. Kal was an inquisitive boy who soon learned of the sacrifices despite his parent's intention of keeping the event's secret. But he knew that his best fried Fillip had been taken away. At first he wondered where he was and why everyone avoided his questions. Then he overheard his father and mother and all became clear.

Twelve moons from the day Kallis took power, Hasan decided he could take no more. In the dead of night he loaded their wagon with supplies. He had enough to see them journey many miles, he hoped to be able to secure passage on one of the merchant ships that Kallis had opened trade with from the outlands. His family could be safe. But they were betrayed; betrayed by their neighbors who had witnessed the stockpiling of food. As the family's wagon slowly made way from the city and across the treacherous cliff tops, a small band of tribesmen awaited them. Hassan could see the harbor in the distance, so close was salvation. Hasan was a strong man. He had worked long hours in the fields and his body was like stone. At first he tried to reason with the men, but found them unwilling to talk. They insisted that Hasan and his family return to the settlement. Discussions were ended when a high priest appeared. He ordered Hasan to hand over his son as the price of betrayal. Enraged Hasan struck out at the priest with a spear piercing the priest's side. Then the tribesmen attacked. Kal broke free from his mother's grasp, and ran to aid his father. He drew a small dagger and plunged the blade into the leg of a man beating his father with a club. The man yelled and swatted the boy away. But at the same time he fell from sight over the cliff edge. Laos rose and screamed at the men. The screams died as an arrow pierced her throat and she fell from the wagon, dead. In grief and anger Hasan found new strength. He rose snapping one man's neck like a twig; he did not feel the curved sword enter his back piercing a lung. He swung, using his fists like a mighty mallet, as he crushed the man's throat. But there were far too many. The priest urged them forward, overpowering Hasan, ntil they held him down. The priest calmly walked forward while blood still ran from his mouth after Hasan had struck him. With a swift movement a blade appeared and sliced across Hasan's throat. In despair, he heard his son being dragged from the wagon, screaming as he was led away. Soon Hasan was alone, the life blood flowing from him. His vision cleared to see Kal knealing bedside him.

"Avenge us boy," was all he could say and passed from life.

The rule of Kallis continued for many years. The two great cities were built. A secret police was formed to infiltrate the population and ferret out any who spoke against Kallis. Those that did so, saw their families die horrendous deaths. Many followed in death after cruel torture. The temples of Zocor took on many acolytes. Kallis would frequent the temples. he watched his priests guide those that would take their place. It was on one such day that Kallis watched the teachings during which time he spotted the young man. At once Kallis was drawn by the man's aura, which he perceived as powerful and unyielding. He approached and the man knelt submissively.

"What is your name child?" he asked. The dark haired man looked up and Kallis knew he was no more than sixteen.

"I am Uric my Lord."

"And why are you here? What do you seek?"

"I seek to serve Zocor, my Lord."

"And what else do you seek? Be truthful with me boy."

"I search for power, and the answer to many questions." Uric spoke with fierce power, his eyes radiated emotion such as Kallis had never seen before.

"Then come with me. You are the one I have been waiting upon." And Kallis took the man-boy by the hand and led him away.

Uric was fearful for his life at first, but soon realized that Kallis saw in him the eyes of power. For months Kallis taught Uric from ancient texts. He showed the boy the power of incantation and that knowledge was power. They debated the uses of magic, as well as the properties of the earth. Soon Uric was named as apprentice to Kallis. He was held in great fear. Kallis taught Uric of the power of sacrifice. He was taught that under each alter lies a gem, a bloodstone. These were ancient relics that fed of the force of life, that gave the holder immense power. Kallis always wore a golden gem around his neck. As a gift of his position Uric was presented with a smaller red gem which was cast upon a chain and placed over his neck.

"This makes you as powerful as any man, bar me, that has set foot upon this world," spoke Kallis. Yet Uric desired more. "The age of fulfillment is upon you Uric," said Kallis. "To prove you are my successor you must pass the trials. If you do so, the keys to the earth's secrets will be given."

"I am your servant my Lord. I am ready."

Uric was led to a dark chamber and stripped of all clothes. He was then commanded to drink a dark liquid that sat upon the floor. As he drank the liquid, the room commenced to spin. He fell to the floor to look up at the domed ceiling. He heard the door being sealed with rocks. Though fear was far from his mind, the visions began.

He envisioned a world of machines, and of mechanical birds that brought fire down from the heavens. He saw a world in chaos, yet embraced. He saw a sword of power set in a stone and a King that drews the sword, a man of righteous power. He saw an ancient land surrounded by sand, of rulers that would shape the word. Also seen was a man of legend that would conquer the world and know no fears. The toppling of a continent appeared, and a land that fell beneath the sea. Then he saw himself atop a mountain with great globes of power emitting from his fists. As he cast this power at an unseen foe, he felt the power of his foe and also fear, unremitting fear. Their weapons are thunder and lightning. They use the very elements to battle upon the skies. And he falls. Uric crashes to the ground and the victor approaches. His power is incredible and his aura unfathomable. He hears a name, a single word that casts fear into his heart. Archimedes!

"The visions you witnessed. Splendid were they not? Our rule is forever." exclaimed Kallis after Uric had awoken three days later.

"Yes Lord. We are eternal." The young man laughed, though Kallis sensed his unease.

"I will not ask what you saw my son, but do not fear the power growing within."

Uric spent many moons in study of all the large tombs Kallis kept within his secret library. He scanned for mention of this distant nemesis but found no mention. The fear drove him mad as he knew that he would need all power to face this foe.

Then he made the discovery that would change his world forever. In the secret books of Kallis he found a journal. He learned of the origins of Kallis, from a place far away from which he had been banished. He had discovered buried in a hidden tomb the bloodstones and ancient texts. Kallis had learned the arcane rights and used this to control his people. In revolt they sought to kill him, but his power was too great. Then he had fled for fear of being entombed for life.

After a ceremony of sacrifice, Uric took the bloodstones as usual to Kallis. Here Kallis would draw their power leaving what little was left to Uric. But Uric had studied well and his arts were far more advanced than Kallis knew. Using one of the incantations he had learned, Uric drew the power into himself. He cast a very different spell upon the stone and waited. One by one Kallis drew the power into himself. All that was left was the stone upon which Uric had cast his spell. Kallis placed the stone upon his forehead and began to incant. At first he felt the normal surge then something very different happened. He tried to pull the stone away but could not! He cried in anguish to Uric who merely sat and smiled. A terrible wrenching sensation ran through Kallis' body and slowly his power was drawn into the stone. As the stone fell to the floor, it glowed red and hissed as it struck the floor. Kallis fell back.

"What have you done?" he whispered as he fell to the floor as he reached for the stone. Uric stepped forward and took the stone into his hand then placed it into a small pouch.

"I am preparing for my vision Kallis. Your future has changed. One comes that is mightier than us, and I must be ready."

"But..." Kallis fell back confused. "Give me the stone. I forgive this. You are my son." he begged.

"Son? Son!" Uric screamed viciously kicking the prostrate Kallis. "I had a father, a mother and a sister! My name is Kal-az Umar. My family was butchered under your command, I am here to avenge them!" he spat.

"Liar." laughed Kallis as he struggled to his feet. "You are here for power. Whatever reason you tell yourself that is what holds sway now! The blood you seek to avenge, you draw power from now. We are the same!"

Uric paused as he considered the words he heard. He looked at the stone he had removed from the pouch. His sisters' life had been taken for such power. He wanted to smash the gem; to end this outrage. But he could not.

"We may be alike, but your dreams are petty. I seek to rule this world, to find answers to all questions."

"Let us do that together my son; there is much I can teach you." Kallis sensed that Uric could be swayed. "I will be your master no longer, merely a guide."

"I think not," muttered Uric. "For where I go you have not yet traveled, your false prophecies a means to control. Your God is but a tool to make all subservient to you. I will rule under no such pretense!"

"Then you shall be outcast like I was!" said Kallis.

"Perhaps, but you shall be dead." As Uric stepped forward, he rammed a long dagger into the stomach of Kallis. A small bloodstone encrusted in the hilt lit up as the blade cut home. As Kallis fell, Uric grabbed his hair and dragged the dying man to the chamber where he had seen his visions. "You shall die, where I was born." He threw Kallis to the floor, then stepped outside the chamber. He waved his hands in concerted movement and at once a wall appeared sealing Kallis to his fate."

Thus, Uric began his rule. Gone were the temples of Zocor. They were now simply sacrificial chambers. Uric demanded more blood to fuel his stones. To increase his power, two sacrifices were made every third day, be it man, woman or child. The Rasonites grew more fearful. Uric expended little power to hold the population in check. He needed to retain all the power he could. Soon desertions began and instead of ordering the capture of those that fled from Uric, the sacrificial offerings were increased.

But the power was growing too difficult to wield. Several times Uric had dreams that the cities would suffer earthquakes. Several speakers emerged denouncing Uric, even stating that Zocor was angry at Uric for deserting him. In a catastrophic event, Uric grew angry at hearing of a planned uprising. Such was the force of his power that a massive energy bolt flew at one of the cities, killing thousands. And soon the people marched upon his palace.

Uric sent bolts of lightning and boulders of burning rocks against the Rasonites, but still they came, driven by their faith in Zocor. Years later Uric would smile at the irony that the tool used to cower the people had also given them the strength to overthrow. As his anger grew his felt the power rising. He had drunk all the power he could from the stones. His body shook with the power he held. He ran to the courtyard of his palace having decided that he would flee to the sea. All he needed were the stones that he kept guarded on his person. As the tribesmen broke through the palace gates, Uric screamed defiance, while energy lashed out, cast from every pore of his body. The tribesmen screamed as they fell back in agony. Uric was at once upon his horse. He concentrated hard as he scanned the swelling crowd once more. With a scream he rode forward, and as almost by an invisible hand, his path was cleared as men were thrown into the air. Soon he was on open road and on his way to the harbor. He easily used the gentle persuasion of his power to gain access to a ship. Even the crew was soon under his control. Uric looked back at his homeland as they sailed away, and his thoughts turned to Hasan, and to Petra. A single tear fell down his face.

"I am sorry father." he whispered, yet his hand grasped the stone around his neck, the stone that had belonged to Kallis. As he grasped the stone, dark power coursed through his blood. "I will return, I will use guile and deceit. I will find my foe and take his power as my own." And as the power took hold Kal-az Umar was lost forever.

The knocking on the door awoke Uric. On his command of 'enter' a soldier appeared.

"Lord, the King wishes attendance."

"Very well. Leave me now." Uric commanded. He stood. As he watched the fire, his face, once more, grew solemn. His long fingers entered the pocket of his robe and found their treasure. He grasped the bloodstone fiercely.

Chapter Seven

Lionus sat slouched on his throne, the goblet of wine tipped to the side sending splashes of the claret liquid to the marble floor. A hand maiden stood nearby. Her first instinct was to rush forward and tidy the spill but times had changed in the palace. A mere whim of the King could see someone flogged or even worse, executed. She felt her heart stop as the King raised his head and fixed his uneven stare upon her.

"Get out girl." The words were barely a whisper. "You have no need to be in fear of me." Relieved, she curtseyed low and quickly departed. "No need to fear," he echoed as she left.

It had been six months to the date that Percius had left. Still, he had no news and saw deceit at every turn. Argentous was still unfound. Some called him traitor, while others believed him dead at the hands of Percius. Fewer still believed him dead at the hands of the traitors that sought to defame Percius. Lionus had thought all these thoughts, unable to believe any for a period of time. He was slowly unhinged. Cheris had tried to comfort him, the bitter conflict having died to indifference. Lionus had simply pushed her and his son, Archimedes, away. Lionus had grown to fear the boy. The power he had exhibited had finally persuaded the King that he was possessed. Only Uric kept his council now, and that was strained at his failure to locate Argentous and bring Percius to justice. How Lionus yearned for the return to war. He desired only that he would lead his men onto the field once more. But the glory was diminished; his desire to see his greatest General with his greatest hero ride into battle alongside their King was no more. In truth, he desired death, an end to the cursed thoughts that ran through his mind.

"Mama look!" Cheris looked up from her thoughts. The little girl Dianu ran towards her holding a bright purple flower. Cheris smiled. How quickly the child had taken to calling her mama. She marveled that she knew the fate of her parents yet she instinctively took Cheris as a surrogate.

"What a pretty flower. Where did you find this?" she said yet she knew full well this was in her gardens.

"Archimedes helped me pick it! He said that it was your favorite!" she giggled happily. Archimedes stood at the door, the smile on his face an open relief to Cheris. He had been so sullen these past months. The girl, Dianu, had slowly changed that as she was his first real friend. They were inseparable now.

"And so it is." Cheris took the flower and kissed the girl's cheek. "Are you not late for your lessons Archimedes?"

"I hate them mother. Father has withdrawn all my tutors in favor of Uric. He scares me sometimes. And he is always there!" By he, the boy referred to Janus. Their once strong friendship had been broken upon the mistrust surrounding Percius and Argentous. Although Archimedes would never have believed that Janus could do such things, his mother had sworn that the lies spread about her and Percius had been Janus' doing. She hinted that he may not be acting alone, but he was responsible. Thus Archimedes withdrew from the offered friendship. At first Janus had tried to appease the boy but soon discovered the boy's love and devotion to his mother far outweighed his pathetic attempts at reconciliation. Janus now treated the boy as everyone else did, with fear and discomfort.

"You must attend for me, and your father," she added as an afterthought. "I will not have Uric running to me complaining again." The rebuke was soft but to the point. Archimedes sighed and left. Dianu shouted after him and then ran to be at his side. Cheris laughed as they clumsily held hands and left for Archimedes' schooling. Alone with her thoughts again her mind turned to Lionus. How had things gone so awry? Their marriage had been consummated on strengthening his hold on the land. But they had learned to love one another. Cheris knew that she was never one to play the submissive wife. Yet Lionus had come to love her qualities, those of seeking advice when alone in chambers, or most definitely her opinion. Now that was all gone, destroyed by poisoned whispers. Her thoughts turned once more to the man who had been caught in events, whose life was in peril, if indeed he was still alive, Percius.

"Percius, May God grant you safe passage." she whispered. A crash from behind her startled the Queen. Lionus lurched through the door, his eyes blurred and beard stained red with wine. "You are not welcome here Lionus, in such a state or not!" Her voice was calm but her heart raised several beats. His face contorted in silent anguish. Words seemed to form at his mouth but could not form. He twisted to leave but Cheris heard the faintest sound.

"I am sorry." Before she could move he was gone. Her heart begged for her to follow but the memories of recent events were too strong. She stood and walked slowly to the door then gently closed the world away.

Janus sat watching Uric. The normally calm advisor was pacing his chamber floor, a concerned look upon his face.

"I cannot understand how he escaped, how we have no word of the man!"

"He is just one man Lord." answered Janus, although the question was not put to him.

"One is all it takes sometimes. One man can unite a people, I have seen this." Uric pounded his fist down upon the table. The goblets shook and fell to the floor. "He is a hero, Janus, a man of the people for the people. Our subtle ties will have no effect on them."

"He is a traitor and deserter. His fleeing proves his guilt to many. With Argentous dead and most believing Percius killed him he has lost most of his support, and the King."

"The King!" interrupted Uric. "The King lies in a drunken stupor all day. The support he had is dwindling, and there are doubters now. There are those that believe he was unstable before the seed of doubt was planted."

"But what does it matter? Lionus is finished."

"Finished? I don't need him finished, not yet. I needed Percius vanquished and Argentous the same. But I need the King strong. The war is what feeds me, the blood, the hatred and fear gives power to the stone. The King must be strong to dispel invasion. I need bloodshed not conquering. The stones grow weak."

Janus nodded, Uric had told him little of his power, but he knew the importance of the stones.

"How can the King become strong again?" Janus queried.

"I have arranged for this. Conavar has sent a force of pirates from the north. They shall be here in mere days. I need the King to see his country under attack. If this does not bring him from his malaise nothing shall. Then we shall ride to war."

"Yes my Lord. I have sent hunters to all the provinces. If Percius appears we shall know and they shall see him dead."

"Perhaps, Janus, perhaps." Uric mused.

"Archimedes you must concentrate." Uric snapped. The boy had great power but such little control. He only held semblance of control when under moments of great anxiety.

"But this isn't what my other teachers taught me!" complained the boy. He smiled at the giggle that came from Dianu in the corner of the study. Uric cast a black look and she withdrew into the shadows.

"Boy, I am not an ordinary teacher, nor you an ordinary pupil. Inside you is great power. If this is not harnessed there is no telling the damage you could do." Archimedes blanched at his words. "You could kill your Mother and the little girl. Is that what you want?" Archimedes swallowed hard and shook his head. "Then you shall learn your lessons well and pay heed to me!" The boy nodded. "Good. I have faith in you boy. You are destined for great things. Your achievements will dwarf those of your Father."

"My Father thinks me possessed." Archimedes whispered.

"There are things we cannot speak of boy, things your Father must never know. He fears you. He fears the things that you can do and the man you shall become. We must be careful as your Father is a man in great despair. If word was to reach him of this talk we could both be killed. Do you understand?" Archimedes nodded. "But Uric shall show you the way to unlock the power within your body, so you need never be afraid again. There is much said about me, boy. Much is true much is not. Believe me on this. I desire to see your power flourish and for you to take your rightful place upon the throne. I need your trust, is this given?" Archimedes thought for some time, he then looked Uric squarely in the eyes.

"I give you my trust."

Youanis sat upon the crow's nest of the Alinara. He had been a proud first mate for several years since joining the navy. He was never happier then when at sea, often volunteering to stay on board when they were in port. Times had been difficult recently. He yearned to return to open voyaging rather than the scouting missions along the coast as had been their want over the past months. He could see the crow's nest of the frigates Westrom and Killano in the distance. He knew that only a skeleton crew remained on each ship. The captain had argued against such decisions but Youanis couldn't see why. No one would dare attack Samothrace as there were six garrisons of battle trained soldiers nearby and a heavy contingent of naval crewmen all within a few miles of the dock.

The evening was still and the waters had a deep mystical appeal. The sea breeze gently caressed his face and all was calm. He heard movement below the nest and presumed that one of the crew was taking in some air. He leaned over the side to call down for a flagon of ale. As he did, an arrow spun through the air and before he could react the arrow took him in the throat. Youanis fell back. He tried to sound the alarm but his mouth filled with blood. With his dying gaze he saw them coming. A swarm of black shapes were swimming into the bay. The pirates were here.

Lionus walked the ramparts. He had dismissed his personal guards, as he hoped that the night air and the solitude would do him some good. He stood watching the bay. The sound of the gentle surf brought forth better memories of the times spent here with Cheris when they were first wed. Tears formed in his eyes as these memories clashed with the recent events and his striking the Queen.

"You have been a fool. One man can have everything, but it is nothing without being able to share." And then he saw them, silent and swift emerging from the water. At once he knew who they were; at once he knew why they were here. "Alarm!" he bellowed. "Sound the Alarm! Pirates!" His guards appeared and rushed to his side.

"Sire, get to safety." In the background a horn sounded. "We must keep you safe."

"Safe lad? There is no such place. My place is beside my men. Fetch my sword and breastplate. Send word to the watch commanders that the beach has been taken." As the two guards scurried off, Lionus felt blood surge through his veins. The months of inaction, the treachery were all forgotten. The battle King had returned!

Lionus raced down the ramparts. By now the horn had alerted most to the danger. Seasoned veterans ran from the garrisons and formed a shield wall before the palace. Lionus quickly donned his breastplate and shield once his guards had returned. Together they ran through the palace corridors, to be joined by the palace guards. Lionus saw Cheris clutching Archimedes and Dianu to her waist.

"My Queen, we are under attack. Take the children to the throne room. There are guards aplenty that I am informed will protect you." He turned to leave then halted. "Cheris. I…" Before the words were spoken Cheris lay a finger upon his lips.

"I know my King." she whispered, Lionus stared down at Archimedes and saw the cold expression. He shivered inwardly. Then he was gone.

"Damn in Sullies', what they are waiting for." Biar said to his skipper. The pirates had slowly taken their formation on the beach. In all, there were around five hundred. "What's the bastard waiting for? We are easy pickings, we are!"

"Shut up Biar." snapped the bull necked man. "We do as we are told. We wait!" Giant pyres had been lit around the palace. The light illuminated the beach, and the cover of night was no longer an ally. "He'll bite. Don't you worry. Just be ready to give the signal." At once Biar saw that the Aislan infantry moved forward, Lionus as always, was at the front. They numbered well over five thousand, more than enough to defeat the pirates. "Soon me pretties, very soon."

Lionus was on edge as the men surged forward. Something was not right. This scum would be slaughtered. Pirates were not known for open warfare Surely they had no chance at all. Had hunger driven them to such desperation? No, there were other cities that did not house such a force as Samothrace that they could attack? As the men increased pace, a murmur of their battle cry began to rise. Lionus ran with them but his mind raced. He looked to the beach, then to the cliffs overhanging the bay. Then he looked to the beach again then the bay. Thoughts continued to race through his mind. A trap! They were running into a trap.

"Halt!!!!" he screamed but for some, the roar of their cries were deafening. Lionus saw a burning arrow pierce the night sky. From the cliffs above small flecks of light appeared, hundreds, thousands, like a beach of burning sand. And then the arrows took flight. Lionus had managed to halt a good deal of his men. Yet there were many, crazed with battle lust, who were mercilessly cut down.

"Gods... how many are they?" asked a soldier beside him.

"Not nearly enough!" Lionus summoned his messengers and ordered two regiments to attack the cliffs. He knew that fighting archers on higher ground would be perilous. However, he had little choice as he needed them occupied so he could reclaim the beach. In the distance he saw long boats steaming onto the beach, and although it was dark he recognized the emblem on the flag that flowed from the boat, the flag of Ames, Conavar! Then Uric appeared and as always Janus was not far behind.

"Majesty, we have discovered eight long ships off the coast. On estimate with full crew there could be as many as three thousand men in the cliffs and on the beach."

"I don't care. Kill them all! Where are the regiments to attack the cliffs?"

"They are approaching from the western and eastern fronts. The ground is lower but the killing ground is less."

"We need them in action soon. Look, they are forming a wedge." Lionus pointed at the beach. The pirates had taken back stage and the Amesian soldiers were forming an attack position. "I need our men in single file. Form a shield wall!!" Lionus bellowed. Echoed by the orders of his officers, the men linked shields. "They shall break upon us as the sea upon rocks!" he hissed as he formed his part of the wall. "Uric, oversee the defense of the palace. And remember, no survivors but one, an Amesian officer!" Uric nodded. As Janus turned to leave with Uric, Lionus words spat out. "Not you! Your place is with the men."

Janus merely nodded and linked into the shield wall. Roars from the cliffs told Lionus that his regiments had engaged. This was a sign he had waited for. His sword rose into the night sky. "Forward, for country!!" he bellowed and the men forwarded as one.

The Amesian soldiers reacted as one. The wedge ran forward with a splitting cry. Lionus watched the approaching mass, as he anticipated impact. With a thundering crash the divided forces met. Lionus' sword lanced forward and took a man in the chest. A blade glanced off his chest plate. He took the man down with a vicious repost. Blood flowed freely from a cut to his scalp. All around he saw men dying, dismembered and bleeding. A surge of power flowed through his body. A beheaded Amesian fell before his sword. The battle had lost all form of control, and all that remained was frenzy. He turned to look for more foes.

Uric watched silently from his chamber. The small stone around his neck throbbed as Uric drank from the bloodlust of the battle. Twice now he had seen the King falter and he had used vital energies to sustain the man.

"What is happening?" a small voice asked. Uric spun round to see Archimedes.

"What are you doing here boy!" he hissed, alarmed that he had not felt his presence.

"I came to find you. What is happening to you?" Archimedes pointed at the robe under which the gem could be seen glowing.

"Nothing to do with you boy! Get back to your mother!"
The boy nodded, but he looked older, wiser, as if he knew all of Uric's secrets. He stood his ground, as if daring Uric to command him.

"I will go and find my mother then." And he was gone.

Illian, a Captain in the army, approached the King.

"Sire we have routed them. They tried to retreat to the sea but they could not cast off against the tide. There are no prisoners."

"Good. And what word from the cliffs?" Lionus replied.

"The eastern face has been cleared. Again none were left alive Sire. The western face has small pockets of resistance but they won't last long. Lord Uric has taken custody of the captured Amesian General Corel."

"Very good. Our losses Captain?" Lionus asked surveying the dead.

"Early estimation is around three hundred dead with another four that will not be fit for duty again."

The King cursed, "Very well, I will be in my chamber if needed. Once I have washed the blood from my body I will attend to the questioning of General Corel. Send word to Uric that he is not to question the General without me. And tell the surgeons that they need not attend to me until those of greater need are taken care of." Illian saluted as the King departed. He noted the man stopped to talk and embrace many of his fellow survivors along the way. How wrong could rumors be he thought. It was only yesterday they had heard he was a broken man.

"Never further from the truth!" muttered Illian and set about the tasks he had been set.

The General Corel lay in a pool of blood upon the floor, the sword jutted from his stomach like an unholy testament to his death. Uric stood watching the scene. All had developed as he had desired.

The moment interrogation began Uric sensed the tension in Lionus. In planning the attack with Conavar, the plan was for the General to be taken alive, to tell his story and be set free. Both Conavar and Uric knew this would never happen. He knew of the relationship between the two of them, and no one else did or ever would.

When Lionus had questioned the General as to where information had come from regarding the positioning of the ships in the bay, the General had told him in practiced form of a man named Percius selling the information for free travel through Ames to the far north. Such was the anger in Lionus that he had struck the man down, branding him a lair, then finally driving his sword through the unarmored General's stomach. Uric had soothed the King, and finally made him accept that Percius had betrayed him once more. Then he cast a small spell so the King became drowsy and had left to sleep.

Uric pulled the blade from the body of the General. He laughed at the man's arrogance that he would be allowed to survive.
"Percius, wherever you are, you have aided me once more."

Youanis watched the men close. Scum, most of them, he thought. Yet even here there were good men, fighting the good cause. Youanis had been forced to leave the infantry when he lost his hand in a skirmish with the Amesian cavalry. He had argued that he could fight just as well with his left arm but the General was adamant, and stated that an impaired soldier could seriously endanger his comrades. So at fifty three the former Captain returned to his village. It soon became apparent to Youanis that his fight was not over, Nomads roamed the land, attacking villages and the smaller cities. Worse still, the damned pirates attacked the harbors with ease. News was that they were even traveling inland now.

Youanis, always a man of action, quickly formed the home guard. Most were old men or young pups not wanted by the army. However there were few that for their own reasons were not at war. Cowards? Hardly, he thought. They saw action on a daily basis now, and all fought well. They lacked discipline was there only shortcoming. They also disliked taking orders from the nobles. Some were criminals or deserters that had a change of heart or conscience. Youanis prided himself on the fact that he could tell. But then Regnak had joined up. The man was skilled with the blade; more skilled than he let on. Youanis had watched the man fence. He was holding back all the time, just doing enough to be victorious. His quiet manner could not disguise the fact he was educated. His mannerisms told Youanis that. And of course he always wore the headscarf. The man also sported a dark beard. It was clear to Youanis that he was in some sort of disguise.

Youanis soon made Regnak his second in command. The respect he commanded from the men was a joy to Youanis who struggled at times with the more loutish of his force.

"Regnak, a moment." The man walked over. Youanis noted the lightness of his feet, the balance of a soldier born.
"Aye sir?" Regnak questioned.
"I've had reports of some movement near the coast. Seems that a fleet of ships are moving down coast."
"Down coast? A fleet? Pirates don't move in groups; they are more liable to cut each others throats as ours."
"Well, from what is reported there are a few pirate galleys. The rest are Amesian." Youanis saw the concern in the man's eyes.
"Traveling south? They must mean to attack Samothrace. We must send word of warning!"
"Now boy, you know there is no way we can outrun warships. But from what I gather there are a few bodies encamped around the bay. Amesian spies more than likely. They will be waiting for pick up and probably have some information that's needed."
Youanis read Regnak's mind. "I suppose it is our duty to stop them from getting this information. You seem keen to me?" Regnak nodded.
"How many on the beach?"
"Scouts say only three."
"Well if they are to be taken aboard it might be worth my while getting on board. I could scupper a ship if lucky." Regnak smiled but Youanis saw the glint of determination behind that smile.
"So be it."

The night grew cold; it always did by the sea. Youanis and Regnak had crept as close to the tents as possible. An almost inaudible whistle told them that the others were in place. With a quick nod the two men leapt over the rocks and landed gently upon the sand. Youanis notched an arrow to his bow and let it fly. The single hooded figure that stood outside the tent turned into the arrow. The point pierced his heart. Before a sound was made Regnak pulled the man down and silently finished the job. Then he pulled the hood clear of the dead man and noted his complexion.
"Amesian," he mouthed to Youanis who nodded understanding.
A brazier stood outside the tent. It was unlit to prevent it being spotted thought Youanis.
"Take them alive boys!" he whispered and at once eight men descended on the tent. Youanis and Regnak stood outside and heard the startled cries and then thudding sounds as the two men were clubbed unconscious.

Regnak saw the bodies dragged from the tent. One was Amesian but Regnak was shocked to see the other.
Youanis noticed the expression on Regnak's face but said little. Regnak rushed into the tent and Youanis quickly followed. He saw Regnak rifle through several bundles of papers before turning and rushing from the tent. He quickly grabbed hold of the non-Amesian man searching pockets until he found a scroll. Regnak quickly scanned the document and turned with rage upon the man. The figure groaned and opened his eyes. Youanis watched as the prisoner evidently recognized Regnak and tried to crawl away in terror.
"Traitor!" Rek screamed and drew his sword. As he advanced, Youanis grabbed his shoulders. But such was his rage he pushed the older man away. As the prisoner got to his feet Regnak rammed his blade into the stomach. Slowly the body slid to the floor. All who watched did so in stunned amazement. Regnak turned to the glowering Youanis.

"We need to talk, alone and now!"

"Damn right we do boy, and it had better be good!" he spat in undisguised anger.

"I have deceived you Youanis," he stated alone in the tent. "My name is not Regnak. To tell you the truth might put you in danger. But believe me I am not a deceitful man." Regnak held up two scrolls. "That man was a personal guard to Lord Uric. He carried messages that proved he has been playing nation against nation, a traitor to our King and country." Youanis merely nodded, taking in every word his companion said. "These are reports concerning our troop deployment at Samothrace, the Capitol and the borders. They state exact figures and plans for the coming months. They are signed with Uric's seal." He held up the wax embossment. "This further scroll dictates the movement of the Amesian cavalry and the whereabouts of Conavar and Roman. It seems that Uric is playing both sides against each other."

"But why?" questioned Youanis.

"I have no idea, but he must be stopped."

"How? He is the King's eyes and ears!"
"Without going into detail I cannot travel to Samothrace. I need an ally. Though Conavar is a cruel man I am sure he would be displeased to learn of this duplicity. However Romen has been an unwilling pawn. I am sure I can convince him."

"But he is deep in enemy country. You would be cut to pieces before you even got near him!"

"Not so. These reports state he is camped within a mile of the border. I could infiltrate their camp and seek him out."

"Tis madness! They will think of you as an assassin and have you killed."

"No! Romen knows me, he knows I am no assassin."

"Knows you? Who are you lad?"

"I wish I could say, truly I do. It states here that our friend out there was not to take ship but was to ride to the border and seek Conavar out with this information. Whilst the information regarding Conavar and Romen was to travel south and kill the Amesian then bury the bodies, I have to travel north."

Youanis looked at the man and knew argument would settle nothing. With a nod he declared the matter concluded.

Moments later Regnak's horse was saddled. Youanis stood before him. "Ride along the coast before cutting in. The bastard Nomads don't like the water. It will be a safer journey, though I still say it is crazy!"

"These are crazy times my friend." And he was gone.

The journey in the end was uneventful. Regnak rode by night and slept by day to avoid the perils of darkness and sleep. Only once did he meet a group of deserters intent on robbing him. These men, though, were cowards and soon departed after two of their party had lost limbs.

Regnak thought long and hard about the route he should take. He knew that approaching the Aislean border would be dangerous. He was well known amongst the troops. Disguised or not, he would soon be recognized. Had news traveled of the lies put against him? Though many might not believe him capable of such deeds, there were plenty that would sell him on profit of reward. And no doubt the King had offered handsome reward.

So Regnak set upon the route he had chosen initially. He crossed the Aislean range, a treacherous path into the mountains that would lead him to the heart of Ames. From there he knew that he could approach the Amesian border and hire on as a mercenary.

As he stood before the path leading to the mountain range, his breathe was taken away by the distant snow-capped peaks. They shone gloriously, and the beauty transfixed his glaze. For the first time in so many months he felt free.

He realized that his horse would never be able to make the crossing. So he unsaddled the mare and set her free. As he freed himself from all unneeded artifacts he began his journey. At first the road was easy, but as he climbed higher the path degenerated to almost nothing. Before nightfall, he found the path no longer existed and each step became a clumsy haul. The night came in and with it came the freezing winds. Regnak took shelter in a cave but this gave little resistance. Using his tinderbox, he fashioned a small fire, which unfortunately gave scant warmth. With the morning, after a restless night's sleep, Regnak set off again.

Day after day he climbed higher. The altitude made breathing difficult. The first flurries of snow melted against his face. As the snow worsened, Regnak had no choice but to seek shelter in a newly found cave. He scrapped together what kindling he could hold steady, and with his shaking hands, he lighted a fire.

Suddenly a great roar startled the warrior. He turned round, his sword instantly in hand. A giant bear lurched forward, its massive paws swinging in the air. His weather torn reactions failed to react and the bear's massive paw smashed into

Regnak's chest. He flew through the air and out of the cave. His hands groped almost lazily for the edge of the path but found nothing.

He fell heavily for what seemed like an age as he crashed from one outcrop to another. He knew he was dead. His body finally met with an over-hanging tree. Blood poured from his broken mouth. Regnak felt the painful scrapping of broken ribs. Soon, he passed into unconsciousness.

He awoke to flame and heat. The cave was huge and illuminations flickered across the ceiling. Regnak saw that his body had been wrapped in heavy woolen blankets. He gingerly felt for his ribs. As he gingerly explored the area, he was astounded to feel no pain. He quickly pulled up his shirt and saw not even a bruise remained.

He looked up as he heard the approach of his mysterious benefactor. An old man approached with a wide smile on his face.

"My thanks for your aid. How did you heal me?"

"I can do many things, young Percius." At the sound of his name he jumped up.

"Who are you?"

"Who am I? I have been called many names, as I can do many things. I can give you your heart's desire. And you can fulfill my dreams of vengeance."

"I am no manstool. Or whatever else you are!"

"Be still Percius and listen to what I have to say. I have many names, but I was once called Kallis. I was rich with power and wealth. I was betrayed and left for dead. And he that betrayed me took all that was mine. He has grown. He is powerful beyond your ken and beyond your power to harm. I speak of Uric."

"Uric." whispered Regnak. "If what you say is true, then I cannot harm him. How can I help you?"

"As you are now you could not. But I can arm you with weapons of great power."

Regnak sat and looked at the old man.

"Very well, speak on."

Chapter Eight

For eight years the war continued. Each side was evenly matched. Whenever ground was won, it was rarely held for long. The land was too large for sufficient forces to occupy without areas left open for reprisal.

As the troubles continued there came tales of the man Regnak, a hero in the Northern infantry. He had quickly risen to General. His skills with both blade and spear were legendary amongst his men.

When Lionus returned to the Northern borders he heard of such tales and immediately requested the presence of the warrior.

So many years had passed, Regnak thought, so much has changed. Yet, there was so little he could remember. The last night in the caves with Kallis, the old man had died, but not before giving Regnak such gifts. With a touch of his hand Regnak's hair became a golden brown, and his eyes faded to a grey color. Minor differences in his face would mean Percius would never be recognized again. And then there was the blade. It was a weapon that would never dull and that cut through stone like butter. Regnak only saw one purpose for this wondrous weapon, that the blade could kill Uric. Kallis had told him all. Regnak knew that Uric was beyond human. He was the personification of a vampire feeding off of the dead, and those that lust after death. He had agreed to meet Lionus. he hoped in doing so that Uric would be there. As he approached the King's tent his hand automatically gripped the sword's hilt tightly.

"Halt!" came a voice. "Who are you?" snapped a man. Regnak looked upon the face of Janus. His seething hatred of the man could barely be held in check.

"My name is Regnak. I have an audience with the King," he answered, barely keeping the anger from his voice.

"So you're the hero, aye?" sneered Janus, "Seen plenty of those turn to crow food."

"Tell the King I am here!" he replied as he noticed that Janus closely inspected his face.

"Do I know you? You look familiar," remarked Janus.

"No, I would remember I'm sure." lied Regnak.

With a wave of his hand Regnak was led into the tent. For sometime, as he conversed with Regnak, the King had no idea this was the man he hunted for so many years. Lionus praised Regnak and embraced him when they had finished. He commended both Regnak's courage and command. Regnak felt ill composed. For some time he had first hated the King, and then pitied the man. Once, he sought to travel south and kill Uric. However, he had encountered an Aislean regiment and wound up enlisting. He knew his skills were needed. Now in the presence of the King, he again felt pity. The once tall and proud man was laid low with the wounds of war. As he left he noted the portrait of Cheris sitting upon the King's table, his heart skipped a beat. He realized that he still felt the same.

As he left, Janus approached him.

"There is something about you I don't like and I am sure I know you." he spat.

"I know you not at all and I see plenty to dislike already," Regnak retorted.

"Do you know who I am, bastard?" Janus ranted, angrily. "I am Janus, the King's champion."

"Yes, I have heard of you."

"Do you feel fear?" taunted Janus.

"Only from the smell that comes from you!"

"Watch your mouth and be careful next time you see me!" whispered Janus as he moved closer to Regnak.

"To see you would make a change. From what I hear most of your enemies have been struck from behind."

Janus reached for his sword, but the icy steel gaze of Regnak held him in check. The two men stood in silence for some time but eventually Regnak moved on. He much regretted not removing Janus' head straight away.

"I know you," whispered Janus to his back. The stare had rekindled distant memories that he was not able to recollect but knew he soon would.

In the morning Regnak was returning from breakfast when two men accosted him. They each held knives, and sought to kill rather than rob. With ease he disarmed them. But before he could question them, they were dead with bolts through their skulls. Regnak knew this action was Janus' doing. However, he could prove nothing. He needed to know what Janus suspected — was it just a grudge or was he recognized.

Regnak journeyed down to a river to wash and swim. As he approached the water he noticed a figure closing on him from behind. He turned and faced Janus.

"I knew that I knew you." The face is different, the name is different, but you move the same. Don't you Percius!"

"Percius? Janus, you are mistaken. I am Regnak!"

"You can lie all you want but I know it is you." Regnak moved to unsheathe his sword but Janus raised his crossbow. "Death finally comes to you."

And then it started. Like a low rumbling both Janus and Regnak looked up. Through the trees in the distance they came, a whole host. The enemy fast arrived and there were thousands of them. Janus was transfixed. Regnak jumped to one knee, and came to his senses. Janus fired his crossbow. The bolt flew over Regnak's head. From his boot, Regnak pulled a long thin knife. In one swift moment the blade was free and buried in Janus' neck. As he fell, Regnak leapt forward and pulled the blade free.

"You are right you miserable scum, it is I. Know this… if I had my way your death would be so much slower!" As he hissed these words, he drew the blade across Janus' throat. The approaching forces were getting close now. Without hesitation, he ran back to the camp to raise the alarm.

Within seconds the enemy was in the camp. Tents were scattered as foot soldiers began to panic. Regnak and a small force of men armed with iron hook spears stood their ground against the onslaught. Carnage reigned as horse and rider fell. More and more Aislean infantry found their feet and began to drive the raiders back. From the swirling dust, a thundering march could be heard. And then, from the mist, Lionus emerged and rode forward, sword in hand screaming in attack. From the enemy pack a rider appeared. Regnak recognized the plume of Romen and the two Kings met in battle. Romen's huge battleaxe thudded against Lionus' shield which toppled the Aislean King to the ground. But before a death blow could be landed, Regnak leapt forward. With a spring, his blade sliced through Romen's stirrups. The King fell heavily. Regnak regained his footing as two raiders were upon him with dazzling speed. However, with an enchanted blade, they both fell, screaming.

He turned to see Romen about to drive his axe down upon Lionus. Lionus kicked out which took Romen's feet away. As they both struggled to their feet, the weight and slow speed of Romen's bigger weapon proved costly. Lionus thrust his sword through the stomach of the invading King. The axe fell to the ground. Then, as Lionus ripped the blade out, Romen fell head first to the ground. A retreat signal was heard but the Aislean troops had recovered now. Their retreats were blocked and the slow extermination of the enemy began.

Regnak looked into this distance. Although his eyes may have deceived him he saw a lone figure standing upon a distant rock formation. The man was Uric.

He rapidly saddled his horse and dashed through the trees.

Lionus struggled back to his tent. His valet stripped the armor from his body, and began to press cold compresses against his many wounds.

"Boy, are you ready to go home," he smiled to his valet. "I think I am," was the reply.

The King returned triumphant as word of the death of Romen spread. Only Conavar remained now to challenge the rigors of war that had been savage. The population had dwindled. Once great cities lay in ruins. Lionus knew that come next summer he needed to rebuild rather than destroy. He would seek a truce with Conavar, giving both leaders time to rebuild.

Lionus' thoughts though were now directed towards Cheris. How he desperately missed her, her council, and her love. He had been back in Samothrace for three weeks before he saw her again. She was polite but distant. Her hostility had been directed at him when he ignored his son, and Lionus disliked and feared the fey boy.

"Cheris, I know that you cannot forgive me easily, but Romen is dead. The end to the war might have finally begun. All I desire is to rebuild — rebuild our country, rebuild our lives. Please let us put past indiscretions behind us. We can be happy again."

Cheris looked upon the King. It seemed that without doubt he was sincere. But the love she had once felt had diminished. The duty she felt towards her country was a distant memory. The events surrounding Percius, so many years ago, still plagued her thoughts. The King's attitude towards Archimedes had never changed. She knew that she would never feel safe again in the King's company.

"Lionus, long and hard have I thought on this. Though my heart might tell me different, my head remains as ever steadfast. We have been through too much for things ever to be the same. Your future lies in the field of battle rather than by my side, or by the side of our son."

"The boy is a demon!" he hissed, "You saw what he did to me. How can you deny this?"

"He is gifted, nothing more, nothing less. Even your snake Uric says so!" Lionus rose in anger, his hand as ever snatching the flagon of wine to his lips.

"One day you shall come before me and beg forgiveness Cheris. On that day I shall remind you of this conversation!"

"I shall never lie prostrate before you again!" Cheris shouted as the King departed.

The kiss was sweet and long. Archimedes felt like he was floating on air. Delyse held him tight, in her arms. He felt no fear and the many questions that plagued his thoughts were gone.

"In your arms the world seems such a peaceful place. One would never know of the war."

At the mention of the war Delyse stiffened. At sixteen, Archimedes would soon take his place in the recruits. As Prince he could withdraw. But Delyse knew Archimedes would never do this, not to shame himself or to give his father more cause for consternation.

"I feel like I love you my princess." he whispered. A sudden clasp of his shoulder made Archimedes turn. Dianu stood and watched them with tears running down her face. She turned and ran. Archimedes looked at Delyse.

"Go to her Archimedes. You need to talk to her now." With a nod and a quick kiss he was off.

"Dianu wait!" he shouted, his athletic frame caught her with ease.

"Leave me alone; go back to your strumpet!" she cried as she wrestled from his grip.

"Do not speak of Delyse that way. It is not her fault I feel as I do."

"Why! You know I love you." she sobbed against his chest.

"And I you. You are my sister, my best friend!"

"But no more than that!" she said between gulps of teary breath.

"I have never felt that way; I have never knowingly given that impression."

"You have, you have! Mother said so!"

"Mother knows of the love I feel for you. She also knows of the love I feel for my sister, be it blood or of the heart."

"But I need more. I love you Archimedes! If she wasn't here, you would feel the same! I know it!"

Archimedes took Dianu's head in his hands.

"Dianu. However I feel for Delyse does not change how I feel for you. You are my sister. It can be no other way." Dianu tore away from his hands. His heart felt hollow as the girl spun away crying. He thought about calling after her but realized he had little choice. She needed time and space. He saw Delyse walking through the gardens. As ever his spirits were lifted.

Lionus struggled along the long winding passageway and lurched from wall to wall. The wine he had consumed drove him on. The burning shame of rejection fueled his every step. Through a parapet he saw Dianu running across the gardens. The sight of her young lithe body sent shivers through him. Anger and lust overcome him. He would have her, if the Queen was to deny him, and no other would. He crept along the wall and watched the girl climb the steps then enter her chamber.

"I feel so bad." muttered Archimedes. Delyse took his hand.

"You have to tell her, for her sake, as much as your own. Her illusion may be shattered but at least she has her future now. If her misconception had continued you might have robbed her of that. If anyone should feel bad, Archimedes it is I. I am the one who has robbed her of her dreams, of her love." Delyse head bowed. Archimedes saw the moon sparkle in her eyes and as ever he was captivated by her beauty.

"I will seek my mother's permission for your hand." With her father slain in the war he knew he needed only his parent's approval. "She will convince father. I fear he would deny me any happiness."

"It is his fear speaking, Archimedes. He knows of your strength."

"It is far more than that my love. He is a changed man. Though we were never close, the man of the people is long gone. I fear for all our futures."

Delyse leaned forward, as her lips brushed against Archimedes. She felt his body relax.

"What is it my Prince?" Archimedes began to shake in her arms. The trembling was accompanied by a glazed look in his eyes. Then at once it was over. He slumped forward. Delyse took hold of his body.

"Dianu," he whispered, "She is in great danger." As he regained his strength, he lifted from Delyse's embrace. "I must go now! Fetch my mother now to Dianu's rooms." Delyse's mouth opened to speak, to question, but the earnest look in his face gave her all the answers she needed. Archimedes ran from her into the night.

Lionus crept along the corridor, and with every step, lust invigorated his body.

"Why I am skulking?" he asked himself aloud. "Am I not the King!" he shouted angrily. Two guards were walking along the walkway. He commanded them as he spoke. "I am entering these rooms. No one is to enter, no one, on pain of death," he slurred. While the guards shot quick glances at each other, they quickly nodded in salute. Lionus walked to the chamber door and smashed it inwards.

Dianu sat by her dresser brushing her hair. The tear tracks of her bitter parting from Archimedes had now washed away. But the stains on her heart would never fade, she thought. A sudden crash startled her. She turned to see the King striding towards her.

"My Lord," she began as he struck her violently.

"Shut up whore. You and my bitch wife spend many hours talking and laughing at me behind my back no doubt. You have shown me little respect since I took you into my palace. It is time for you to earn your place." Lionus hissed and pulled the girl to her feet.

"Lord, what ill have I caused?" she cried.

"Nothing your body cannot put right!" He grabbed the neckline of her dress and ripped it away. Outrage replaced fear in the young girl. With all her strength she dug her nails into the Kings face. She ripped her nails downwards and drew long lines of blood. She screamed at the top of her voice, as she pleaded for help while she tried to avoid Lionus' clutching hands.

Outside the chamber, the two guards looked at one another. Each dsplayed grim expressions. Each was in despair. One reached the handle of the door but the other simply placed his hand over the handle and shook his head. They knew their place. With any interruption on their part, the King would see them hanged.

"Whore!" bellowed Lionus as her threw a mirror at Dianu. The edge cracked off her head which caused her to fall as the mirror shattered at her feet. Lionus was upon her half naked form. He ripped at her corset. He slapped her hands away and then he slaped her face, Dianu's hand grasped for a piece of the broken mirror. As she twisted, mirror in hand, she drove the shard into the King's arm. He roared in anger then grabbed the girl around the throat and lifted her into the air. He threw her to the bed, with his hands still around her neck. His hands throttled the life from her.

Archimedes ran towards Dianu's quarters. In despair he saw the two guards and heard the commotion within.

"Move." he ordered, his voice dark and cold.

"We cannot," stuttered one of the guards.

"Move now or I shall send your soul screaming into the netherworld," Archimedes spat. Neither guard disbelieved the Prince as they moved aside. Archimedes burst through the door. His breathe was frozen in anguish as he saw his father lying over Dianu with his hands choking the girl.

"NNOOOOOOOOOOOOO!!!!" he screamed. He grabbed his father and threw him to the ground. He saw the dark bruising around the girls' neck. He drew from his memory and the healing of Janus as Archimedes knelt before the girl. But as his power surfaced, it was immediately dispelled. His healing powers were of no use here. His sweet Dianu was already beyond even his power. The girl was dead,

"Dianu, please come back. You can't be dead. I'm sorry. I love you. We can be together. Please come back...don't be dead, please." The pitiful whimpering was followed by slow tears falling from his face to Dianu's. He finally just whispered, "I'm sorry."

"Now you know pain boy," chuckled the drunken King. "Now you know suffering."

Archimedes rose to his feet. The distress and fraught emotion were replaced by an uncompromised, cold anger. He felt his body tense. This time his body welcomed the righteous hatred that flooded through his very being.

"Pain, father? I will show you pain." Archimedes raised his hand and Lionus was lifted into the air. He floated there, a small whine of fear emitting from his mouth. As Archimedes closed his fist a terrible cracking sound reverberated around the chamber. Lionus' body went into spasm as his bones began to break. "Is that pain, father, is that suffering!" Lionus' face contorted in pain as he tried to speak from his shattered jaw. "Now die you bastard!" Archimedes brought down his fist which then thundered against his thigh. Blood exploded from the eye sockets, ears, nose and mouth of Lionus. The dead body of the King fell to the floor. The two guards rushed in. They stood frozen as they look at the ruined body of their King. Archimedes' cold stare lay upon them.

"So you would stand guard over this? Is your duty to your King so precious you would see this girl murdered?"

"We did our duty." stammered one guard. "It was a King's order."

"Very well. I am your King now, and I request one thing — your lives." The words were devoid of emotion. With a piercing stare the guards both clutched at their throats. As Archimedes clenched his jaw both men fell to the ground. A gurgling sound escaped as their throats were crushed and the life torn from their bodies. "Know that this is my justice."

Cheris and Delyse burst into the room. Both stood shocked at the scene before them. Archimedes did not notice their arrival. He knelt before Dianu and gently covered her body.

"I am sorry. You are free from hurt now." he whispered.

Chapter Nine

Cheris and Delyse were surprised to see the body of Lionus crumpled and dead lying on the floor. By the death of Lionus, Archimedes would now be the King. While he continued to tenderly rock the body of Dianu in his arms, Archimedes looked up at his mother. He whimpered, "I didn't mean to kill my father, but when I saw what he did to Dianu, I could not control what I did. I loved my father. Yet he had no right to take the life of Dianu, even if he was King. He killed something I dearly loved, so now I guess I will take my punishment like a man." He said all that while tears streamed down his face like an uncontrollable fountain of water.

Cheris and Delyse looked at each other. Then Cheris said, "I can't allow anyone to know the truth about what happened here. You know as well as I that Archimedes was justified in his actions and Lionus was wrong. He took an innocent life so we must hide the truth of what happened here. Archimedes is King now, and we must take action to protect this. "Delyse, help me drag the body of Lionus to the terrace, and we will throw the body over the terrace. Everyone will think he fell. With his drunken ways, no one will question this."

So, Delyse and Cheris both grabbed a leg, and dragged the body of Lionus to the terrace where they threw the heavy body over. After that was done, Cheris cautioned, "What happened here today must be forgotten, never to be spoken of again. This must be a secret we are to carry to the grave!"

Delyse then ran to Archimedes, as he still cradled the body of Dianu. Delyse put her arms around Archimedes and said, "My King, I know you are hurt, but now you have greater responsibilities to face. You are the King now! So, take my hand so you can leave this awful scene of death. Everyone will know Lionus killed Dianu while trying to rape her. When he realized he had killed her, he tried to get away in a drunken stupor. In his haste he fell and the fall killed him. So come my King!"

Archimedes stood still as he looked down at his beloved Dianu and said, "In a way this was my fault. Dianu loved me and I could not return the kind of love she had for me. I loved Dianu like a sister. My father had no right to do what he did. I am not sorry for what I did. I was his judge. He got what I think he deserved!" Then Archimedes took the hand of Delyse, and along with Cheris, the three left the room.

The first order of business for the new King was to prepare for the funerals of Dianu and Lionus. It is an Atlantean tradition that their bodies must be presented to the God within forty-eight hours. So it was decided by the new King, that the bodies would be offered to the God at the same time, murderer and victim together. They would be set a sail, one behind the other. The funerals would occur first, then the coronation of a new King would take place.

The next day, Cheris went to the quarters of Archimedes to escort him to the ocean where the funerals would take place. Cheris requested, "I know this is hard for you my son, but you must speak. Your subjects will expect this of you, my King!" So, Archimedes, escorted by his mother and Delyse, went to the ocean.

He stood on a scaffold and was cheered by his subjects. One could see the pride as it shone on the face of Cheris. Archimedes first spoke over the body of his father. "My father, the King, was a very worried man. What he did was wrong. He was not the man he once was. War and the fruit of the vine got the best of this once great man. He can't be held accountable for his actions. He was a sick man, and now he is released from all that plagued him. Now, I present his body to the God." On that, the body of the old King was set ablaze then put on the ocean.

Now Archimedes looked down on the body of his beloved Dianu. He mumbled softly, "My sister, my friend, my long life companion. So unjustly her life was extinguished by the old King. All I can say is, I present her body to the God and part of my heart goes with her." Then her body was also set ablaze, and set sail across the ocean.

Once done, the royal family headed back to the castle to now prepare for a coronation.

After the royal family got back, Cheris looked at Archimedes and said, "The solemn is over with. Now we plan for a happy occasion, one already scheduled to take place tomorrow. You may think this is fast, but we are at war, and your coronation is badly needed so the enemy realizes you are the true King."

Archimedes looked at Cheris, and replied, "Mother, you are so right! I know my duty to my people and to my country. But it is so hard to be happy after what transpired between my father and Dianu. Yet you are so right! The coronation will take place in the morn!"

The sun shone on the face of Archimedes through the window in his bed chambers, and woke him to his day, as a prince. On that day he took his rightful place on the throne as King. As he got out of bed, Cheris, was already up making preparations for the day. She appeared very excited, because she had waited for that day since Archimedes' birth. Archimedes told one of the servants to get his mother, because with her help, they would choose an appropriate outfit to wear for the coronation.

The servant found Cheris and told her of the wishes of the new King. Cheris made her way toward his chambers, followed by servants with food and drink for breakfast. Archimedes and Cheris chose to have breakfast on his terrace, so they could enjoy some of the beautiful day.

On the terrace, the two had a breakfast of fruit and fish. Cheris said, "My son, on this day, you will make me so proud! You are actually going to fulfill your destiny to be crowned King. I know the coronation is just a formality, but an important one especially because of the war. Your enemies will then know you are truly the King. Your word is as strong as that of your father. The priest of the God had just a short time to prepare for this, but this is a necessary act for your subjects and your country."

Archimedes looked at his mother and replied, "M'Lady, your words are but the truth. I just hope I make you proud, and I hope I am as good a King as my father once was."

The two retired to his chambers so Cheris could find appropriate attire for Archimedes. Cheris looked through the clothes and eventually decided on a red and black outfit. The black was to represent the mourning of those that had passed and the red was to signify strength which was needed for Archimedes to rule his subjects and his country.

After Cheris made her selection for Archimedes, she went back to her chambers to make a selection for herself. The attire was very important, as all subjects would see the royal family.

After a while, Cheris returned to the chambers of Archimedes. She wore a pastel green gown with a light yellow train. She posed gorgeous, regal and beautiful. Archimedes was done in full royal attire. Cheris said, "My son, you already look like the King. This is just a formality. I must leave you now, and take my place in the temple. When the time is right, your servants will take you to your horse and carriage that will bring you to the temple. I am very proud of you, my son!" And with a kiss on his forehead, Cheris departed.

Soon, a knock sounded from the door of Archimedes. He told them to enter. Then the servants escorted him to his carriage which was white trimmed in gold and pulled by six white horses. It was open so that the subjects could see Archimedes as he made his way to the temple.

Upon arriving at the temple, the coach stopped right in front. As Archimedes, stepped down from the coach, he was met by a cheering crowd of his subjects who threw flowers as he walked by. Once inside the temple, he was led to a room to wait for the ceremony to begin.

Soon, one of the temple workers came to get him. The ceremony had already begun. The procession began first. Leading the procession was a boy about twelve years old who carefully carried an ornate crown. After the young boy, came some of the priests of the temple followed by Archimedes himself. Above the procession in the royal box, a proud Cheris looked on with Delyse by her side.

Archimedes reached the altar to the God. Here, he bowed in reverence, as the archbishop took over. The high priest began the ceremony:

Sirs, I here present unto you

King Archimedes

your undoubted King

Wherefore all you who are come this day

to do your homage and service.

Are you willing to do the same?

Archimedes kneeling said to the high priest, "Yes, I do in the name of the God!" The high priest continued,

Sir, is your Majesty willing to take the Oath?

Archimedes answered,

I am willing,

The Archbishop shall minister those questions while the King, having a book in his hands, shall answer each question as follows:

Archbishop: Will you solemnly promise and swear to govern the People of Atlantis to any of them belonging or pertaining, according to their respective laws and customs?

Archimedes: I solemnly promise so to do.

Archbishop: Will you to your power cause Law and Justice, in Mercy, to be executed in all your judgments?

Archimedes: I will.

Archbishop: Will you to the utmost of your power maintain the Laws of God and the true profession of the Gospel?

Will you to the utmost of your power maintain in Atlantis, established by law?

Will you maintain and preserve inviolably the settlement of the Temple of Atlantis, and the doctrine, worship, discipline, and government thereof, as by law established in Atlantis?

And will you preserve unto the Bishops and Clergy of Atlantis, and to the God there committed to their charge, all such rights and privileges, as by law do or shall pertain to them or any of them?

Archimedes: All this I promise to do

Archimedes then rose and accepted a sword from the archbishop. Then he said:

Our gracious King:

to keep your Majesty ever mindful of the law and the Gospel of God

as the Rule for the whole life and government of Princes,

we present you with this Book,

the most valuable thing that this world affords.

And the archbishop shall continue:

Here is Wisdom,

this is the royal Law,

These are the lively Oracles of God.

As the book of the laws of God was handed to Archimedes, the ceremony concluded with the crown being placed on his head. Archimedes then looked at all his loyal subjects in the temple. Then, as the new King, he made his way back to his carriage.

As he reached his carriage, his subjects outside the temple cheered the new King. On that day there would be a celebration throughout the land.

Several weeks passed since the coronation of Archimedes. He inherited everything in the kingdom from his father, including his father's personal advisor, Uric. If there ever was a 'yes' man, his name would have been Uric. He told the new King everything he wanted to hear, while all the time, secretly, Uric planned the demise and stress for the young King. Uric was now the personal advisor to King Archimedes which was just where the swine wanted to be.

Cheris knew the true actions of Uric, but only based on her feelings. She had no legitimate proof of any of this from the man she so distrusted and disliked. All she could do was try to warn her son of what she suspected, and try to guide her son against his personal advisor. Still she protected her son like a mother lioness would protect her young.

One of the days of the new King's reign, he decided he wanted to take Delyse sailing, even though there had been warnings of an impending storm. Yet as he looked out from his terrace, Archimedes saw no storm clouds, only the beautiful warm sunshine. Archimedes said to his mother, "Delyse and I will be fine. Stop worrying mother, I am skilled in sailing, and there is not a storm cloud in the sky. And even Lord Uric said I should take advantage of this beautiful day!"

Cheris looked at the King and replied, "Son, I know you think my worries are uncalled for and I am just your mother, but men coming in from the sea have said, it is a miracle they are alive and that they survived the massive storm they encountered. They even took the time to come tell us this at the palace. Naturally that poor excuse of a man, Uric, would tell you to go. When are you going to learn not to trust that swine? But, you are the King, and I am only your mother. I am sure you know best!"

Archimedes was King, but he, like any other boy that made his own decisions for the first time. So, with a quick kiss on the Cheris' cheek, he took his leave to get Delyse. They would make their way toward the docks.

Archimedes found Delyse in the royal gardens. He told her of his intent, and together they headed for the docks. Over the last few weeks Archimedes and Delyse had become very close. Even many subjects had noticed the closeness between the two. Some wondered if maybe there might be a new Queen on the horizon.

The pair soon reached the docks where Archimedes' sail boat lay in wait. When they arrived, Delyse carefully helped him into the boat. Then a very confidant Archimedes sat sail. As they sailed past the harbor, Archimedes' heart skipped a beat as the warm sea breeze blew through the long dark hair of Delyse. Archimedes thought to himself that Delyse had the beauty of a goddess. He couldn't help but notice the outline of her thin body, as her guaze-like attire blew in the breeze.

Archimedes had thought long and hard about asking Delyse to be his Queen. Yet he hesitated because he was also engrossed and caught up in the awful war that now plagued the whole continent of Atlantis.

But for now, Archimedes just thought about the situation at hand as he looked toward a smiling Delyse. While the two were enjoyed each other's company, they hardly noticed the black storm clouds starting to billow in.

The once calm seas became violent and savage. Horizontal rain came in torrents, stinging the skin as the two searched for a way out. Sharp lightning sparked over the dark stormy sky, while the thunder made a deafening sound. By now, the small sailboat was being thrown side to side. Archimedes did his best to keep the boat afloat.

Then like an answer to a prayer, the two saw a small island on the horizon. Using all his might, Archimedes tried to sail the small boat in the direction of the island. Visibility was down to a minimum because of the torrential rain.

Suddenly they heard a big thud as the small boat ran ashore.

They thanked God they were still alive. The two left the boat, hand in hand as they tried to find some sort of shelter. It seemed they were lucky enough to find one of the small uninhabited islands which was just outside the Bay of Atlantis.

They walked for awhile and sought shelter for themselves under trees. Then they saw what looked like a cave. They headed toward the cave for the shelter they desperately needed. As they entered the dark and damp cave, Archimedes realized that for the moment he and Delyse were finally safe and at least out of the storm. Both were wet and cold, but alive. They stayed near the entrance of the cave, so they could take adantage of whatever daylight was left.

They both collapsed into each other's arms, exhausted. Now all they could do was wait for the storm to pass. After they slept for awhile, the two awakened to the sound of rumbling thunder, that signaled that the storm wasn't yet over. Delyse got as close to Archimedes as possible. She was cold so she used his body warmth to stay as warm as she could.

Archimedes was so proud of the fact that he could help Delyse as he held her close. He looked at her beautiful face, and once again his heart skipped a beat. He felt as tall as a mountain as he held his possible Queen in his arms.

Delyse still shivered as she looked at Archimedes and said, "I thank you Sire, for trying to keep me warm. You are such a good person. You know, I could stay like this forever. I guess you know I am starting to fall in love with you?"

Archimedes looked at Delyse, and smiled ear to ear. Then he said, "Delyse, I think you know I feel the same without saying a word! I trust you as I do my mother. But one thing really troubles me. Sometimes this power that I possess really scares me. Just as my father did, I become so enraged that I have no control over what I do. This really scares me! I like to be in control, but it seems at times, this power I possess is in control instead."

Delyse looked at Archimedes and replied, "Sire, this power is part of you. I am sure in time you will learn how to control this thing. The power makes you unique in who you are. I am starting to love you wholly and completely. And as this is being a part of you, how could it be bad?"

Archimedes kissed Delyse on her forehead as he embraced her. Suddenly they heard a noise outside the cave, like footsteps. Could it be a patrol coming to find the King and Delyse? Archimedes motioned to Delyse to be quiet. He told her, "I am going to sneak outside to see if they are forces from my army or the forces of your father the duke, or just exactly who they are."

Archimedes left a knife with Delyse. He quietly crept outside so as to not let on to those outside that they were in the cave. It was still raining, but it had slowed a bit, making visibility a little better. He was very careful not to make any noise as he made his way through the brush and foliage to see what he could see.

Then, in an instant, Archimedes saw a group of men. They were wearing rags and very dirty, so he knew they're not of his forces or that of Delyse's father. He recognized these men as cutthroats and pirates. He also knew he must get back to Delyse to protect her. He knew that if these men found her they would do unspeakable things to her. He knew he must do his utmost to protect her.

As he tried to get back to the cave through the brush, Archimedes got caught. One of the men displayed himself to be the leader as he exclaimed, "Now, what do we have here? From the looks of your clothes, you are royalty. Holding you should bring a tidy sum!" Then one of the other men joined them with Delyse in hand.

The leader said, "Well now, an added touch just for our pleasure!" Then another of the scoundrels grabbed Delyse by her hair and roughly kissed her. Archimedes was enraged as he shouted, "I am warning you for your own good to let her go!" The leader casually replied, "Just what exactly do you think you are going to do? You are but one man against all ten of us. It seems we have the advantage!" Without another word Archimedes drew his sword and began engaging the nomads in battle. He then yelled to Delyse, "Run! Hide until everything is all right!" Delyse did not need to be told twice. She did as she was directed without any hesitation.

Archimedes was an excellent swordsman. As such, he tried his best to threaten the ragged tagged men off, but there were just too many. A nomad's sword stroke hit the side of Archimedes' cheek, drawing blood. Archimedes felt the blood as it trickled down his cheek which caused him to become really angry. With Delyse looking on from the brush, Archimedes became a different person.

No words were uttered. He didn't move any part of his body. But five men flew into the air. Their bones broke just like Lionus' did. Then they fell to the ground like a crumpled heap of clay. Next, the other men were thrown against the rocks that made up the cave, which instantly killed them. Delyse saw that they was no more danger and ran to the protective arms of her King.

Then they heard their names called, and ran toward the sound. It was the forces of Archimedes. He and Delyse now knew they were really safe. They had survived their incredible ordeal.

Meanwhile in the country of Ames, Regnak had just discovered the reason he went into hiding, was no more. King Lionus was dead. The threat no longer remained. He could now reclaim his true identity as Percius. No longer did he have to hide. All those years, the passion and love he felt for Cheris still burned within.

The news had really caught Regnak off guard, as he had consumed himself in battle strategies and the war. The longing he felt, the nervousness of the anxiety over the thought of Cheris, surfaced once again. He knew that Archimedes was now the King, and that the two of them once shared a special friendship. Archimedes had once loved Percius, and Percius knew the new King would not harm him.

With that thought in mind and from that day forth, Regnak was no more. He now claimed his true identity as Percius! He decided he would go back to Samothrace because he so wanted to see Cheris again. Something he once thought to be impossible, could now become a reality.

The love and passion he embraced for Cheris was like an unending fire within his soul. He knew he must take his chances and go to Samothrace. He prayed that Cheris still felt the same. Percius remembered the passion from the last kiss the two shared when he was forced to flee for his life.

Percius now summoned his second in command, a man named Dimitri. This warrior had been loyal to him since the beginning. Dimitri came into his tent and saluted him because he was his superior. Percius said, "Dimitri, you have been a true friend to me since the beginning. You know of my true identity. It has been an honor fighting beside such a formidable warrior, but I must take my leave. King Lionus is dead and I must go to Samothrace to see the Queen. I must learn what fate has in store for me there. I turn the men over to you. I know you will lead them in the right direction."

Dimitri bowed to Percius and said, "It has been my honor to serve with you, and I hate to see you go. But you must follow your heart. I have a wife and my love for her is deep, so I know how you feel. I will tell the men you were called away my friend. I will do my best to lead the men in the right direction. My Lord, it has been an honor! Be careful and God speed to you!" Then the two warriors grabbed each others arms, as that like a warrior's hand shake. Then

Percius took his leave.

Percius quickly mounted his steed and he was on his way back to Samothrace.

He took a path along the shoreline. While he was admiring the beauty of the ocean, he saw something that appeared out of the norm. He rode his horse to the top of a hill for a better look.

From the top of a hill, Percius couldn't believe his eyes. On the ocean was a fleet of at least one thousand ships. He tried to see the mast flags that would tell him of their loyalty.

It appeared that the ships were flying a red flag with a black crow in the center. The flag looked very familiar to Percius, but he just couldn't place it. This really bothered him, as he thought, 'what on earth were all of those ships for?'

Still staring at the ships, Percius tried to search his mind in an effort to remember where he had seen that flag before. Whoever those ships belonged to had a mighty powerful force.

Percius decided to move on as the anticipation of what awaited him in Samothrace had his stomach in knots. As he continued his journey, it suddenly dawned on him where he had seen the flag before. A red flag, with a single black crow was that of Uric, the swine of a man, who was responsible for his downfall. Uric was the evil one who had put untruthful ideas into the head of King Lionus. If Percius had his way, he would strangle the life out of this traitor with his bare hands.

So it seemed that those ships were loyal to Uric and were probably there to do his evil bidding somewhere. The burning question in the mind of Percius was where were they from and where were they going?

If only he could figure that out! If only he could tell the new King what Uric had planned. Percius ran words through his mind to himself. He would wait until he got to Samothrace, then he would personally confront Uric.

Chapter Ten

Now that Percius saw that all the ships flew the flag of Uric, he decided he couldn't leave the country of Ames. He was a key witness to identifying all those ships that evidentially were going to try to invade the country. He felt a responsibility to Ames as this land had been his home for a number of years. Because he was the man he was, he sensed that if he left now, he would be leaving the country in a vulnerable situation.

Percius had the utmost faith in his second in command, Dimitri, and knew he was more experienced as a warrior in a leadership position. He decided to put his journey back to Samothrace on hold for a short time. If he were to leave Ames now, and an enemy of the country attacked and won, he just couldn't live with himself.

So, he decided to return to his troops in the north, and help them one more time. It's not that he didn't think that Dimitri wasn't qualified, but there were so many troops. To beat all of those forces would require certain expertise, the expertise of a leader. That leader was Percius. So he mounted his horse once more and headed back to his troops.

As Percius approached the encampment, he noted that the troops were prforming their everyday chores. Dimitri spotted Percius when he arrived and followed him into the tent to make strategic war plans. Once inside, Dimitri questioned him. "I thought you were off to Samothrace. Why m'Lord did you return?"

Percius looked at Dimitri. "I was on my way until I saw a massive fleet of ships, apparently loyal to Uric. I believe that were sent to invade Ames. I just couldn't leave our troops. There were so many of the potential enemy! If we were to engage these troops in battle, it would be a lost cause. It would become a blood bath just waiting to happen. I just couldn't leave you or the men at this time. I came back to have the men withdraw. I realized that facing all these forces, would surely mean death. Our men would be outnumbered easily three to one. I want the men to withdraw."

Dimitri replied, "You think the only course of action is to withdraw?"

Percius answered, "You didn't see what I saw. There were thousands of ships, carrying thousands of troops. To engage these forces would mean inevitable suicide. My men have families and lives to go back to. Falling in a fair battle is one thing. But to send the men to a sure death — I couldn't live with myself. Yet I have another idea which may benefit us in the future."

"If I can make Lord Conavar join our cause, fight with us side by side, we just might have a chance of beating the troops of Uric. I will seek to end the differences between Lord Conavar and myself. This move may very well benefit our cause." Percius then summoned a courier to take a message to Lord Conavar regarding his intentions.

Meanwhile in the main tent of Conavar's encampment, the worries of the war were starting to get to him. In the middle of his tent, was a table with papers strewn everywhere. He poured over the papers and maps trying to come up with a new battle strategy.

Suddenly he heard a commotion outside. It was Percius' courier. Ogden, second in command to Conavar received the message and brought it inside. As Ogden entered the tent, he uttered, "M'Lord, it is a message from Regnak. I am curious to see what this renegade wants."

Conavar read the note aloud. It said that Regnak wished to create an alliance. Conavar wadded up the note and threw it to the ground, laughing as he did. "Regnak takes me for a fool. An alliance? What type of trickery is this? Conavar thinks that Lord Uric is sending troops to his aid, when in reality the troops of Uric are coming here to invade."

Conavar trusted Uric. He had no way to know of the deception Uric presented. But Conavar still had faith that Uric would send troops to help him. With the extra troops expected to come, that would surely mean a much needed win for Conavar. He thought that the note he received was part of some elaborate plan to ensure a win.

So Conavar inadvertently paid no attention to a truce offered from Percius. Why should he when he thought that Uric's troops were coming to help him.

Percius waited to hear word from the courier he had sent to Conavar. Soon the courier came back and reported that Conavar had disregarded his idea for an alliance. Percius shook his head from side to side, as he guessed Conavar was a fool. All the while, Percius and his men were getting ready to flee.

Percius had done little research on the flag the forces were flying. He was not familiar with the design and the yellow flag displayed at half moon. He found out soon that they were Jahir, warriors from a land far from Atlantis. It was a land once ruled by Uric.

He had heard of their way on the battlefield. They took no prisoners. They killed all except for the women and children, which they took to serve as slaves. Since his forces would be outnumbered and considering their reputation for being merciless, Percius figured the best thing to do was to retreat. There was no shame in hiding.

Percius figured to move his troops south, far away from the Jahir. He had no way of knowing that some of the Jahir had already come ashore and were making their way inland.

He would not be apprised of this until the scout he sent returned. Percius also had sent a courier to Archimedes to warn him of the impeding danger from the Jahir. He sent the courier as Regnak. It wasn't the right time to tell Archimedes his true identity.

Soon he heard his scout's horse coming to the encampment. The scout dismounted and went directly to Percius. he saluted and said, "M'Lord, the enemy troops have landed and they are making their way inward. It seems they are headed north. That is all I saw. I have no idea what they are up to!"

Percius thanked the scout for his keen observations. He had no trouble figuring out what they were going to do as they headed north. The forces of Conavar camped toward the north. So, it was very clear what their intentions were.

He thought to himself, what a proud and stupid man Conavar was. But since was now quite certain of what the Jahir were up to, he contemplated the possibility of an ambush, maybe near Conavar's encampment. Maybe with the forces of Conavar, along with his own forces, they might have a slight chance. Withholding the element of surprise was a mighty powerful advantage. Percius knew what was about to happen. He planned to help Conavar whether he approved it or not.

He knew the encampment lay between two cliffs, somewhat as in a valley. A Jahir ambush would be perfect for this would slow down their attack. Possibly it would give Conavar and his troops a little more time to escape, or to grasp a battle strategy.

Percius summoned Dimitri. With Dimitri at attention, Percius said, "There has been a change of plans. Instead of us retreating, I have decided that we are going to help Conavar. You know his encampment lies between two cliffs. Get the men ready to do battle. Part of the troops I will take and plan an ambush from one of the cliffs. I want you to take the other half of the men, and prepare to attack the enemy from the other cliff."

Dimitri saluted smartly and replied, "M'Lord, I hear and will obey! I will get the men ready for battle!"

With that invitation lingering, Percius went to his planning table and sat down to figure out his battle strategy. In a few minutes he walked outside. At that point, he was ready! Dimitri had informed the men. Percius mounted his steed with half the troops lined up behind himself. His forces also were equiped with four catapults to help them in their endeavor.

The troops stood loyal with him, as they marched into an ambush formation. They knew not whether they would emerge dead or alive.

Meanwhile, in the camp of Conavar, all his troops were relaxed as they awaited orders for their next encounter. They had no idea what was about to transpire. Lord Conavar himself, in the privacy of his tent, drank of the fruit of the vine, but found no shape to face what was about to happen.

On the facing cliffs, Percius and Dimitri strategically placed their troops with two catapults on each side. They might not stop the Jahir, but they would surely slow them down.

Soon you heard the sounds of horse's hooves, echoing like the rumbling of thunder. Ogden, Conavar's second in command, heard this monsterous noise and immediately raced toward Conavar's location to inform him that the troops from Uric were arriving. A very drunk Conavar tried to get himself together to greet the friendly troops, or so he thought.

The approaching Jahir were armed and ready as they rode into an unknowing ambush. Their swords and shields glistening in the sun. Once they were positioned between the cliffs, Percius and his forces attacked. Conavar and his men heard the commotion. They were caught totally off guard. They thought it was the Jahir.

Conavar and his men still hadn't gotten ready for war until he heard a voice yelling, "The Jahir have come to kill you!" It was Percius trying to give Conavar a little warning. Then he shouted to his men, "To arms! To arms!" as he tried to get himself ready to do battle.

The Jahir were now between the cliffs. They were met by arrows, large and small rocks, as well as burned rocks. The ambush seemed to be working, but the troops just kept coming. Some were killed, but some managed to get through the ambush to attack Conavar and his troops.

Conavar's men had deployed themselves into a phalanx, a wall of overlapping shields and layered spear points. They did so to protect themselves as best as they could. The Jahir, now in the camp, showed their ruthlessness. They were armed with shields and short spears. They began killing men with no remorse. You could hear the sound of clashing swords and the sounds of men as they died.

By forming a phalanx, Conavar thought he could block the Jahir, but he was wrong. The Jahir killed the forces of Conavar almost like little stick men. Conavar watched as his men were stabbed and run down into the ground, one by one.

Percius tried to get to Conavar's troops to help from the cliffs. But, it took a few minutes to get to them. During those few moments, Conavar's troops were almost wiped out.

When he finally did reach Conavar, the damage had already been done. There were dead men lying everywhere. The brown mud ran red with the blood of warriors. Percius saw Conavar crouching outside his tent. He dismounted and approached Conavar, now a broken man. Percius put his arm around Conavar, as the man wept like a baby.

Conavar looked at Percius and said, "Regnak, my comrade, I was a stupid fool of a man for trusting Uric. I thought he was an ally. Now look around. All this is of my doing. I should have trusted you. You even risked your own life to help me."

Percius knew as well as Conavar that the Jahir were liely taking a reprieve to get their troops better assembled. Because the unexpected ambush really caught them off guard, before the kill, they had to get the troops and their wits better assembled. Unfortunately, the Jahir would probably return better organized to finish the job.

It seemed that all hope was lost for both Percius and Conavar. Then, once more they heard the hooves of horses and became more fearful of what lay ahead.

The Jahir had fooled them yet again for they were already back for the kill. But instead of a single rider that rode into Conavar's devastated camp, their prayers had been answered for it was Archimedes who now arrived!

Archimedes looked around at the massive devastation of war and said, "It would appear that I arrived at a good time. I received word about the Jahir and their intentions. I thought it best for my troops and I to come and personally help you, Lord Regnak. I asked travelers on the road where your camp was. But when I got there it was abandoned. Yet I could hear a battle in the background, so I followed the noise which led me to you."

Percius looked at Archimedes and said, "You are an answer to a prayer, your Highness! The Jahir have retreated. I fear they will reorganize their troops. They shall return! But when they do, they are in for quite a surprise!"

Archimedes regarded the man he knew as Regnak and replied, "I will need time to organize my troops for battle. Can we use your tent Lord Conavar? I need to structure a decisive battle plan!"

Conavar agreed to the request of Archimedes. So together, Conavar, Percius, and Archimedes entered the tent to work out a strategy plan. Inside, Archimedes just stared at Percius then said, "Lord Regnak, your reputation as a warrior proceeds you. But there is something about you that is very familiar. Have we met before?"

Percius glanced at Archimedes and replied, "Sire, I don't think so!" Percius' appearance was disguised by virtue of his beard. He didn't think it was appropriate at the time to tell Archimedes the truth. They all had to use all their energies to concentrate on the matter at hand.

After a while, the sound of a single rider was heard entering the camp. A scout loyal to Archimedes arrived and announced, "Sire, the Jahir are on their way back. I would say they are less than a mile away." The scout dismounted and bowed to the King then he went his way to join the other troops.

Archimeded knew of the dense forest behind the camp. It was here that he placed some of his troops amongst the foliage. He also told some of his troops to hide in the tents. He believed that the Jahir might think the tents would be abandoned after such a fierce battle. The rest of his troops took their places around the encampment and prepared for a fight.

Soon they heard the horses of the Jahir. As the forces went into the camp, they were attacked by the warriors hidden in the tents deep within the forest. Percius' men had the catapults set in strategic places around the camp. The catapults threw burning rocks at the enemy troops, and caused many warriors to be wounded and fall to the ground. Some were being burned alive, while others were hit by boulders.

Some of the troops, as they made their way into the camp, were surprised by the additional troops of Archimedes. The sound of clashing swords echoed everywhere. It was a veritable blood bath! Soon the Jahir sounded retreat, for they realized that their defeat was at hand. Then, with nothing further to be gained, the Jahir pulled back.

The three leaders looked around at the awful bloodletting that had just taken place. The very ground itself had turned red from the spilled blood of warriors. Conavar scanned the scene before his eyes and shook his head. Then he said, "All this was because of my arrogance. How many died today that didn't have to? All this because of an arrogant stupid man! Just about all my men lie on the ground dead! They were husbands, sons, and fathers. They fell in a battle that could have been prevented! I should have died with my men!"

Without saying another word, and before either Percius or Archimedes could stop him, Conavar unsheathed his sword, and fell on it. He was dead almost immediately. He had been taught that it was the honorable warrior's way to die. Yes, he would die with pride and honor.

Meanwhile on the border of Alisia, Lord Uric joined the Jahir, taking his rightful place as their leader. Here, more troops were assembling, just awaiting orders to go into battle.

Both Percius and Archimedes wanted peace. They were both sick of the war and the toll it took. Conavar, having taken his own life, was indeed another casualty of this unneccesary battle. Another great warrior and leader was lost because of Uric. A courier had been sent to Alisia to give the leader of the Jahir a message. The message said that Regnak and Archimedes wished to discuss the possibility of a truce and an alliance.

The courier arrived at Uric's camp. He tethered his horse then walked directly toward Uric and handed him the message. The courier said to Lord Uric, "M'Lord, a message from King Archimedes. I was to hand deliver it to only you!" The courier then retreated outside.

Uric opened the message and began to read its contents. But as he did, he laughed aloud. As he reached the part where the alliance was mentioned, he mumbled softly, "An alliance...well so be it! They don't want to mess with me. I will show them an alliance!" Uric then summoned his own courier to his side. As he did so, he almost dropped the blood stone which gave him his powers. He carefully placed the stone back in his pocket. He believed he would soon see battle and thus he would need the stone as it drew its power from bloodshed. He took time to write a note. Then he handed the written note to his courier to take to King Archimedes. It simply indicated that he was willing to meet.

Percius and Archimedes had just left the funeral pyre which had consumed the body of Conavar. Archimedes made sure that Conavar was sent to the afterlife, from a warrior's life. Both men were still a little shaken from how Conavar so suddenly took his own life. They walked back to Percius' camp.

As they entered the main tent, Archimedes said, "Conavar was a great leader and warrior. He will surely be missed! He just couldn't accept the fact he lived after so many of his men had died. He was truly a brave man. His death will be remembered. I hold the Jahir responsible for this. But, there must be a cease fire. So many died during the last battle!"

Percius replied, "Sire, I agree! He will be missed!" Percius now realized that he was alone with the King and perhaps now was the time to tell the King who he really was! "Sire, remember when you asked me if we had we met before? I lied. We have indeed met before, and what seems like another lifetime ago, we were rather close. I remember a small boy that longed for a friend. There was a man that befriended you. He was a man you confided in and a man that was a true friend. And he remained as a friend until the boy's father was brainwashed by untruths. It was only then that the man had to flee for his life! The lies told made the father issue an order for the capture of that man for treason. Archimedes, do you remember?"

Archimedes looked at the man in front of him. He was momentarily in shock. Then he exclaimed, "Percius? Percius? I thought you were long dead! Is it really you?" Archimedes then hugged the man he had called Regnak. There were tears in the King's eyes, as Archimedes said, "You were my best friend. I never forgave my father for the heartache he caused you. You must come back with me to Samothrace. There is no one now to hurt you. I never believed the accusations of treason. When you left, my mother took it very hard. You were her friend also!"

Now, and finally again, Percius could go back to Samothrace. It was a dream come true. He could see his sweet Cheris once more. Percius inquired, "Your mother, how is she? Yes, I am Percius, and I will go back with you. But there is something I want you to know. Your mother, to me, is more than a friend. The truth is that I have loved her for many years. Your mother and you have always been in my heart. I want you to know, she was always faithful to your father and to her duties. Further, she never did anything to disgrace your father."

Archimedes replied, "Percius, I think mother loved you too! She is just fine! This will really surprise her. And as long as I am King, the charges of treason are null and void. Percius can once again take his rightful place by my side."

Then the sound of a horse announced an approaching rider. Percius walked outside of the tent, and saw that it was a courier from the Jahir. Percius took the message, which told them that the leader of the enemy was willing to meet. Percius then told the courier to tell his leader that King Archimedes accepted his invitation.

When they arrived in the encampment of the Jahir, Archimedes and Percius stood in awe at the presence of all the troops. They both dismounted from their steeds and entered the leader's tent.

Once inside, Archimedes and Percius were in for a shock. Seated at the table was none other than Lord Uric. The man supposedly so loyal to Archimedes, was himself a traitor.

Archimedes was angry. he shoued, "You! You are a man I thoroughly trusted. If not for the need of an alliance, I would kill you myself! But we need some kind of cease fire!"

Uric, with a lecherous look on his face responded, "Do sit down! Am I seeing a ghost? Percius, I thought you were long dead! I am so glad to see you are alive!"

Percius said, "I see you haven't changed at all, Uric. You are still the untrustworthy swine of a man you always were, and I am sure my well being was not one of your major concerns."

Archimedes added, "We need to talk about the matter at hand. All ill feelings will be resolved in time. The peoples of Ames and Alisia are at their wit's end due to all the blood shed and death from the war. I would like to give these people a reprieve, a time for them to get a grasp on their lives!"

Uric continued, "These so-called people, peasants most of them, are most insignificant. If I agree, what's in it for me?"

Percius then stepped in and said, "Always thinking of yourself I see. You never changed. For your part of the alliance, the King and I will spare your life! You can just walk away! Send the Jahir back to their country. The King will not order your arrest!"

Uric uttered, "I don't need any help from either of you to stay alive, but I am sure my men would like to see their homeland once more! I will agree to your terms! But why couldn't the King himself, offer this? Is he weak as his father was? You know his father never loved him? In fact his father feared him! I agree to your terms Sire. But hear this — when the time is right, you and everything dear to you, I will destroy!"

Percius noticed that Archimedes' eyes were starting to change color and he quickly commented on this to Archimedes, "I see you still have your gift. But please, not now Sire. If you did hurt him, we would never leave here alive. I feel the same as you about this swine, but not now Sire. He is trying to provoke you, to bring your gift to the surface. Highness, please, not right now."

Archimedes answered, "Then our meeting is over. But Sir Uric, know this, your threats don't bother me. You know what I can do. This time you were saved by Percius. But there will come a time I will face you alone, and this idea keeps me going. I just wait for that day."

On that note, Uric stood up, bowed to Archimedes and left the tent. Archimedes and Percius followed with a thousand questions about the fate of the future going through Archimedes' mind.

Chapter Eleven

As both Archimedes and Percius vacated the camp of the Jahir, Uric watched their backs as they left. They both knew they could never trust this man, and they thought nothing was beneath this snake. Before the end of their meeting, Uric agreed to send his forces back to their homeland, but there was a hint of doubtfulness in the air. The two men agreed that a scout should be sent, just to make sure Uric kept his word.

Once back at Percius' encampment, the King summoned one of the warriors. Archimedes gave him orders to go watch the ships of the Jahir until they had departed. He warned the scout to stay out of sight because the King was worried if the scout was captured, he would likely be tortured and killed.

In the tent of Percius, Archimedes sat down. For the first time in a very long time, he could just sit back, relax and enjoy a good drink of the fruit vine. The King knew if Uric pulled his soldiers, the war would come to a conclusion, even if only for a brief moment. That would give the people time to catch their breath.

As he relaxed, the King spoke to Percius, "If everything goes as planned, we can send the men home at least for awhile. We can also go home to Samothrace as soon as we know for sure that the Jahir have departed. You can meet my wife and children and of course, mother. Are you afraid?"

Percius was also enjoying a glass of wine. He said to the King, "Sire, I consider it a great honor to meet your family. As far as your mother is concerned, I could never be afraid to meet with her. My stomach is actually in knots, but I would presume that is nerves. In truth, I can't wait to get back!"

The scout that was sent by the King watched the Jahir ships from the top of a hill, while hidden by the bushes and trees. So far, it appeaed as if the Jahir were preparing to leave for the ships were raising their masts. The scout could see the men on the ships scurrying around. Soon the ships actually began to depart, one by one, each ship creating a single line as the moved away from the shore.

The King looked at Percius and said, "It is time to tell your men they can go home and be with their families for a while. This means we too can go home!"

Percius called all his troops together and commanded, "Men, you have served the King and I well! No leader could be more proud of his men. All of you are gifted warriors. Now the time has come for us to disband, at least for a while. I am relieving you of duty, and you are all free to go home to your families until we need you again! God speed, and the King and I thank you for your sacrifice and service!"

After saying this, Archimedes and Percius walked back inside the tent, as the troops cheered them. You could hear the excitement fill the air, as the anticipation of going home became strong in the air. You could also hear the troops cheering the names of Archimedes and Regnak.

Back inside the tent, the two men started preparations to go home to Samothrace. As Percius prepared, feelings of anxiety and anticipation of seeing Cheris once more filled his entire being. These feelings he thought were long dead. But now they again erupted to the surface. He again realized that the eternal flame of love still burned within his soul for his sweet Cheris.

As they prepared for their departure, Archimedes said, "You have never met my wife, Delyse, or my twin children, Aoleon and Arion. I myself can't wait to get home, to have my wife and children in my arms once more. It seems as if I have been away from them for a lifetime. I'm sure you can't wait to see Mother!"

Percius hinted to the King, "The thought of your mother and my love for her burns deep within my soul. It has been so very long! I don't think the realization that I am actually going home has truly hit me yet. But, I will admit I am nervous!"

Soon the camp was disbanded, and the troops were on their way home. Archimedes and Percius made their way back to Samothrace. It was about a five hour ride to get to Samothrace, so it was likely that they would arrive in Samothrace on that very day. The weather was beautiful. There was nothing to slow their ride.

As the city appeared on the horizon, Percius began feeling very nervous. He just couldn't wait to see the love of his life once more.

Archimedes had no time to send word to his family that he was coming home so this would be a big surprise. One of the peasants saw the King as he made his way to the city. The peasant ran to the palace and announced to all who would hear him that the King was home. The word soon spread through the city like wildfire.

As the King and Percius entered the city, they were cheered on by the masses. They quickly reached the palace where both men dismounted from their steeds.

Delyse and the two children greeted Archimedes with open arms, after welcoming the King home. Then Archimedes announced to Percius, "This is my Queen, Delyse, and my two children, Aoleon and Arion. Please meet my lifelong friend, Percius."

Percius bowed to the Queen in respect saying, "Your highness, it is my pleasure to meet you. I am your humble servant."

Then Percius saw Cheris. His stomach was instantly in knots with a lump in his throat. She was just as beautiful as the day he left.

Cheris walked up to her son and welcomed him home. Then Cheris saw Percius, and cried out, "I thought you were dead! This is a surprise!" Cheris' heart was beating so fast, it felt like it was coming through her chest. She bowed to Percius then turned and walked away.

That act really hurt Percius. He was so excited to see Cheris again, but she greeted him with such coldness.

Delyse had the cooks prepare a special dinner in honor of the King's return. After a few hours alone with Delyse, the King made his way toward the dining hall, Delyse at his side. They were closely followed by their four year old twins, Aoleon and Arion. Cheris was already at the table. Percius shortly joined them.

As they ate their meal, there was a lot of small talk, mostly consisting of the weather and the adventures of the King's escapades while he was gone. After the meal, the twins played on the terrace adjoining the dining hall, until it was time for bed.

Cheris called the nanny and told her that it was the twin's bedtime. But then a very small voice was heard to say, "Do we have too? Father just got home!" It was the voice of Aoleon.

Cheris answered her. "Yes, it is bed time! Your father and Percius have had a long journey today, and I am sure they are very tired! It is bedtime for us all!"

The twins kissed their parents good night. Then they were off with the nanny. Everyone else also went their separate ways to their chambers.

All had retired for the evening, except for Percius. Before he could rest, he had to have some answers from Cheris as to why she was so cold.

After making sure everyone else had retired, Percius headed toward the chambers of Cheris. Although there were guards outside the chambers, the guards had heard rumors of a romance between Percius and Cheris before the death of her husband. So, the guards really didn't think it strange as Percius made his way to her door.

Percius stood outside Cheris' door and softly knocked. Inside, Cheris thought it might be her son so she called out 'Enter.' When Cheris saw that it was Percius she lowered her eyes toward the floor. She made sure to not look directly at him.

Cheris said to Percius, "I was wondering when you would try to get me alone, to talk with me. Really I have nothing to say except we were wrong."

Percius then became mad. However, as he did not want to show his anger, he softly said, "Wrong? Do you know what I have gone through over the years just for loving you? I put my very life on the line because of my love for you!"

Cheris replied, "I just can't imagine what you have gone through, and for that I am sorry. But don't you realize it was because of our forbidden feelings for each other that it was the very reason Lionus died? I could not be a wife because of my feelings for you. It was my feelings for you which caused Lionus to act the way he did. Archimedes saw Lionus hit Dianu. Then Archimedes got mad and could not control his gift which caused the death of Lionus. Because of our feelings! His death is something I have to live with the rest of my life, because of our feelings!"

Percius spoke softly, "Cheris, that was not your fault that Lionus went mad. How can you blame yourself for whom you love? So you are now telling me you don't love me? Look me in the eyes and tell me that! You can't, can you?"

Cheris answered, "I never said I did not love you. It is simply that I could never be happy with you because of what happened, because of our love!"

Percius believed a person's eyes were the window to one's soul, so he told Cheris, "You can't even look at me! Look me in my eyes and tell me you don't love me! Tell me you do not wish to be in my arms!"

Cheris now crying, replied, "Oh, Percius, you know I can't do that! Because I do love you, and because of my love for you, I brought death to the palace! I could never be happy. There is a black mark on my very soul!"

Percius lifted Cheris up from her chair by her shoulders. Then the two embraced and shared a long passionate kiss. Cheris then asked Percius to leave and Percius complied.

Percius had no way of knowing after that night, it would be a very long time before he saw Cheris again.

The next morning, even before the sun rose, Cheris made her way toward her son's chambers. She hadn't slept all night. Her mind was full of thoughts of Percius. But because of a guilt ridden soul, she couldn't deal with what she wanted. She was scared that if she remained in the palace with Percius, she would eventually give in to her strong feelings of her love.

She reached her son's chambers and softly knocked on his door. The King was already awake, "Enter!" Cheris opened the door and entered her son's chambers. Archimedes was up and dressed, sitting on his terrace, to watch the sunrise. He asked his mother to join him. Cheris kindly obliged her son, and sat down on the terrace with him.

Archimedes replied, "Good morning mother. You look troubled! Have you been up all night? Your eyes are red! What on earth is wrong?"

Cheris answered her son, tears already starting to stream down her checks. She cried, "Son, Percius came to my chambers last night! He came to me to tell me of his love for me. Son, I will not tell an untruth, I love this man, like I have loved no other, but I can't succumb to these feelings. This is why your father went mad. It was the very cause of his death. With this on my conscience, I could never be happy with Percius. I could not stand to have him in the palace. I must go away. Son, I beseech you, let me go away! There is an order near the coast, the order worships God. So I beg you, send me there! Maybe then I can learn how to live with myself!"

Archimedes was shocked. He stood up, walked over to his mother and hugged her saying, "Mother, stop crying. I can't stand to watch you hurting. I know how you and Percius feel about each other! I don't want to see you go away. But if you feel you must, I will make the arrangements this very morn! All I want is to see you happy."

Archimedes summoned one of his servants, and told him to prepare a caravan to go to the coast. He asked that his mother be brought to the religious order. Then he told his mother, "Are you sure about this? You really want to go away?"

Cheris, still crying, answered, "It is not my wish to leave you, Delyse, and the twins, but I must. I don't trust myself around Percius, and I can not give in to my feelings. I believe being in a place of God, I can learn how to live with the fact of your father's death. I love my family and I also love Percius, but I just can't give in to my feelings!"

Then Cheris took her leave. She walked back to her quarters to prepare for a journey she wished she didn't have to take.

Delyse walked on to the terrace and saw her troubled husband as he watched the multi-colored sunrise with tears in his eyes. He told Delyse of his mother's plans. Delyse cradled her distraught husband in her arms, and tried her best to console him.

Then the moment was interrupted by the twins coming into the chambers to wish their parents good morning. Archimedes got himself together because of the twins. Even though his heart was breaking, he had to put on a smile, because he was the King.

The King, Delyse, and the twins strolled into the dining hall for breakfast. When they got there, Percius was already there with a big smile on his face. He said happily, "Good morning! I am so happy Archimedes! Your mother still loves me and my heart feels as light as a feather! I have planned the entire day for your mother and me."

Archimedes told the twins to go play on the terrace until the food arrived. He didn't want his children to see a broken man. He replied, "Percius, I know you and mother love each other deeply, but mother came to me early this morning! She wants to go away! I am sorry but I also love my mother! When she came to me, she was hurting. I can't stand to see mother hurt. She has been through so much! So, I granted her wish. She is leaving. I am so sorry."

On hearing this, the smile faded from the face of Percius and was replaced by tears of frustration. Percius tried his best to keep his composure in the presence of the King and Queen. He stood up, bowed to the King and said he understood. Then he said that he needed to be alone and he took his leave.

Percius walked into the courtyard with his pain as he tried to make sense of what just occurred. He just couldn't accept the fact he and Cheris would never be together. That great warrior was now a broken man.

Ten years passed since that day Archimedes and Percius came back from war. The once small twins were now inquisitive fourteen year old teenagers. Delyse still held her breathtaking beauty and Archimedes couldn't ask for a better wife.

Ten years had gone by since Archimedes banished Uric from Samothrace. Ten years passed since Archimedes found out his personal advisor Uric was a back stabbing traitor. Percius now had the title of personal advisor and best friend to the King. Archimedes trusted Percius with his very life.

It had been also ten years of peace for all of Atlantis. Uric had not been seen or heard from during that time. During this period of peace, Archimedes had helped rebuild the countries of Ames and Alysea. He had made Samothrace his capitol. Archimedes had earned himself the title of the great King of Atlantis.

Life for the past few years had been very good. Archimedes tried his best to see Cheris as often as possible, but, it was not easy. Cheris finally seemed to be able to accept the fact that the death of Lionus wasn't her fault, but she still refused to see Percius.

On that particular day, Archimedes and Delyse enjoyed a midday meal on their terrace, as the twins were in another part of the palace attending to their daily lessons. Soon their meal was interrupted by Percius. He had a solemn look on his face, not the smiling face he usually had.

Archimedes stated, "Percius, you usually join us for our meals. I was starting to worry. Is there something wrong? You have a look of worry on your face!"

Percius bowed to the King and Queen saying, "Sire, I do hate to be the one to deliver this news, but I have just heard from the leader of our troops in the north. The enemy troops have come ashore and they number the thousands. They are making their way toward Samothrace, killing anyone and everything in their path. It would appear that the sweet rewards of peace have gone away. I am afraid we will have to do battle once more. It seems, Sire, their leader is none other than Uric."

Archimedes then told Percius, "I leave it to you to organize the troops. Never will I allow Uric and his troops to take Samothrace. Ten years of peace and now this. For some reason I knew Uric was not dead. I can feel his ungodly presence. I just wondered when he would make an appearance. Now I know."

Delyse looked at her King with tears in her eyes, "I guess this means you will go away again, leaving me to worry each day, whether you are alive or dead!"

Archimedes clasped the hand of Delyse and replied, "My Queen, my beautiful Queen, dry your tears. I will not be harmed. Haven't I always returned before? I will also return this time! Do not fret!"

Delyse, still with tears in her eyes said, "Yes, Sire you have always returned! I will have to tell the twins. I will do everything in my power to keep my composure for the sake of our subjects and the twins. It's just when you are gone, Sire, I miss you so much!"

Archimedes replied, "My Queen, I can always depend on you to hold things together while I am gone. I am the King, and as much as I would like to stay, I can't! If I stayed now, how would that look to my subjects?"

Delyse answered, "I know, sometimes I wish you were not the King, but I know you must go. It is your duty!"

Archimedes kissed his Queen then he left with Percius by his side. They marched into the war room which had not been used for ten years. Here the two men would work out a battle plan.

Archimedes was very tired from his day of planning yet another tedious war. He retired to his chambers with Delyse. While Delyse went directly into their bedroom, Archimedes remained in the sitting room of their chambers. He took this opportunity to relax and enjoy a glass of the fruit vine.

Snuggled alone in the sitting room, Archimedes sensed a powerful feeling of doom. He had no idea as to why this was occurring. It was the same feeling he used to get when he would know of the presence of the evil Uric. Yet it had been ten years since Archimedes had seen Uric. However Archimedes just couldn't shake that feeling.

All of a sudden, a white mist formed in his quarters. The white mist took on a human form. It was Uric.

Archimedes just couldn't believe his eyes. After ten years he appeared to him. Archimedes said, "Are you real? I thought you were long dead! I thought the world was rid of such a festering evil! Why appear to me now?"

Uric looked at Archimedes with contempt in his eyes, and an evil grin on his face. Then he said laughing, "So you thought I was dead. I am too powerful to die! I have been laying low for ten years, as my troops did battle, I was also there basking in all the death and blood, feeding the blood stones that give me my power. I was becoming stronger and stronger."

"I am very strong and powerful. I intend uniting your powers with mine. Then I will be the most powerful being on earth and no one or nothing will stop me!"

Archimedes looked at Uric and said, "I don't even know the source of my powers. What makes you think you can take my powers? You are an evil power hungry being! Your death would benefit many!"

Uric laughed, "I will find the source of your powers and they shall be mine! Every being on earth will bow to the name Uric. I will be King of the entire world! I will have unending wealth and you or anyone else can't stop me!"

Archimedes stared at the disillusioned man, "Uric, you are mad! No one will bow to your evil ways! Everyone will know of your madness!"

Uric replied, "Archimedes, I will tell you this: death and destruction will be yours, starting with your dear mother. I will make sure there will be strife and destruction in your life!"

Upon hearing that, Archimedes couldn't help himself. His eyes began to change color. Then suddenly a lightning bolt struck the place where Uric had just stood. But it was too late, Uric was gone.

Meanwhile, outside of Archimedes' chambers, Percius had something to ask the King. He overheard everything, including the threat against Cheris.

What Percius just overheard made his blood boil. He was blinded by rage and not thinking rationally. He raced outside into the courtyard, mounted a steed and quickly headed for his Cheris.

He thought of nothing but Cheris. Percius didn't care it was a moonless night. He didn't care how hard it was to see. It was as if he was being led by pure instinct to get to the women he loved. She was the only woman he had ever loved and he had to get to her as quickly as possible. Rationality would have told him to wait until daylight, but the anxiety within his very being, drove him to get to Cheris.

It took Percius a couple of hours to get to the refuge. But when he arrived, what he saw, made his heart drop. Could he be too late?

Even though it was a moonless night, Percius looked down on the compound, from a vantage point in a nearby tree. He could see what seemed to be assassins all over the ground, inside and outside. The cutthroats ran rampant.

Percius used this to his advantage, as he moved with stealth on the compound, hidden by darkness and shadows. He tried to be as quiet as a mouse, as he tip-toed inside the compound.

Soon he was well into the compound. Some of the assassins heard a noise, but before they had the time to look for the source of the sound, Percius in a blind rage, appeared from the shadows, sword in hand. He cut down all and anything in his path. Leaving a trail of assassins' blood. Then deep within the bowels of the compound, he saw his sweet Cheris, her body crumpled on the floor, as she lay in a pool of blood. Percius screamed, "NNNNNNNNNNOO OOOOOOOOOOO!", as he raced to her side.

With tears running down his face, he took her in his arms and said, "You just lie still. I will try to stop the bleeding. I will go for help after I move you to a safer place."

Cheris took the hand of Percius, within her own blood stained hand and stuttering, "My love, your efforts are so appreciated! I know you truly love me now! But you know, as well as I, it is too late! I am dying. But before I die, I must tell you I was wrong! I was driven by guilt to shut you out of my life and I was wrong. I never once stopped to think, how much Hell I must have put you through. Please forgive me, I was so wrong. Percius, I love you, unlike any I have loved before!"

Percius looked at his dying Cheris with great sadness. "My love, don't talk of such things as death. I will get you back to Samothrace where you will be safe. As for your guilt, I understand! You just made me the happiest man on earth, by knowing you truly love me!"

He leaned over Cheris. He embraced her in his arms, and kissed her. Then her body fell limp. He knew she was dead! Tears streamed down his face as he looked at her. He painfully cried, "I promise you this — I shall avenge your death! Uric caused this and he is a dead man!"

With hatred now in his heart, he left the compound. He headed north with one thing in his mind and heart, the demise of Uric.

Chapter Twelve

A whole year had come and gone, since Archimedes lost his dear mother, Cheris, to the cutthroat Uric. He missed her terribly. He missed her motherly love and advice, the touch of a mother's hand, and her always being there to reassure him. The memories of his mother were one thing the murderous Uric could never touch.

Archimedes sat at a table in the war room that was closed for so very long. It was used last when everyone had tasted the sweetness of freedom. That was before Uric made another appearance sending Atlantis into war once more. He was reading a papyrus scroll from his confidant Percius. The content was anything but good news.

It seemed that Percius had acquired employment aboard a Jahir vessel which traveled to the Jahir homeland with one intention in mind — to destroy Uric. Percius, being a master of the blade, kept it always by his side, hoping to find Uric one day and end his evil existence. The blade he carried was the one that was blessed by the teacher of Uric, which might also end Uric's life.

Another thing Percius did, being within the rank of the Jahir, was to listen to other Jahir as they spoke of their plans of war strategies and other things of importance to Archimedes. Then Percius reported his findings to the King. The reports Percius sent were never good news. His findings helped the King prepare for battles, giving the King an advantage.

On that particular day, the King tried to focus on the problem at hand. However, he had a hard time concentrating. He heard the noise beneath his terrace from the war room. In the courtyard, the twins now fifteen were playing. It seemed they were playing a game of tag, just as they did when they were small. Aoleon and Arion's playing and laughing shattered the King's concentration.

Archimedes moved toward the terrace with that thought in mind. He intended to tell them to be a little more quiet. When he saw the two having such fun with each other, he didn't have the heart to spoil their fun. He watched his children as they ran and played around the fountain in the middle of the courtyard.

Shortly after that moment, they stopped running and playing around. The King could hear their conversation. He heard Aoleon say, "I bet my power is stronger than yours! Watch this!" In the blink of an eye and without moving a muscle, a little puppy appeared in the courtyard.

Arion said, "That was nothing! Watch this!" Suddenly there was a kitten in the courtyard. The little puppy instantly chased the kitten away. Aoleon replied, "We must never let mother or father see us use our powers! You know how they feel about that. We would surely be in trouble if that happened."

Archimedes watched his children and memories began to flood his mind of when he was a child and how his own father thought he was cursed and a demon. This left a scar his soul. Now he couldn't help but think that his children might be cursed just as his father thought he was.

Archimedes still had no clue from whence his powers came. He still searched high and low at that nagging question, which burned within his very soul. He realized that he had passed that misunderstood gift onto his children. Not as strong as his power, but just enough. He prayed his children were not doomed as he was, by his own father.

Archimedes exited the terrace and returned to his work on battle strategies. He was interrupted again by his beautiful Queen, Delyse. She had come to get the King for their midday meal. She immediately saw a look of concern on her husband's face.

Delyse sat beside her husband and, "Husband, I see the look of worry on your face. What is it that bothers you so?"

Archimedes looked at his Queen and said, "I have just seen the twins at play! I saw them play and using their powers which I prayed they would not have. They were acting like the power itself was some sort of game. They're too young to recognize how they were cursed! They do not know how much strife that power will bring to their life!"

Delyse replied, "Sire, our children are most fortunate to have a father that understands this thing. Your father merely condemned you, saying you were cursed and a demon. You understand! You would never do to our children as your father did you! So, my King, do not be concerned, our children are strong and as they get older, they will learn about the gift, and how to use it in the right way!"

Archimedes continued, "My Queen, my beautiful Queen, you always say the right things to make my concerns seem trivial. I tried to lead our children in the right direction and they are strong. I just pray others do not shun them because of the power!"

Then the King and Queen left the war room, hand in hand. They made their way to the dining room for their midday meal.

Percius, now very weary, was in a strange new land of the Jahir. He had traveled far on a Jahir ship for six months. He had endured six months on the open seas and six months of being on a ship with his enemy. His feet were ready to touch land once more, even in the unknown land.

Traveling, and compiling information for his King, and under the disguise of another cutthroat Jahir, he quickly learned their ways and customs. He could blend in and travel amongst those who ended the life of his sweet Cheris. The main thing on his mind was simple. He had to avenge the death of the woman he so loved.

On the ship, it had been his job to help with the mast. He mostly kept to himself among those he so hated. Yet, he always stayed alert to learn anything he could and to send such news back to his King. His goal was the total annihilation of the Jahir and their twisted leader, Uric.

Percius was very tired. Yet the fire of revenge within his soul kept him going. He hoped that one day he would face Uric, one on one, to destroy the sick, demented, power hungry, Uric.

But now, in the land of the Jahir, he must be on his utmost guard. If anyone found out his true identity, it would surely mean his death. He had to live to finish his one job and destroy Uric.

Percius descended the ship that brought him there and set foot in this strange land. The harbor looked to be bigger than the Bay of Atlantis. As he stood on the dock, he watched as the ship unloaded its supplies, while he listened to the constant buzz going on around the docks.

He then left the docks and walked to a strange city. He had to find a place to sleep. The city was crowded with people everywhere. There were all kinds of buildings and shops lining the cobblestone streets. Most of them seemed to be abandoned. He noted that the war appeared to have taken its toll on the Jahir population.

Then Percius finally found a tavern that was not abandoned. This place had rooms for rent. He walked inside the small tavern and noticed the art on the walls. He thought that the tavern owner must be very wealthy because the place was decorated by many things that spoke of great wealth.

Percius spotted a very big man standing behind the bar in the tavern. He assumed that was the owner. He made his way toward the bar then spoke to the man, "I see you have rooms to rent. I would like one while my ship is in dock."

The big burly man looked at Percius and remarked, "You are new to this land. You are not dark like the rest of us, you are fair! Where are you from?"

Percius stated, "I am from Atlantis, but I sympathize with the cause of the Jahir. So I joined them to do battle and whatever is needed of me to help their cause."

The big man responded, "Then, my friend, you are welcome here! Since the war began, business is slow. Take the room at the top of the stairs!"

Percius walked into his room to rest for a while before he went back to the pub to have some food. The room was simply furnished with just a bed, a chair, and a table with a wash basin.

After an hour or so, Percius returned back to the pub to have some food and some ale. He sat at one of the tables in the pub, enjoying some ale before his meal. Across from him, at another table, sat three men that looked like warriors. He couldn't help but overhear their conversation as the three men seemed to be a little intoxicated from drinking.

One of the men uttered, "Let's enjoy this because it may be the last ale we have for a very long time. Who knows, we might not survive fighting in a battle with King Archimedes and his troops. They say he is a very formidable enemy!"

One of the other men replied, "Before we go to do battle in Atlantis, remember we are to go to the castle of Lord Uric right outside of town, to get our orders, because he has something special for us to do."

Percius could not have been luckier as the three men had unknowingly disclosed the location of Uric's castle. With this information in hand, Percius decided he will pay Uric a visit, under the curtain of nightfall.

In the dead of night, Percius made his way to the fortress of Uric. After making his way across a very deep moat around the castle, he saw a big tree right beside a balcony that he hoped would help him gain access into the castle.

He climbed the tree, then jumped to the balcony. It turned out that he was on the balcony right outside the room in which Uric was located. Percius hung onto the balcony for dear life as he saw there were several men in the room with Uric. Percius knew that he had to be very quiet if he were to catch any of their conversation.

He saw Uric sitting at a table, going over papers with the other men. Percius heard one man say, "With you controlling several countries, my Lord, and your troops in the thousands, King Archimedes, will be much outnumbered. I bet he has never seen such a vast number of troops all willing to do your bidding my Lord Uric!"

"We already have a number of ships on their way to the northern territories, and within days another will be ready to go to the southern territories!"

Uric spoke, "I hope Archimedes will take his troops to the north, and with the troops in the south, there will be no means of retreat. Then he will realize he is outmanned and outmaneuvered! Once he realizes this, I hope he will surrender! Remember, we will take no prisoners, except the King, himself."

As Percius still hung onto part of the balcony, he found himself in quite a predicament. He knew what he just overheard, needed to be communicated to Archimedes as quickly as possible. He also knew that one of the many ships in harbor was scheduled to leave for Atlantis first thing in the morning. That ship was not his of course, but he knew if he left the Jahir homeland on this ship, his cover of being loyal to the Jahir might be compromised.

Percius pondered the decision to warn his King, for whom he had an undying loyalty, or got the revenge that burned deep within his soul. Since the heart of Percius lay with Atlantis, he jumped back to the tree. He lowered himself carefully down to the ground, then quickly made his way back toward the city. He had to be ready to board the ship that would be bound for Atlantis first thing in the morning.

Unbeknownst to Percius, Uric knew he was on the balcony, Uric could feel his presence. Uric knew he must stop Percius from making passage on the Atlantis bound ship.

Uric realized he had to use his powers to stop Percius. So, without hesitation, Uric, began his incantations to summon two things: the shadows, and those ungodly things come from the fiery pits of hell. He acted as if he was in a trance, as he swayed side to side, repeating the same incantation, over and over. A huge ball of fire suddenly appeared. Then instantly, the fire then changed into the shadow creatures.

The two creatures were taller than the average man, ebony in color from head to tail. Each had large, leathery wings which were folded to their side. They had no facial features except for a black mouth, which displayed the sharpest of teeth.

The creatures bowed before Uric. Uric then said, "Find the one called Percius and then destroy him." The creatures then flew off to do Uric's evil bidding.

Percius, now outside the city, was thinking he had made it without being detected. Above him he heard a screeching sound then the flapping of wings. He looked up and saw the two creatures. They were headed straight toward him. He looked around surveying his surroundings, looking for a place to hide. He found none. The reality of him having to do battle with those things from Hell dawned on him. He knew those things were not ordinary creatures. He figured they were sent from the evil Uric.

Percius knew those creatures were the creation of black magic and thus he realized one must fight magic with magic. Always by his side, was the sword that was blessed by Uric's teacher, blessed with the magic to kill Uric. But Percius also knew he must use the magic in the sword to fight those awful creatures.

He pulled the sword from its sheath and stood courageously steadfast, ready to do battle. The creatures swooped down from the sky, trying to get Percius within their grasp. Instead, Percius faced them swinging the blessed sword. As the sword moved, it emitted a strange soft glow. He swung at the first creature, cutting off the first creature's head. Instead of bleeding, the creature disappeared.

However, the second creature remained. It swayed at Percius from behind, causing him to fall to the ground. Percius landed on a sharp stick which resulted in a chest wound. Wounded and bleeding, Percius staggered to his feet. Then the creature plunged straight toward Percius.

He ducked the grasp of the creature. It swooped over Percius, and Percius knew the creature was going to come straight for him again. But this time Percius was ready. When the creature was almost at the point of grasping Percius, he again swung his sword, hitting the creature in his chest. Then this creature also vanished.

The magical sword that Percius carried now felt slightly heavy and its glow wasn't as bright. But Percius had no idea the power of the sword had been drained somewhat by battling the creatures sent forth by Uric.

Now the revenge that was in the soul of Percius surfaced. He could no longer ignore the feeling, even knowing he might die. He just didn't care. He decided to go back to Uric's fortress, to face the evil man. But he also knew he must make his report to the King before he would face Uric.

Back at the castle, Uric sat at his desk. He was so engrossed in what he was doing he didn't notice the black figure coming up behind him. Usually Uric could feel a presence, but his mind was on other matters.

The shadow behind Uric was none other than Percius. Percius, with his magical sword in hand, put the blade in Uric's back. The blade exited Uric's front. Amazingly enough, this action didn't even phase Uric. Uric stood then turned, striking Percius to the floor.

As Percius got to his feet, he watched Uric yank the sword from his body. The sword had lost some of its powers from the battle with the shadow creatures.

Uric looked at Percius and said, "You know my powers are strong. You cannot destroy me. Your very presence sickens me!"

Percius held steadfast and bravely faced the powerful Uric. Uric raised his hand, and Percius was gone. Brave and valiant Percius was no match for Uric. No mortal man was.

Chapter Thirteen

It was a hazy morning in the city of Barrowmere, about sixty miles north of Samothrace. The sun was peering through the clouds, indicating this would be another hot summer day. One of the residents of Barrowmere, a man by the name of Omin, was awakened by the rising sun. He and his family were sleeping on the roof of their mud brick home because it was so hot.

Omin turned over as he looked into the face of his beautiful wife, Petra. Her long dark hair framed a face which had skin of alabaster. Omin found a string near by, and he chuckled as he dangled the string playfully in her face. Petra stretched, just as playfully pushing her husband's hand out of her face.

Soon the two were joined by their four year old daughter, Dahlia. She saw her parents were playing, so she jumped on her father's stomach, thinking they were all going to play. Omin started tickling his daughter then looked at her saying, "Daughter, I must get up and get ready for another long day. I have to bathe and eat, so let's go inside the house."

Petra had already gotten up, and gone inside the house to prepare their morning meal. She made a meal of fruit and fish. They were going to drink the milk from the cow that was outside in the back of their house. Then Omin and Dahlia joined Petra at the table outside the kitchen.

As they sat at the table enjoying their morning meal, Omin said, "Seems it is going to be another hot sultry day. It is really going to be hot at the cliffs, but I have a duty to relieve the night guard at the outpost. So while I am gone, what are my ladies going to do for the day?"

Petra looked lovingly at her husband, and said, "Dahlia and I will clean the house and prepare a wonderful meal for you that will be ready for you when you return from the outpost. Dahlia is learning how to become a good wife for someone, one day."

Then little Dahlia looked at her father and replied "Father, mother is going to let me cook for you today. I will try really hard, so you will be proud of me."

Omin looked at his daughter who was the spitting image of her mother. "Dahlia, you make me proud, no matter what you do. You are my little monkey!"

Then Omin told Petra, "My commander told me yesterday that if I keep up with my duties the way I have, I will make it to captain of the guard. That would mean more money and more time with you. So, I am going to try very hard so I can take care of Dahlia and you better."

Petra said, "Husband, I will stand beside you, no matter what. But being with you more would be very nice!"

Then the family having finished with their morning meal began their morning tasks. Petra left the table in order to start her daily routine. Dahlia walked outside to play, until her mother called for her, and Omin started toward the outpost to relieve the night guard.

It took Omin about an hour to walk to the outpost. The outpost was located above the ocean in steep cliffs which were used to protect it. Omin noticed his surroundings. He stumbled through a green meadow which, as he got closer to the meadow, turned into rock. Omin had to walk high within the rocks to get to the outpost.

Once he arrived at the outpost, he was hidden within the rocks. The outpost itself, was built on two rocks near each other, it was made of wood. The night guard was very glad to see Omin because it meant that the guard could leave.

The ocean had a mist upon it because of the heat. This would make it a little difficult to see anything on the ocean, especially farther out to sea. Omin took his place within the outpost. He would remain until the night guard returned at sunset.

After a couple of hours or so, Omin thought he saw something within the mist. But it had to get closer to shore before he could make it out.

Once this something did get closer to shore, he made out a lone ship. He wondered to himself, why this ship was on the ocean. It looked like a galleon, a warship. He could even make out the massive catapult on the deck of the ship. This really had Omin in awe.

Omin was not concerned about one ship, but then he saw a few more and more. By that moment, he saw hundreds of war ships as they made their way through the mist. Now he was greatly concerned. It was his job to sound the alarm so others in the guard would know to go to arms.

He knew this could only mean one thing: an invasion. He was expected to stand and fight with the other guard, yet his head filled with thoughts of Petra and Dahlia. So, he was in quite a quandary. He had to choose between his duty to the guard and the duty to his wife and child.

Omin knew if he remained to face the enemy, it would surely mean death for his family. If anything were to happen to them, he could not live with himself. He decided to not sound the alarm. Instead he quickly ran home to get his family and leave.

When he arrived home, Petra and Dahlia were in the living area. Omin tried to keep his composure so he would not alarm Dahlia. He told her to go outside for a while. He then confided to Petra what was going on. He told her to gather what she could. Then they would head south to Samothrace because Omin knew how well fortified the city was.

Omin called Dahlia. Once she was inside, he mentioned to her they were going on a little trip to Samothrace. Dahlia knew Samothrace had all kinds of things that the city of Barrowmer didn't. Dahlia was very excited to go. They became a family that would flee the inevitable.

After a very long voyage, the massive fleet of warships finally reached the shores of Atlantis, just outside the city of Barrowmer. The first to set foot on the land of Atlantis was Hasan-bar, a man with a heartless reputation. He was the General and second in command to the cutthroats of the Jahir. He only answered to the evil Uric.

Hasan-bar stepped from a small boat and lead the troops which numbered almost three thousand. He watched as more Jahir troops set foot on the Atlantean shore. Uric had chosen his second in command wisely. Hasan-bar was ruthless. He killed with no mercy, no remorse, and no conscious as a living demon from the fiery pits of hell might kill.

After enough troops were on land, he ordered some to move upwards, blocking the retreat of the poor souls of Barrowmere from the doom and gloom, they were about to face.

Hasan-bar took the lead of some of the troops and gave them the order to burn and destroy all in their path. Ruthlessly, his troops did as they were told. This was his troop's actions. The troops followed his orders exactly as he gave them without question or hesitation.

The troops hadn't gone very far inland, and had not met any of the enemy as of yet until now. On a path just outside the city of Barrowmere, Hasan-bar and his troops encountered a family comprised of a man, a woman, and a child. Hasan-bar was a large and burly man, with a long black beard. Even his appearance scared the child, which caused the child to cling tightly to her father.

As he looked at the innocent family, Hasan-bar and his troops blocked their path. Then Hasan-bar said, "Well, now what do we have here? Seems we have run across some Atlantean scum. They are not worthy to even breathe the air. The only thing good for you is death!"

Hasan-bar continued, "It is my duty to rid the earth of such scum!" With those words, Hasan-bar dismounted from his steed and walked over to the man who was holding the child. He unsheathed his sword and plunged it into the man and child. As he did, he yelled, "Now, that is all Atlantean scum are good for!"

The man and child still clung to each other as they collapsed to the ground dead. Only the woman remained alive. By now, the troops were having their way with her, as many troops raped her over and over again.

Hasan-bar then shouted to his troops to stop. He turned to the woman and said casually, "My pretty, do you have a name?"

The woman, who by now was battered and bloodied, answered him. "My name is Petra, I do not worry for myself, but you just killed my husband and child! I have no reason to keep living! You just destroyed my world!" Petra told Hasan-bar this because she thought since he had stopped the Jahir troops, Hasan-bar might spare her life.

However, with absolutely no hesitation, he told Petra, "Atlantean women are only good for one thing. So allow me to honor your wishes, my pretty!" He grabbed Petra by the hair, held her head back and then he slit her throat, ear to ear, to make sure she was dead.

Once Petra was dead, Hasan-bar mounted his steed and lead his troops further onto the continent of Atlantis. Whatever lay in their path would surely be destroyed.

On that day of evil, death and destruction were now on the continent of Atlantis.

Meanwhile back at Samothrace, the capital of Atlantis, an ill King Archimedes had not yet been appraised of the happenings outside the city of Barrowmere. He had taken to his bed as he seemed to be very sick. The royal physician just announced that Archimedes had a malady of congestion of the body but with a few days of rest in bed, he should be as good as new.

The royal physician told the King that it was very important that he get as much rest as possible. But Archimedes couldn't sleep and rest as he was told. Each time he closed his eyes, he began to dream. His dreams were not pleasant either. Instead, they were dreams filled with violence and premonition. He dreamt that Uric, the evil man, was spreading horrendous evil and propaganda through the entire land of Atlantis.

The beautiful Queen, Delyse, stood beside her husband, doing for him what she could. At this particular time, as she watched her husband's troubled sleep near the terrace, Delyse could hear the twins as they ran and disported in the courtyard. She was afraid the noise from the twins would wake Archimedes, so she walked toward the terrace and called to the twins, "Aoleon, Arion, you know your father is ill! Have you no respect? Be quiet, as not to wake your father!"

Delyse heard her husband, "My Queen, I am awake. The twins have not woken me. No, I am awake rather by the violent dreams that plague me!" Upon hearing this, Delyse returned to the King's side and said, "Husband, you know what the physician said. Please rest!"

Archimedes replied, "Rest? How can I rest when my mind is plagued by these forsaken dreams? I dream of war. I see the whole of Atlantis in total disarray and worst of all the deaths of you and the twins! But please don't let my words make you fret as they are just dreams!"

Delyse looked lovingly at her husband with a caring expression. "Sire, your words do not cause me any worry! I just wish the dreams would stop, so you could rest my Lord!"

Archimedes worried over his dreams and the message that they might present. At one point, he tried to get out of bed and go to the war room to moan over some battle strategies. But he was stopped by Delyse, telling him to go back to bed.

Archimedes complied and returned to his bed. Just then there was a knock on his chamber doors. Delyse called out, "Enter." A high ranking palace guard stood at the threshold and said he has some rather urgent news. Delyse tried to stop the guard from bothering her ill husband, but Archimedes then spoke. "My Queen, you know I must hear this news for it is my duty as King!"

He looked at the palace guard and told the guard to relate the urgent news. "Sire, we just got news that the Jahir have once more landed on Atlantean ground. They have troops numbering in the thousands, and they are making their way inland toward the city, leaving a path of devastation and destruction behind them! Sire my apologies for bringing such bleak news at such a bad time!" The guard then bowed and exited the room.

Upon hearing that, Archimedes felt he must go to his war room to figure out a strategy which would prevent the Jahir from entering the city. As the King got to his feet, a very concerned Delyse uttered, "Sire, I know what you must do, and I stand behind you as any wife should. But I can't help be greatly concerned for you! I love you so, and Sire I do not know what I would do in the event something should happen to you!"

Now on his feet, Archimedes said softly but firmly, "My Queen, I love you also. However, please don't be concerned about me! I will be fine!"

Archimedes stumbled slowly to the war room along with two of his Generals, to make a battle plan. They hoped to ensure the demise of the Jahir. As the trio went over maps and other documents, Archimedes and his Generals arrived at a plan. Archimedes figured he and his troops would travel north and surround the borders of Alysea. Here the passageways were very narrow, and from here he hoped to capture and slaughter the enemy.

After coming up with this plan, Archimedes looked at his two Generals and ordered, "Get the troops ready. We shall pursue this plan within the hour!"

In an hour or so, an ill Archimedes met his troops outside the palace. He walked outside, with Delyse and the twins beside him. As Archimedes prepared to mount his steed, Delyse grabbed him by the arm. Archimedes faced his wife and saw she had tears in her eyes.

Archimedes looked at his wife and children. He sensed a feeling of doom. But he could not understand the message his feelings were trying to tell him. He bent down and picked up each of the twins separately. He kissed each of them and assured both of them he would soon return. Then he faced Delyse, as she tried to maintain her composure as the graceful Queen, while her heart was literally breaking.

Delyse was trying so hard to be the Queen who was in control of her emotions. But when Archimedes took hold of her in his arms, the tears started to flow. Archimedes stood in front of his Queen and wiped her tears away, while he tried his best to assure her that he would be home soon.

Delyse looked at her husband and said, "Sire, I know you must go, and you have always returned, but I have this feeling I will never see you again! This feeling is eating away at my very soul!" Archimedes answered, "M'Lady, don't worry. I shall return. Now dry your tears!" Then Archimedes mounted his steed and he was on his way. Delyse and the children watched until he disappeared from sight.

Archimedes figured their best bet was to do battle from The Plains of Dormanu. Dormanu was a piece of land just outside the border of Alysea. In that area, there was a hill. Archimedes planned to fight the Jahir from this hill to give himself an advantage.

On their way to Dormanu, Archimedes and his troops surveyed what they saw the closer they got to the plain. They saw what used to be farmhouses that were now burned to the ground. They saw dead bodies, still out in the open, perfect for food for the vultures,

As Archimedes looked at all that death and destruction, he just shook his head side to side in disbelief at all the devastation the Jahir had caused.

Soon, they were on the plain, near the place in which Archimedes planned to do battle. Here was the place that his troops should set up camp. A signal was sounded, and camp setup was begun.

Constructing the camp took awhile since Archimedes commanded several thousand troops. The troops were all abuzz as they unpacked their equipment from packed horses. When all were almost finished, there were tents as far as the eye could see. In many ways, the sight resembled a small town.

The servants of Archimedes set up his tent. The King was very glad as he felt really badly. He went inside his tent to rest for awhile. As he stepped just inside, Archimedes literally collapsed from exhaustion. He still had a fever which made him feel very weak.

As he relaxed in his tent, the ill King was soon startled by the presence of a scout. The scout delivered the news that the Jahir troops were only about a mile away. In fact, some had even broken across the border. As the scout departed, it was now clear to Archimedes that he and his troops would probably have to do battle sooner than expected.

Archimedes knew the enemy was close so he ordered his troops to build a wall and a ditch around the encampment. Using the earth and stones obtained from digging a huge ditch, the troops constructed a rampart or wall. The wall ranged from five to twelve feet high and from six to ten feet across. It was made of stout wooden lumber from the trees that were four feet high, waffled and battlemented. This afforded protection to the archers. With enough time, it was also possible to cover the sides of the embankment with sod to brace the earth and also with bundles of brush and sticks. The wall was quite steep on the outside. This assured the troops that it would not be washed down by the rains. It also gave better access to the troops. He strengthened it on the inner side by sloping it gradually so that steps of brush or logs could be constructed. Further protection was made possible by the ditch around the camp.

This act would give the encampment the protection it needed. The small hill, from where Archimedes wanted to make his attack was outside the encampment. In this case, time was the enemy, as there was not enough precious time to build a ditch in front of the hill.

The typical battle strategy during this time in history was for both rivals to face each other and then charge from a hill. This simple maneuver gave the troops an easier walk because of gravity. It generally might seem to the enemy that the troops were being drawn to them. This also gave them a better optical advantage.

With the enemy just minutes away, Archimedes gave the order for his many troops to position themselves in battle stance on the little hill. When the enemy was just within sight, Archimedes and his troops were ready.

The enemy was marching in a straight line in battle mode. When the enemy neared the Archimedes and his troops, an "approach formation" was taken up in which the packs and saga were laid aside, shield coverings removed while helmets and crests were put on.

Archimedes ordered them to charge down the hill to meet the enemy head on. Archimedes and his troops showed nothing but bravery as they clashed with the Jahir. In the air you could hear the cries of men, some as they attacked others and some as they died.

Whether it was enemy or Archimedes' troops, you could see the sun reflecting off all the swords that were doing battle. Archimedes on horseback, cutting down everything in his path.

The King swung his blade, side to side, thinking of his family as he did so, which empowered him and made him even more determined.

Catapults had been put in strategic places so their flaming contents could do the most damage. The archers made the air fill with a rain of deadly arrows.

The ground that was once only rocky, now ran red with the blood of all the men that had fallen in battle here. Archimedes still moved forth swinging his sword in hand. Suddenly he felt a hand on his foot, pulling him to the ground. As he fell, he dropped his sword.

As his golden armor glistened in the sun, he knew he had to quickly fulfill his task. The Jahir warrior that pulled him to the ground tried to run Archimedes through with his sword. But Archimedes quickly rolled over and the Jahir just missed him.

Archimedes saw that the Jahir warrior was going to try again as he lay on his side. Archimedes pulled out a dagger, and deftly caught the Jahir with his dagger in the warrior's midsection, immediately causing the warrior's death.

Now on his feet again, Archimedes looked on the ground at one of the dead Jahir, and he spotted a spiked mace. He picked it up and continued fighting.

The bloody battle continued and slowly moved the Jahir back to the border. At the border were more of Archimedes' troops. Their presence caused the Jahir to retreat.

Archimedes looked around. On the blood red ground, there were bodies of men everywhere. He thought to himself that he never wanted bloodshed. But he knew that all this was because of a power hungry, evil Uric.

Archimedes and his troops returned to their camp. The lower ranking men had to rest awhile before they began the gruesome task of burying the dead.

Archimedes was very happy that this moment, for they had a victory. Yet soon his happiness was clouded. Shortly, a scout reported to him that several thousand more Jahir were approaching the border.

Back at the Samothrace palace, a very lonely, worried Queen, sat in the garden,

OF ATLANTIS

outside the palace, watching her children at play. She could see so much of her husband in her twin boys. That just made her heart yearn more for the man she loved.

Archimedes had always returned from his battles, but this time she felt something was different. She couldn't shake this feeling she had; one of impending doom. Being wife to the King, Delyse understood his duty to Atlantis, but this feeling, caused the Queen to feel rather depressed.

The boys had just finished playing a game of tag. Aoleon noticed the troubled look on his mother's face. The golden haired child walked up to his mother and taking her hand, said, "Mother, don't worry! Father promised he would return, and father always keeps his promises!"

A distraught Delyse looked at her innocent son as she picked him up and kissed him. She replied, "Aoleon, don't worry about me. I just miss your father so much when he is gone! I know you speak truth when you say your father will return!"

Arion briefly chased a butterfly. Then he joined his mother and brother. he said that he wanted to stay outside a little while longer at first. But then he too noticed and sensed the feeling of doom that his mother displayed. As he looked up at his mother Arion offered, "Mother, if I pick you some flowers, will you feel better?"

This gesture really moved Delyse. She replied, "You don't have to pick any flowers for me my son, I just miss your father so! But I do love you and your brother very much."

Aoleon, tugged at his mother's hand, "Come, mother, play with us like father does when he is home! You could watch me run, because I run faster than Arion! That always makes him mad!"

An Arion added, "Mother, Aoleon is not faster than me! Come on, watch us run, and then you will see!"

A very weary Delyse stood up as both her boys pulled her toward the tree from which the boys always used as a starting point in their races. As they stood beside the tree, the twins prepared to race. Delyse still felt distraught. But for the sake of the twins, she shouted, "Go!" And the twins were off running in their friendly competition.

Running like the wind, the twins ran to the fountain in the middle of the garden. Then, racing around it, they ran back to the tree. Delyse carefully watched. When the twins reached the tree, they arrived at the same time. Delyse happily spoke, "All right you two, nobody won! You both reached the tree at the same time!"

The twins were now arguing with each other about who really got there first. Delyse firmly informed them, "Aoleon, you are just as fast as Arion. And you Arion, are just as fast as Aoleon! It is time for our midday meal, and after that I feel we should go to the temple and pray to God for your father's safe return."

Delyse and the twins walked into the dining hall for their midday meal. As they moved through the huge corridor of the castle, their footsteps echoed behind them. Delyse sensed that the castle seemed so big and so lonely.

Still a little distraught, Delyse and the twins reached the dining hall where they approached the enormous table, and sat down. For the sake of the twins, there was always a table setting for their father. Delyse did this hoping, that if this eased the twins missing their father, it would be for the best.

As the three sat at the table, servants attended to the Queen and the two princes. The trio dined on fruit and beef. The royal cook, Andrid, had a special relationship with the twins. Sometimes, he took time away from his many duties just to play with them.

This day Andrid had prepared something very special for the boys, apple dumplings. The twins looked on this dish as a treat. In fact, they were very excited about the desert.

Aoleon said loudly, "Mother look! Apple dumplings! I know Andrid made these especially for me and Arion. He is really our friend!"

Arion then blurted out, "Yes mother, Andrid is our friend, but he likes me more than Arion! See, I got the biggest dumpling!" Then Arion stuck his tongue out at Aoleon.

At that point, Delyse stepped into the argument. "All right you two, I'm sure Andrid likes you both the same. If you two start fighting amongst yourselves, you will be punished. I'm sure you don't want me to send you to your rooms!" After Delyse threatened them as a mother might, the two settled down. Instead, they looked at each other each trying to stare the other down.

Delyse then asked, "Are you two finished eating? I feel we must go to the temple to pray for your father's safe return! If we pray to God, I am sure he will watch over your father!"

OF ATLANTIS

After the conclusion of their meal, Delyse and the twins headed toward the temple on an upper floor of the castle. Delyse hoping that talking to God would ease her heavy laden heart.

The trio walked up the striped stairs to to the temple on the upper floor. Then Delyse pushed open the heavy wooden door which opened on to a place of defined beauty.

They entered into a room whose walls were enlaced in gold. A massive light fixture hung in the middle of the room. On the sides of the walls were places for one to place a candle, as Delyse did at that moment. At the end of the room was a beautiful altar, covered with a plush purple material. There too was a place to leave a small sacrifice to God. It was here that Delyse placed a small emerald crested pen belonging to Archimedes.

The priest wasn't here. It was his duty to collect the sacrifices for God and to teach the twins about God. Delyse reasoned that it was proper to bring an article belonging to the King, since she and the twins were going to pray to God for Archimedes.

At that point, the twins began to act up. So Delyse angrily spoke, shaking her finger at them, "What did I tell you before? SSSSSSSHHHHHHHH! You boys pray to God about your father. In this place, you are always on your best behavior."

The trio bowed before the altar, as they prayed for the safe return of their father. On her knees, Delyse was almost in tears, as she beseeched God to protect the man she so loved.

After their prayers were said, the trio left the room. Aoleon said, "Mother look, steps to the tower. From there we can see ships in the bay. Mother, we have been good. Can we please go to the tower so we can watch the boats? Please... please...please?"

Arion started tugging at his mother's skirts, more or less begging her to let them see the boats. Delyse finally gave in and the twins began the long climb on the narrow staircase, to the tower.

The tower room had a few chairs scattered about the small area. The room itself wasn't really used for anything. The three stood at the tower window and watched the ships in the bay, as they came and went.

While Delyse watched the ships, she recalled when Archimedes once said that when he was young, his mother, Cheris, would bring him here to watch the ships, when his father was also gone. Now, just like their father, the twins looking at the ships and tried to guess where they were going. Perhaps, they wondered, if one of the ships may be going to where their father was.

Delyse was also playing the little game with her sons, but then she saw something that could only mean trouble. A fleet of ships flying the flag of Uric was approaching. She knew the ships carried the murderous Jahir. She watched as the boats moved into the harbor and finally made their way to the shore.

Almost at the instant when the ships hit the shore, the Jahir jumped from their ships and began running amuck in every direction. Delyse then heard the alarm, which called all the guards to arms.

Delyse watched as a great battle ensued. The twins, now sleepy from their midday meal, began to nod off. As they laid their weary heads in her lap, Delyse watched in horror at the plight of the guards. They were tremendously outnumbered. The guard did their best to stop the cut throats, but they were no match for the Jahir.

The Queen now knew that she and the twins were in danger. The Jahir were now infiltrating the castle, itself. All rooms had been built with escape tunnels on the bottom floors. However, rooms of the upper floors was equipped with a secret chamber specially for the protection of the royal family.

Delyse woke the sleeping twins and softly explained to them that they were going to play a game about some very bad men were in the castle, and they were going to hide. The hidden chamber was located nearby, behind a tapestry. Delyse and the twins quickly hid themselves there.

Soon the tower room was overrun by the Jahir. As the trio hid, Delyse heard a familiar voice that said, "I have an idea where they are! The cook was tortured. He couldn't have lied to us!" Delyse knew it was the voice of Uric.

Arion heard what was said about Andrid. The child gasped. Delyse put her hand over his mouth, but it was too late, Uric and the Jahir had heard the boy.

Now Uric knew exactly where they were. Uric pulled the tapestry down off the wall and threw it to the floor, revealing the secret chamber. He grasped the door handle and swung the door open. The trio looked up to find Uric standing over the royal family. "Now, look what we have here!" he said with a sneer.

At this time, about a hundred miles off the shores of Atlantis, sailing on a calm clear ocean, the King and his troops sailed north, in the hopes of implementing a plan to stop the bloodthirsty Jahir.

It was the middle of the night and Archimedes, in bed in his cabin, was jarred awake from an ominous dream. He was sweating profusely as he got up from his bed and poured himself a glass of wine.

The nightmare that woke the King was just too real. It seemed so much more than a dream. Even though he was now awake, the King sensed that what he dreamt was actually the truth.

He tried not to panic. Archimedies kept his composure and sent a message to his Generals. he wanted to confer with them. He just knew within his very soul that something he truly feared had actually taken place.

In his dream, Delyse and the twins had fallen into the evil clutches of Uric. But the ungodly feeling of dread and doom that the King felt in the dream was still with him, he sensed Uric, and he knew what just transpired while he was sleeping, was a dreaded reality.

The King positively knew that his wife and children were in terrible trouble. Archimedes also believed deep within that he and his troops must go back to Samothrace to free his family from Uric.

Now there was a knock on his cabin door. He expected his Generals and so, Archimedes told them they could enter. As they did, each noticed the solemn look on the King's face. Further, for the King to have summoned them in the middle of the night, the Generals knew something really big must be transpiring.

Burbine, one of the Generals said, "Sire, why were we summoned here when all should be sleeping? Have you managed to obtain new information on the Jahir?"

Archimedes looked at them all and replied, "Something very bad has happened! You all know at times I can sense things! While I never know how I know things, I do know for sure that the Queen and the two young princes are in dire straits! Uric is in the city, and my family is with him! He has taken them prisoner! We must return to Samothrace!"

The Generals all looked at each other, and almost shook their heads 'no' in unison. Burbine then stepped forward. "Sire, I think I speak for all when I say, with respect, that going back to Samothrace would be a bad thing to do! If the Jahir have conquered the city, they would run rampant within!"

Burbine continued simplistically. "M'Lord, going back to Samothrace would be suicide! A man can find another wife. He can have more children, why throw your life away! Why risk your life? Your subjects need their King! If something were to happen to you, there would be no leadership, and God help us all if the Jahir and Uric gained control of the throne!"

Archimedes stared at his Generals with solemn look on his face. He replied, "I would do nothing to bring ill will to my life, but this is VERY important to me. Maybe I am truly thinking with my heart, but if something were to happen to my family, I would not want to continue on the journey of life alone!"

Archimedes continued, "Most of you have a wife and children. Think how you would feel if something happened to your family! I know Uric rarely takes prisoners, so their very life is on the line! As your King, I command that we must go back to Samothrace."

Burbine and the others left the King. Burbine sought the captain of the ship to tell him to change course and head toward Samothrace.

Now alone, Archimedes had time to reflect on what he knew was a devastating reality. Uric had his family. And Archimedes made a promise to himself: if Uric harmed his family in any manner, he would find Uric, wherever he might go. Yes, he would be hunted down and be destroyed.

It was a very hot humid day as three lone ships made their way to Samothrace. As they neared the city, the signature of the Jahir's handy work could be seen everywhere.

The merciless and ruthless Jahir, infamous for not taking prisoners, had impaled most Alysea soldiers they had captured. They had left the poor souls impaled in plain view. They were all along the side of the road that went into Samothrace. It was, to Uric, a signature of who now controlled the city.

One of the riders now headed for the city was none other than the King himself. Archimedes shook his head from side to side, as he took in the scene he viewed. He surely thought to himself that he never wanted anything like that to have happened. By nature, Archimedes had always been a peaceful man. Yet now the only word he could think of was 'horrific.'

As the three lone riders got closer to the city, they saw the charred remains of what used to be their homes. They heard the screeching of the vultures as they waited, greedily, for their prey to die. They who feast on the carcasses of the dead waited now. The once lush thriving land was now only a scene of death and destruction.

The three men stopped just outside the city for a drink of water. The three, the King and two body guards, like the wind, heard the sounds of death. The wind carried the sound of death as you heard the cries, of those impaled but were not yet dead. Those were the victims who were mercilessly suffering, wishing for the sweet escape of death.

Archimedes looked at his two body guards. "You have served me well, my friends. But as your King, I have only one command left to give you. I release you from your duties. I want you to try and make an escape for your life. The rest of this journey I must do alone! It is my family that is in danger, and I do not want anymore blood on my hands. I therefore command you to go your own way. Uric is mine and mine alone!"

Simon, one of the guards with Archimedes, and a loyal subject, said, "M'Lord, if you venture into the city alone, it would surely be suicide. It is my duty to stand beside my King, to protect him at any cost. I will not dishonor you or myself by letting you go into the city alone!"

Archimedes took a cloth from his side and slowly wiped the sweat from his face. He turned and looked into Simon's eyes then at his other guard, Lorean. Then he said, "Simon, Lorean, both of you are my true loyal subjects. But if I command, you must obey. Honor me by following my order, and go away from this place of death and doom which has been manufactured by a madman. I must go into the city alone!"

The two men both truly knew they must follow the command of their King. It was with very great hesitation, the two men wished the King Godspeed. Then they mounted their horses and rode off in the opposite direction. Archimedes stood silently still as they disappeared from his view.

Archimedes was all alone now. It was only now that he began to make his way nearer to the city. Strangely enough, even as he reached the outskirts, no Jahir stopped him. This made him believe that this was the way Uric wanted it. He ws truly expecting to face Uric soon.

As Archimedes approached the city's edge, from one of the many hill tops, a Jahir scout kept watch of traffic in and out of the city. The scout saw the King as he approached the city. He also knew he must get that news to Uric as soon as possible.

The Jahir scout jumped on his black as night horse nearby and swiftly headed to the palace to alert Uric of the King's approach. The man expected that he would be greatly rewarded by delivering this news.

Once at the palace, the scout dismounted and quickly ran into the war room which had been taken over by Uric. Now out of breath, he stood before Uric, bowed, and said, "M'Lord, the King approaches. He was alone, just outside the city!"

The evil man knew good news when he heard it. "Brennon, your news pleases me. See your General and you shall be well rewarded! Outside the city, on approach, huh? This gives me time to prepare for his arrival!"

After the scout left, Uric walked across the massive hall to another room, one which held contents most important to the King. In this room were Delyse and the twins, all under lock and key and totally under the control of the madman.

The twins clung to their mother out of sheer fear. Yet Delyse held steadfast in the presence of danger just as a Queen should. As she glared at Uric from the chair to which she was tied, she said "What is it that you want of us? I demand to know!"

Uric, with a lecherous grin on his face replied, "The King approaches. We must be ready to greet him! I have a special surprise for Archimedes, and you shall help!" He then summoned his guards. As he turned away, you could hear a deep demonic chuckle.

A lone rider rode through the streets of a thriving city that once was. All the buildings looked burnt and charred. The cobblestone streets, which were only a short while ago clean and cared for, were now horrendously stained with blood. Although the roads were well populated with Jahir soldiers, not one confronted the King as he made his way toward the palace.

Along the way to the palace, the King noticed one of the barn-like buildings. From the structure, he heard cries for help. At one of the windows he saw a few men, no doubt held by the Jahir. He thought, as he rode, that those poor souls were being held prisoners to only benefit the Jahir in some way.

The cries were soon stopped by Jahir warriors as they shuttered the windows closed. There was not another sound but only an eerie kind of silence, as the King continued to the palace.

Still, on the sides of the street, the King saw the bodies of those victims, impaled by the biddling of the madman. They marked his way as a kind of a warning. Only silence prevailed here as well for evidentially these people had been released from their suffering by death.

Some of the bodies were women and children. As Archimedes passed this grotesque sight, he thought to himself that he was viewing the work of a lunatic. It was evident to Archimedes that Uric had no conscience or soul. The man had to be not in his right mind. No one in their right mind would do anything such as this.

Archimedes made his way deeper into the city, on his journey to the palace. Archimedes was trying to plan a way to stop this insanity. Uric was very powerful. Yet it was evident that his greed had thrown him over the edge of sanity.

Finally, as he reached the palace steps, Archimedes was met by Uric, who tightly embraced a terrified Delyse. He had a small blade at her throat. Beside the palace steps, he heard the cries of his children, as they begged for help. Archimedes looked around the immediate area and saw his two sons tied to a stake. Nearby were executioners who seemed ready to burn the boys alive with just the word from Uric.

Epilogue

Many lifetimes later, Archimedes finally rested in Paris, France, the city of love. He used the assumed name of Jacques Caron. He met a young archeologist by the name of Damien Acton. Acton followed Jacques for several weeks. He believed the man to be special in some way. During this time, Damien kept bothering Jacques to let him be his student. While watching the old man, Jacques seemed to show quite the knowledge of ancient civilizations which were specific to Damien's interest. Finally Jacques agreed to the request, and another adventure in the life of an eternal began:

Be unwearied, unceasing, alive

you and your own true love;

Let not the heart be troubled during your

sojourn on Earth,

but seize the day as it passes!

It was a very sunny afternoon as Jacques and Damien exited Le Biblioteque, the great library in Paris. Damien had given notice at the university of his intention's to end his service. He would work an additional two weeks, and then he would be free to pursue his chosen path.

The university asked Damien to do a special favor for them. They wanted him to give a final lecture on the third dynasty of ancient Egypt. This had been the reason for the pair's visit to the library.

The two men soon reached Damien's flat where they prepared their end of day meal. Jacques looked at Damien and said, "Are you aware that you, more or less, wasted your time researching books and periodicals on ancient Egypt at the library?"

Damien looked at Jacques with inquisitive eyes. "My dear friend, what do you mean? I have always based my lectures on what has been written down through out history. I don't understand what you mean."

Jacques replied, "All right my friend, I will explain. You can't really trust anything you read about ancient Egypt. The ancient Egyptian people were very proud. As a result, the Pharaoh's scribes only wrote down what they wanted you to know, while they always made sure Pharaoh had the upper hand."

Damien asked, "Exactly how do you know this to be a fact?"

Jacques replied, "My dear Damien, I have not completely told you everything. One of my most well known densities was that of Imhotep, genius of the fourth dynasty. I know that certain things aren't true my son, because I was there. I lived it."

Damien responded, "You mean to tell me you were there? Are you telling me that you were Imhotep of the fourth dynasty in Egypt? Well then, you must tell me everything just for my own personal thirst for knowledge of ancient civilizations!"

Jacques exhaled flustered, "Very well then. But most of what I am about to share with you, you will never find in any books or writings from that period in time. What I am about to share with you is the absolute truth, and only for your ears to hear. I will be a lot more honest than the books you research on the subject. So, let me take you back to a time when life was simple and tell you the whole truth."

Damien eagerly wanted to hear Jacques' depiction of ancient Egypt. The two men stood on the small terrace just outside Damien's flat. It was a warm beautiful night and there was an abundance of twinkling stars in the clear night sky. Jacques and Damien pulled over two chairs and made themselves comfortable. Then Jacques began to tell his story.

"I told you about when I lived in ancient Babylon. But what I didn't tell you before I went to Europe the first time was that I also stayed in Egypt for a while. I got work from a caravan that had come to Babylon to do some trading. They had come from Egypt, and the caravan needed some extra bearers. It seemed like a good idea and so I joined the caravan which led me to Egypt."

"We were heading toward Saqqara, which was home to the Pharaoh at the time. Our route took us through the desert. I had never seen so much sand. It took what felt like forever to get through the desert."

"We were crossing the Gaza Plateau, when I saw something my eyes just could not believe. There, sitting in the middle of the Plateau, was the biggest structure my eyes had ever beheld. This massive structure had the body of a lion and the head of a man. My eyes were transfixed! It just looked so majestic and regal in the ancient Egyptian sun, that I was awe struck!"

"I asked one of the other bearers what this huge thing was? The bearer told me that it had been there as long as the sands. The Egyptians held so much reverence for this as it was thought to be a gift from the Gods. All believed that it had guarded the desert and sands. They called it the Sphinx."

"We continued our journey through the hot desert, until we finally arrived at the city of Saqqara. After walking through a massive gateway, we finally entered an ancient city. There were people everywhere, vendors all along the streets selling their wares, with small houses and shops that lined the sides of the street."

"When we finally reached the palace, we stopped while one of the task masters went to request an audience with the Pharaoh. There, he could inspect the riches we had brought with us for him and his country."

"Once we were seated, we were refreshed with some clear cool water. Then we heard a legion of horns that announced the presence of the Pharaoh. A procession emerged. Right in the center, was Pharaoh Dojosher, the pharaoh at that time. He was surrounded by several beautiful women. I'd say they were his wives. There were even several children in the procession, possibly the royal family."

"We were told to bow before our God, Pharaoh, which we did with reverence and respect. Then, strangely, it was as if the Pharaoh sought me out." He said to me, "Why is it that you look different than the other bearers?" I told him I came from a land across the great sea. That was why I didn't look Egyptian. The Pharaoh looked intrigued. He invited me into the palace so I could tell him more of my strange homeland."

"I humbly accepted Pharaoh's most gracious invitation. So I got in the line of the procession, following the man whose life I would change forever."

"As I followed the procession inside the royal palace, once again, I was at a loss for words. In Atlantis, mosaics were a big part of palace decor. But these people had painted colorful depictions right on the wall. I had never seen such beauty as this so masterfully done."

"To my surprise, it was extremely cool within the palace and soon the procession reached the throne room. This room was so ornate. It was completely decorated in gold and jewels. You could tell by the surroundings, that Pharaoh spared no expense."

Once in the throne room for a short time, the Pharaoh took his rightful place on the throne. He looked so regal and majestic, somewhat like the Sphinx itself. Then suddenly there was an interruption. A slave girl came running in, sobbing as she entered. She told the Pharaoh that his eldest son, who was heir to the throne, was playing very close to the banks of the Nile. He lost his footing and fell into the river which was supposed to be the giver of life. Just behind the slave girl, appeared several guards. One of the guards carried the lifeless body of the royal prince. The guard looked at Pharaoh and said grimly that the boy no longer draws breath."

"I looked on the Pharaoh's face. I saw anguish. I knew how he felt for I recalled how I felt when I saw Uric holding the dead bodies of my own sons. I knew I had to do something. It was clear what I had to do. I knelt down over the royal prince. Then, I blew the air of life into his lungs."

"While I knelt, Pharaoh was pacing the floor, shaking his head in disbelief. All of a sudden the young prince began to breathe once again. Pharaoh and his court subjects just could not believe their eyes. As the young prince sat up, the Pharaoh ran to his side and hugged him as if he would never let him go."

Pharaoh turned to me, still holding his son, and said, "I know not where you came from and I really don't care! What I do know is that you brought my son back to me from the land of the dead! You shall be handsomely rewarded! It must be said that the Gods brought you to us! This, I know, to be true!"

"For what you have done for my son, you shall become the royal family's personal physician. And since you not from Egypt, you must have need of an Egyptian name. Therefore, from this day forth, you shall be known as Imhotep. Let it be written, let it be done."

"So from that day forth, I became a part of Pharaoh's household. Any matters that pertained to health, I was sought as council. Soon I would introduce more from my life in Atlantis, to make the lives of these primitive people a little bit easier."

Damien realized it was well past 10 P.M., so he and Jacques decided to retire for the evening. The next morning, the two men rose bright and early. Damien liked the mornings for it gave Jacques the opportunity to tell more of his story.

And so Jacques continued. "It had been a few years since the Pharaoh adopted me to his court. By this time I had the opportunity to show Pharaoh several things I learned from Atlantis. I had also gained several titles bestowed on me by the gracious Pharaoh. A few of my many titles are Chancellor the King of Lower Egypt, King of Upper Egypt, Administrator of the Great Palace, Hereditary Nobleman, High Priest of Heliopolis, Builder, and finally, the Sculptor and Maker of Vases in Chief."

"I was very honored for how the Pharaoh looked upon me. I hadn't married yet, but soon I would meet the love of my life and marry. Although I would deeply love my wife, I would never feel the same extent of love for another woman as I did for Delyse."

"I tried to forget what that troubled soul Uric did to my family in Atlantis. Yet the pain and memory remains. There are always three gapping holes in my heart, one for Delyse and two for my twin sons that were tragically murdered so very long ago."

"I, Archimedes, King of Atlantis, always had to hide my true identity. I also had to be in the service of another which was not an easy task for me."

"One day, while I was attending to one of my many duties, I happened to see a new hand maiden who was attending to the Queen. She was absolutely stunning! I watched her from under the curtain covers as she brushed the Queen's hair. I was awestruck. I could not move. Her beauty totally engulfed my mind, body, and soul."

"My heart was beating so fast, I felt like a young inexperienced boy again. Not since Delyse had a woman so entranced me as did this one. I decided right then and there that I must get to know this wonderfully seductive creature."

"One day, while I was walking through the palace, I happened to notice Hati, the hand maiden to Queen, bathing in one of the many pools in the palace. I couldn't help but stop and watch her. She was sleek as a gazelle as she gracefully moved in the water. She had the body of a goddess. Her tanned skin just glistened. For the very first time in a long time, I felt passion."

"I decided to make my presence known, but not until she had time to put on her robe. I walked up to her and introduced myself. Hati told me she heard of the miracles I had performed for the Pharaoh."

"I asked her if I might show her some of the city of Saqqara sometime. She agreed, but then excused herself to attend to the Queen."

"The next day, Hati met me at the city gates. I felt as giddy as a school boy. I couldn't help but stare at this beautiful creature as her long black hair blew in the wind. I asked Hati to forgive me for staring, but I thought she must be a reincarnation of the goddess, Isis. I thought she was the most beautiful creature my eyes ever beheld!"

"Hati looked as if she were blushing. She told me she was very humbled by what I thought of her. We started walking inside the busy bustling city of Saqqara. As we walked through the narrow streets, I couldn't take my eyes off of this amazing creature."

"Soon, Hati said she thought I was going to show her the city! I asked her to forgive me; I told her just being in her presence made me happy. Once again, she lowered her big brown eyes in humility!"

"After a while, Hati discreetly put her hand into mine. This told me, that she also had feelings for me as well. And then it happened; my lips met hers, and once again. passion was stirred within my soul. After the kiss, I knew Hati would become my future wife."

"There were no words to describe what I felt with her. I think she also knew that in time she would become my wife. Soon, we were once again at the palace, where Hati took her leave."

"But before she left, we shared another kiss and she promised we would be together again. I watched her as she ascended the palace steps, feeling my heart beating so very fast, I knew she was the one!"

"I also knew that Hati was very much the Egyptian. She would not submit herself to me until we were joined. So according to law I had to ask Pharaoh for permission to join with Hati."

"I knew what I was feeling was passion because true love takes time. But I had to have this women that had caused my soul to be engulfed by such passion."

"I requested an audience with Pharaoh which was granted. Then I stood in the presence of Pharaoh. I asked him for permission to be tied with Hati. Pharaoh immediately agreed, but there was a look of anguish on Pharaoh's face. I asked him what was wrong."

"Pharaoh told me he was worried about his soul going into the land of the dead. Egyptians were more concerned about the afterlife than everyday life. Pharaoh wanted a grand tomb, one in which his spirit would have no trouble finding his body. It was most important that he could reunite with it after death. This was really a major concern for Pharaoh."

"Pharaoh knew I had architectural ability. He beseeched me to design a tomb for him. It should be one that mankind had never seen before. It must be one in which, even after his death, he and his power would remain immortal."

"Pharaoh entrusted me with the task of designing him a tomb which was to be unlike anything ever seen. The tomb should be something on such a grand scale, that when it was seen, people would automatically think of Pharaoh Djosher."

"I found it very hard to stay focused because thoughts of Hati were on my mind constantly. I was supposed to meet her in the palace garden that very night. I planned to ask Hati to become my wife."

"I could hardly wait for nightfall to arrive. I rushed to the gardens to meet Hati. When I finally made it to the gardens, she was already there! I had to take a moment just to watch this exquisite creature. There was a full moon that night. I could see the moonlight shining in her hair. I thought to myself, I pray to all the Egyptian Gods that Hati would agree to be mine."

"After watching her for awhile, I made my presence known. When she saw me she ran toward me with open arms. When she reached me, we embraced in a very passionate kiss."

"Afterwards, we walked hand in hand through the palace gardens, taking our time as Hati often stopped to look at the flowers. We soon came to a fountain. Here we stopped and sat on a nearby bench."

I got up my courage, took Hati's hand in mine, then looked into her eyes. Then I said, "Hati, I think you are the most beautiful woman I have ever seen. I know since you are a follower of Isis, you have never known a man. I love you so very much. I want you to join with me in this life and in the land of the dead!"

"Imhotep," she said, "I too love you. Are you sure you want me for eternity? If you do, then I am sure Isis and Hathor, the goddess of fertility, will smile on us. I accept what you ask of me. I know you are not of Egypt, but I want to wed in the Egyptian way."

"Soon the conversation of the entire palace was about planning an Egyptian wedding. I was rather lucky because most weddings in ancient Egypt were arranged. But in our case, we were free to wed because of Pharaoh's generosity. The only rule we had to live by was that until the wedding, we were not allowed to be alone."

"The day finally arrived. our wedding was to be held in the throne room, overseen by Pharaoh and his Queen. I was dressed in a totally white linen toga. And to be terribly honest, for perhaps the first time in my life, I was very nervous."

The ceremony soon began. The first to arrive in place were the Zaffa, a group of musicians. They were followed by Hati in her bridal array. Hati was stunning. She had flowers in her dark hair and was dressed in a gown that looked as if were made of woven stars. She was breath taking. She stood directly beside me. Then I took her hand in mine, looked into her eyes and said,

"It Is Her Love that Gives Me Strength

My sister's love is on the far side.

The river is between our bodies.

The waters are mighty at flood-time,

A crocodile waits in the shallows.

I enter the water and brave the waves,

My heart is strong on the deep.

The crocodile seems like a mouse to me,

The flood as land to my feet.

It is her love that gives me strength,

It makes a water-spell for me.

I gaze at my heart's desire,

As she stands facing me!

My sister has come, my heart exults,

My arms spread out to embrace her.

My heart bounds in its place,

Like the red fish in its pond.

O night, be mine forever,

Now that my Queen has come!

My Queen, my lover, today just like Isis and Osiris, I pledge my love and myself to you.

Forever, in this life and the land of the dead,

I give you of myself. I give you my love. I want eternal happiness for you

And now, forever and a day, I give unto you myself.

You are now forever my wife.

And I am forever your husband.

Together we will overcome any strife.

Together, forever, infinite, just like the Egyptian sands.

"Then I put a ring on her finger, made from a reed of the Nile, the giver of life!"

Then it was Hati's turn. She looked at me and said,

"I wish I were your mirror,

so that you would always look at me.

I wish I were your garment,

so that you would always wear me.

I wish I were the water that washes your body.

I wish I were the unguent, O Imhotep.

I wish I were the beads around your neck.

I wish I were your sandal,

that you would step on me!

I will stand by your side,

For an eternity if I must.

My love, my life, I, Hati now become your wife, your bride.

Oh my love, all the passion, all the love, all the lust.

Imhotep, the man that stole my heart,

Bringing to my life something new.

A new life together, from this day will start.

My heart sings everyday only for you.

I give myself unto you.

Totally, my love is as infinite as the stars.

Each day I promise, with me by your side, will be totally new.

I am your wife, whether you are near or far.

"Then I kissed Hati and that part of the ceremony was over. There was dancing and a dinner provided by Pharaoh. Of course, as it was our wedding night, we didn't stay long!"

"Once we were alone, I could see Hati seemed fearful. So I told my goddess that all would be fine. I had no idea Hati would conceive on our wedding night, but she did!"

"The next day I decided I would fulfill Pharoah's request regarding his tomb. Now that Hati was mine, I could perform my duties with a clear head."

It was time for Damien to go to the university and teach two classes that afternoon. Jacques agreed to continue his story when Damien returned to his flat.

The afternoon was lovely as Damien made his way back to his flat. Only five more days and he would be free to pursue his passion which was to learn from Jacques, who was in reality, the eternal Archimedes, King of the lost continent of Atlantis.

When Damien arrived at his flat, he was met by Jacques. He took it upon himself to order pizza for their evening meal. As both men sat at the dining room table, Jacques continued his incredible story.

"I made sure that Hati was well cared for. I learned that the goddess Hathor, had smiled on us. Hati was with child!"

"While my mind was on my future child I recognized that Pharaoh was so generous. I wanted to fulfill his wish to have a burial tomb unlike any other."

"I considered several options very carefully. Most tombs were not of good construction and were typically made of mudded brick called mastabas. However, they would crumble under any amount of weight."

"So my first thought was to build a massive city constructed from stone. This job was also good for the Egyptian economy and her people. It took 100,000 men, all of whom earned a modest wage. These people were so devoted to their Pharaoh that they would have gladly done the work for nothing."

"One of the many things I had to keep in mind were tomb robbers. To offset this chance, I implemented a descending passage from the north leads to the burial chamber. Underground galleries surrounded the pyramid on all but the south side. In addition, Egyptians were very superstitious. There were several spells that would be etched in stone at the entrance that likely would scare any tomb robbers off."

"One day while I was surveying, one of Hati's servant girls came running telling me Hati was ready to give birth. But she could not find the midwife. As I was naturally very concerned, I ran all the way to be by Hati's side."

"When I got to her she was in so much pain, that I had her lie down, which was unheard of in ancient Egypt. Most women stood upright in a birthing circle to bring forth a child."

"I knew I was going to have to do this on my own. I gave Hati a leather strap to bite down on, but she still cried out in horrible pain. Finally, I could see the child. But it was a breech birth and then I knew why Hati was in so much pain. I had to do a procedure unheard of in ancient Egypt; I had to cut into Hati's stomach if I wanted to save the life of my child."

"But before I put Hati to sleep, she begged me to let her pray to the God Bas for a healthy baby. While she did this, I boiled leaves of willow and quinine. These herbs would make Hati sleep while I did the surgery."

"After I gave her the drink, she went to sleep and I began my work! After a while, I introduced a new life to the world, a son, which I knew Hati wanted to call Ipy."

"While I completed my work, I suddenly noticed that Hati no longer drew breath. To my complete horror, I realized that my beautiful wife was dead. She would never see the child she so longed for, at least not in this world! I ran to her side, frantically calling her name, but I received no response."

"I had to keep my wits about me for the sake of my son. After cleaning up the child, I went to Pharaoh's main wife, showing her the child and telling her that Hati died during childbirth. I entrusted my child to her nurse."

"Ten years passed so quickly. Each day I watched Ipy grow. He was very lucky because, he was taught and reared beside Pharaoh's son, Sekhemkhet. The two boys were growing up together, just like brothers."

"At times I so miss Hati. I try to keep my mind on other things, but my mind has a tendency to wander back to thoughts of her. One of my major tasks was that of the Pharaoh's tomb. I had already put three mastabas on top of each other. I was still not satisfied with the results so the work continued."

"When I finish the tomb, it would be six tiers high. But I would not present it to Pharaoh just yet. I attended to my everyday duties. Yet, there still remained loneliness which only a woman could fill."

"One day my duties called me to the temple of Isis where I saw her, a priestess of Isis. She could have been the Goddess herself. She had long dark hair and moved like a gazelle. She had a perfect body encased in a thin linen dress. She was stunning!"

"As a priestess of Isis, I knew full well that getting next to her would be very difficult. Most priestesses, who were all virgins, shied away from men! I had asked one of the many guards at the temple who this priestess was. One informed me that her name was Kiya."

"I just couldn't help myself. I was bewitched by her beauty. I watched this stunning creature from the shadows where I hid. I felt passion I hadn't felt in a very long time! I really tried to fight these feelings, but I was a prisoner with passion being my jail."

"Finally I could bear it no longer. I mustered the courage to talk to this exquisite creature! I took a deep breath and I made my presence known. It was simple. I merely walked up to her and introduced myself. At first she shied away, but finally she answered back by telling me her name."

Then she asked me, "Isn't your name, Imhotep?" I answered yes. Then I told her to forgive me for staring, but her beauty was breath taking. I wanted to get to know her better. I asked simply if we might meet this night beside the city gates?

"Amazingly enough, she agreed without hesitation. I never really noticed her flirtatious ways. Further, I didn't notice how fast she answered. Later on, I would understand why! But right at this moment, I felt ten feet tall."

"I went back to the palace, to finish the day's work, totally excited about what the night held! I really felt honored that this beautiful priestess of Isis had agreed to meet me!"

"The curtain of nightfall finally embarked. I was as excited as a young boy going on a first date. I carefully tried to be discreet as I make my way to the city gate of Saqqara. The last thing I wanted to do was to get caught meeting Kiya. if I were to be caught, it would surely mean banishment for her."

"Soon, I reached the city gate, and there Kiya stood, waiting for me. She had her face under a veil so she might not be recognized. I approached her and took her hand in mine. I then told her that I had a friend outside the city gate. If it was alright with her, it was where I thought we might go as I totally trusted this person."

"When we reached my friend's tent, I excused myself for a moment and spoke with him. I confided that we desired to be alone! My friend departed leaving this beautiful woman and I alone. Inside the tent I noted that my friend even left a bottle of the fruit of the vine! Kiya and I talked for hours as we drank the wine! Then without a single spoken word, Kiya leaned forward and kissed me! The next step was clear. We let the moment engulf us with several of hours of intense love making."

"Soon we were just lay there whispering to each other as the dawn began to break. It was necessary for Kiya to prepare to sneak back into the temple. Yet, I had to know before I let her go, when I could see her again. She placed her hand on my cheek and whispered to me that when it was safe for her, she would send word."

Damien, who had been listening intently to my story suddenly realized how late it was. So we decided to retire for the evening, "Tomorrow is Saturday, Jacques. No classes. I'll have all day for you to tell me more."

The following morning, both men got a cup of coffee and breakfast and sat once more on the terrace that adjoined Damien's flat. Here Jacques continued his story.

"The affair Kiya and I pursued lasted for a couple of months. Then, one night I made a discovery. After making love that evening, Kiya lay on her side. As I bent over her, I noticed a small tattoo in the small of her back. It was a tattoo of flames not much larger than a thumbnail. This really set me to wondering, because in the small of my back, I had the same tattoo!"

"The tattoo was one from Atlantis! Any person of power or with powers had this tattoo. No matter what one did, or what shape or identity that had been assumed, the tattoo was always there! The thought that came to my mind, made me sick to my stomach."

"I suspected that Kiya was a person of Atlantis! But how? Then it dawned on me that anyone that had certain power, could take on any form they wanted! The first person I thought of was Uric! Could my suspicion be one of truth?"

"When Kiya finally awoke, I didn't let on to what I suspected. Kiya gathered her clothes. Then I kissed her good bye as she once again left to return to the temple without anyone knowing that she'd been gone."

"I decided to see if my suspicions were true, I went to the Pharaoh and told him that I had sinned with a priestess of Isis. I wanted my soul to be cleansed so I could enter the land of the dead after my death. Pharaoh commended me for my honesty. However, for Kiya, there would be a different scenario. Pharaoh then decided that Kiya did not deserve to be a priestess of Isis because of her deception. Pharoah banished her from the temple and from Saqqara."

"After Kiya's banishment, I intended to see her quarters. Maybe in those quarters there would be some proof of my suspicion. I beseeched Pharaoh to allow me to see her quarters in the temple. I told Pharoah that I believed Kiya had taken something very dear to me and maybe she had left it there. Pharoh agreed."

"When I get to her quarters, another priestess showed me to Kiya's quarters. I entered a very modest room, with everything looking as it should. then I spotted the book. Here I discovered that Kiya had The Book of Life, a volume that I knew was from Atlantis. All the answers to all my questions were in this book."

"As I sat down with the book, I became quite excited that finally all my questions would be answered. But even before I could open the book, it just totally disappeared from my hands! I knew at that instant that the swine remembered the book, and with the power Uric possessed, wished it back."

"I realized my suspicions were true. Uric had used his powers to take a shape of a woman and possibly destroy me in that way. But, he could never hurt me any more than he had in Atlantis."

"After my affair with Kiya, I decided I had had enough of women. So, instead I concentrated fully to work on Djosher's tomb, and watch my son, Ipy, grow to be a man."

"Ten years passed since construction began on Djosher's tomb, yet I still wasn't satisfied. I had to make it more grand than ever. I wanted the tomb to be seen for miles. I wanted Dojsher's power to be known forever."

"I had decided earlier that since one of the most awful things the poor of ancient Egypt did was tomb robbing, I would construct a maze of underground tunnels and rooms under the massive structure. I did this with the thought of confusing tomb robbers, so that the Pharaoh's eternal sleep would remain undisturbed."

"Under the structure are galleries which open into shafts above. There were also rooms which could be entered via a staircase or a sloping corridor that was intended for other Royal family members. The tomb itself was 28 meters deep. The layout of the rooms was supposed to depict Djosher's palace in the Afterlife. These rooms are often referred to as The Blue Chambers as they are covered with faience tiles in blue nuances. The decorations are meant to imitate mats and tapestries covering the walls of the palace. Finds were often made in these first shafts. Occasionally an empty alabaster sarcophagus would be discovered or a small wooden coffin with the body of a boy who died between the age of eight and ten, and a sometimes even the hipbone of a girl.

There were also two vessels decorated with gold leaf and carnelian coral. Fragments of alabaster sarcophagi and a seal imprint bearing the name of Netjerikhet were also discovered. In the sixth and seventh shafts some forty thousand stone vessels of varied forms and materials were found, many of them made of alabaster, slate, diorite and limestone. Several of them bore inscriptions by Royal names of 1st and 2nd Dynasty rulers like Narmer, Djer, Den, Adjib, Semerkhet, Kaa, Hetepsekhemwy, Ninetjer, Sekhemib and Khasekhemwy. Also non-royal names were inscribed. A sufficient explanation for this has not yet been reached. Did Djoser take hold of his predecessors' tombs and what was in them? A question that would be left unanswered, for a very long time."

"It finally took nineteen years to complete the whole complex for my Pharaoh's tomb. Upon completion, the structure was six tiers high which could be seen for miles. Finally, I was truly satisfied with the project and effort."

"Djosher would rule for twenty-nine years. My son, Ipy would become a scribe in Pharaoh's Sekhemkhet court. The young boy that my son befriended and with whom he grew, ultimately succeeded Djosher."

"I was very proud of my son being a scribe in Pharaoh's court. It was a great honor. The promise I made to Hati, so many years ago, was fulfilled. I watched our son grow to be a man. It seems I had managed to guide our son in the right direction."

"The people of ancient Egypt grew to look at me with the status of Pharaoh, himself. They revered me as half man, half God, because of all the things I did for Egypt and her people."

"For over twelve hundred years, after my supposed death, they worshipped me. Shortly after the death of Djosher, I felt it was time for me to take my leave. To do so, I had to stage my own death."

"Only the priests and embalmers would know the truth. My mummy would not be of me."

"I wasn't worried about those that knew the secret. Because Egyptian people were very superstitious, it was easy for me to swear them to secrecy. I told them that if they exposed the truth, bad luck would befall them, and they may even die. I sealed this promise by performing a few incantations. By doing this I knew my secret was safe."

"So, from that existence, I went on to a different life. But of course, that is another story. Even until this very day, I know my secret is still safe. As of today, has my tomb ever been found? Has the mummy of Imhotep made a debut? Now, my dear Damien, you know the truth."

From the deepest part of Western Europe

A young child will be born to poor people.

Who will by his speech seduce a great multitude,

His reputation will increase in the Kingdom of the East.

(Century 3, Quatrain 35)

Beasts ferocious with hunger will cross the rivers,

The greater part of the battlefield will be against Hister.

Into a cage of iron will the great one be drawn,

When the child of Germany observes nothing.

(Century 2, Quatrain 24)

In the year very not far from Venus,

The two greatest ones of Asia and of Africa.

They are said to have come from the Rhine and from

Hister Cries, tears at Malta and the Ligurian sea-coast.

(Century 4, Quatrain 68)

Liberty will not be regained;

It will be occupied by a black, proud, villainous and unjust man.

OF ATLANTIS

When the matter of the Pontiff is opened,

The republic of Venice will be vexed by Hister.

(Century 5, Quatrain 29) by Nostradamus

Finally, Damien had the time to pursue his passion for spending time with his mentor Jacques. The two men, together, searched for the answers to the questions asked at one time or another by any man: who, what, and whys of mankind.

While searching for the answers, there had been many obstacles in the way over the centuries for the man known as Archimedes. At times he was so close to his answers. Then it seemed fate ripped them away so that the man had to start his quest yet one more time.

Jacques still lived in Damien's flat. Jacques once more reminisced about a time in history that was so brutal. The time was bloody because of one man's twisted quest for total domination and power.

Jacques told Damien, "We are going to run across all kinds of obstacles in the way as we search for our answers. I want to tell you about the most horrific time I experienced in my quest through time."

"The most trying time I ever endured was what you know as the twentieth century. But, it was also a time before you were born. Instead it was time where most people were struggling to just survive. You were fortunate to have escaped the period known as World War II."

"I tried very hard to escape, what would become a most critical part of your history. It was the start of yet another massacre of brother against brother. I decided to try and get as far away from it as I could. I settled in Greece for the madness had not yet reached there."

"I chose an island known as Cepallonuia which was a most beautiful place! It was dotted with picturesque mountains, and beautiful ports. It was a place one only dreams about. I knew we were close to a war and I wanted to escape. During my long life I have seen so much bloodshed."

"Before I made my getaway to Greece, I had resided in Italy until what I call a mad dictator made his presence known. His name was Mussolini. To one of the most historical places on earth, here with him, the madness, as I call it had made its way to Italy. So I came here."

"This part of history, in my long life, I felt was the craziest mankind had ever seen. At this time the threat of war was everywhere. I quickly realized it had made its way to my little island retreat."

"One day I was sitting in the sand of the beach, just watching the tide. I was thinking about nothing in particular, when I heard the motors of planes passing overhead. When I looked up, I recognized them as German. I already knew Germany would play a big part, if there was war. This is when I realized that my little island had been violated."

"Then all of a sudden, it was as if I went into some sort of trance as I stared out at the ocean. Because of my powers at time, my mind would uncontrollably see visions; visions of things yet to come."

"I saw massive suffering and bloodshed. Once again I saw brother against brother. Then in the midst of all this, I saw a man, a pathetic little man. I saw a crazed little man who had dreams of total domination; dreams of a superhuman race. I also saw mass genocide resulting from this madman's insane dream."

"I saw into the mind of this person who was named Hitler! He actually thought he was a perfect person. Furthermore, in order for one to be perfect, they had to be born of pure Arian blood. In this man's twisted mind, to be perfect, he thought you must be a descendant of Atlantis."

"Now, with the reputation of Atlantis being at stake and all the bloodshed I had seen in my vision, I decided I had to do something to stop this maniac. I had always made it a point not to become involved in mankind's petty differences, but this was different."

"This puny little man held the destinies of so many in his grubby little hands. I just couldn't allow this to happen. This is when I decided I would go to Germany, and meet this charlatan, face to face."

"Even his ideas on Atlantis were absolutely absurd! Never would I have let my society commit the atrocities I saw that this man would. All the murder, all the suffering, all the bloodshed... the more I saw in my vision, the more enraged I became. I had the power to stop this. Yet, I went back on my own words that I would not interfere with mankind's natural evolution. But I would go back on my words! I just couldn't sit back and do nothing!"

"After a while the whole island was occupied by German soldiers! This once heaven on earth, was now under the control of the devil's apprentices. There were German soldiers everywhere! There was no escaping their grasp of lunacy!"

"I tried not to even associate with these lunatics. But I couldn't achieve this, because of their mass occupation. Every where I looked I saw the vermin of Germany!"

"Before the occupation, I admit I admired the Greeks defiance. But in the end the occupation occurred. There was war here now as the Greeks tried to resist the Germans."

"After the war, there was mass devastation during the occupation. The once beautiful beach I would go to just to meditate, was now filled with German boats off the coast. The once gorgeous countryside that was covered with farms was now more or less a wasteland."

"One day, I was outside the little house in which I lived. On the road in front of my house, I saw a man walking down the road. He walked, just minding his own business. On his arm, he wore a yellow band that signified that he was Jewish. Then, walking in the opposite direction on the road, came two German solidarism."

"At the time I really wasn't paying attention. Suddenly I heard some one crying out for help. The cries were coming from the road. As I looked toward the road, I could see the two German soldiers, beating the Jewish man with their guns. The man was no match for the two German devils."

"I just could not do nothing and watch as this innocent man was being beaten to death. I was outraged! Then that old feeling of uncontrollable rage occurred in me. Without thinking, the two German solidarism were lifted high into the air, and flung onto the pavement of the road."

"I reached the man and then helped him to his feet. As I neared him, I extended my hand. Bloodied and bruised, the man got to his feet. Then he thanked me for his rescue. I asked him what he did to deserve such treatment. He told me that he had done nothing. The Nazi soldiers attacked him because of what he was, a Jew."

"I began to feel my blood boil. It was then I decided it is time I went to Germany. I asked the plagued man was there anything else I could do. He told me pray for a miracle to stop this insanity of genocide."

"The man then shook my hand and continued on his way. I went back into my house to find a way to book my passage on any ship or train that would bring me to Germany."

"I found passage on a tramp steamer that was still making it's way between the major ports of Greece and the southern coast of England. Amazingly enough, this unsightly ship from the thirties, managed so avoid the U-boat offence of the German navy. So I made my way to one of the still active ports to catch the steamer that would take me to war torn England. From there I planned to make my way somehow to Germany and face this egotistical monster. I made sure I had my passport and all other papers routinely demanded by the Nazis. There were Nazi soldiers everywhere who seemed to only live for the joy of checking passports and papers."

"When I arrived and found the que for this inspection, I casually watched a woman and her three children who were next. The officers checked the woman's papers and evidently didn't like what they saw. Without a word, and at gunpoint, they whisked the woman and her children to a truck almost filled with dozens of similar people. You could hear the cries of the women and the wailing of children, as they were forced to face an unknown fate."

"My papers were checked and I was allowed to board the ship. I thought about what I had just witnessed. There are no words to describe the sorrow I felt. At the time I didn't realize that the people in the truck would be sent to a concentration camp."

By this time, the storyteller and his audience realized, once again, how late it had become. They agreed to retire for the evening.

The next morning, both men took their breakfast on Damien's small terrace, so Jacques could continue. By now, Damien hung on every word that came from Jacques' mouth.

"After boarding the ship, I went to my small, modest cabin. It was dirty, and smelly but it was a cabin of sorts. I unpacked my light suitcase. Then I decided to go on deck to get some real air."

"It was an overcast day and it looked like rain. On deck, I could smell the salty air of the ocean which I loved so much contrasted with the odor of my quarters. I simply mused that beggars couldn't be choosers. Even at that moment, as I gazed out over the ocean, I sensed a presence I could not shake. Staring at the calm water gave me a feeling of inner peace and tranquility amidst the insanity going on in the world that day."

"All of a sudden, my thoughts were shattered by the sound of a young woman's screams. I looked down the deck, and saw a young woman being man handled by a typical gangster-like German soldier. Well, knew I just had to help this poor timid creature. She was so tiny, that she reminded me of my mother from Atlantis, when she was young. So, without a word, I flexed my powers and lifted the German in the air and threw him over board."

"The young woman seemed so relieved. She thanked me and introduced herself as Sabine. As she was introducing herself to me, we noticed the ship came to a complete halt. Then we then heard the words, 'Man Overboard.' It was evident that someone heard the cries for help from the German solider that was thrown overboard. Sabine and I watched just like all the others that were on deck. The only difference was that we watched in silent humor."

"I then introduced myself to her. I took her hand in mine, I bowed, and kissed it. She was curious to know how I did what I did. I told her I was born with a special gift, the gift of telekinesis which simply put was the ability to move objects with my mind."

"I was curious about her status as to why the German had been so violent with her. She told me she was not just any Jew but rather one seen as quite dangerous. She was a member of the resistance. This certain German had thought he had recognized her and was therefore trying to arrest her. Again she thanked me for my assistance. She just had a feeling that she could trust me, and she was right!"

"As we watched the crew of the ship fish the German out of the sea, I asked Sabine to go inside and join me for a drink. I had a small bottle of scotch I hid in my suitcase for those occasions that I needed it to unwind from the images that crossed my mind constantly. She gratefully accepted. Inside we headed towards a rough table in a dimly lit corner and took a seat. A crewman wandered by. I took the opportunity to ask if he could find a few glasses.

The fellow was most agreeable and managed to locate two water tumblers of questionable cleanliness. It seemed acceptable at the moment.

"As we shared what I had left in my private stock, I asked Sabine what she was doing on a ship like this. Surely she would qualify for a regular fancy passenger liner. She then explained to me that she was trying to make her way to London where the resistance was based. Here, she thought she would be safe from the grasp of German insanity. She had done a lot of work for the resistance. The Germans were aware of her efforts. So the resistance was sending her to London."

"I then told Sabine she would not have to worry about making it to London alone. I hoped she would consider me a friend and her new traveling companion. I would see to it that she arrived London safely. She just reminded me so much of my mother, Cheris. Her small frame, her long dark hair, and big blue eyes, in a way, reminded me of a puppy that needed adopting."

"Sabine was flattered I would go to the trouble to make sure she would get to London safely. She was curious as to why I made that promise. I just simply told her that she reminded me of my mother when she was young."

"We just sat there talking and casually sipping our drinks. All of a sudden, the small open area was invaded by German soldiers, with weapons drawn, demanding to see everyone's papers. I managed to stop another crewman who was rushing by. I quickly asked him if there were another way out?"

"The waiter nodded his head and told us to follow him. So I grabbed Sabine by the hand, and we followed the waiter through the kitchen, then through an adjacent door, which led us to the hallway."

"I turned and thanked the waiter and tried to give him a little money, but he refused. He said there was no problem for anything he could do against the Germans was enough pay for him. He bowed, and then he was gone.

"Sabine and I both agreed that the safest place would be in my quarters, so that is where we headed. As we walked quickly but calmly towards the cabin, a thought occurred to me. It was clear that Sabine was receptive to my power of suggestion. I had the power to control her mind so any illusion I created would be perceived as reality to her. This seemed like the perfect time to initiate that approach.

I told Sabine there was no need to worry. I was a gentleman. Then I impressed upon her mind that instead of this poor excuse for a ship, we were instead traveling First Class on a modern passenger liner. She acknowledged the suggestion of my will and the rest, I felt, would make the voyage easy.

"What a lovely cabin," she said upon entering. To her it was now mahogany paneled with a sweet scent of lavender hanging over the air. Sabine sat on a steel bunk and exclaimed that my mattress was so soft. I smiled with acknowledgment. Then she asked why I was going to England."

"I explained to her that I was going to see an uncle there that had been ill. I made sure I didn't look her directly in her eyes because I was always such a terrible liar. I did not want her to know of my plans to go to Germany for fear that I would scare her and she would not trust me."

"During the whole trip to England, I remained steadfastly by Sabine's side. I was there for her to make sure she would get to England safely. She told me she looked at me as her guardian angel. I knew I was no angel. But I also knew I wasn't a devil Nazi either."

"We continued our sea voyage thankfully with little interruption. The illusions I created helped to make her otherwise uncomfortable journey almost pleasant except for the occasional rough seas. In a few days we were scheduled to dock in Portsmouth. We would hopefully be able to make our way to London, where I would escort Sabine to safety."

"That night aboard the ship there was very little to do. I got tired of looking at walls that had not been scrubbed in years. Therefore, to make the final night even better for Sabine, I suggested that there might be dance being planned for the evening and that it would be wonderful event to attend. I felt that no matter what my situation was, it would be a kind gesture on my part to help her to enjoy a few hours of leisure since she had seen so much hell! I thought she deserved at least that much even if it was all created at the bidding of my mental powers!"

"I had to act fast if I was to maintain the illusion. I located one of the female crew, a cleaning woman. I asked her for one of her extra uniforms and suggested to her mind that it would be a fine donation to the war effort if she gave it to me. She stared with a glazed look at me as she handed me the outfit."

A little later that evening I made my way to Sabine's cabin. I knocked softly on her door. When she opened it, I offered her the uniform and asked her to wear this lovely blue gown, to the dance. Of course she gladly agreed as she held the uniform up to her body and confirmed that it was close enough to her small size to fit. Then I returned to my cabin to change clothes so I could impress her with a mentally created tuxedo I'd be wearing."

"When I returned again, I was met by a surprise. Sabine answered the door wearing the cleaning woman's uniform. But in all other respects, she had magically transformed herself into a beautiful woman. She was stunning! Her long dark hair was put up and her face glowed with youth and beauty. I took very special pains to compliment her on how the gown fitted her after all. I told her that the way the silk wrapped around her body was magnificnet in every way. She smiled and agreed as she blushed and thanked me. Even dressed as she actually was, I felt the fire of passion."

"I really did not want this to happen because I thought Sabine looked at me as a father figure. I tried my very my best to hide my emotions. I bowed to her and then I presented her with a corsage I created from wildflowers I had found in the kitchen earlier.. Before I could say anything, she flung her arms around my neck in gratitude. I was speechless, as my arms wrapped around her small frame."

"Then, hand in hand, we proceeded to the ship's mess hall which tonight would serve as our ballroom. When we arrived, the room became exquisitely decorated. For a time, everyone illusion of other attendees would help Sabine forget about the lunacy in the world."

"We were met by a staff member who escorted us to a table. Through my power of suggestion, the table wasn't steel with stains of years of work but rather a fine mahogany dining table covered with a lace tablecloth and set with the finest of silverware and stemware as well. I pulled a chair out for Sabine and sat across the table from her. Tonight was to be special so I ordered champagne. The mess crewman brought two bottles of the best beer he could find. My powers did the rest. Tomorrow, reality would set back in, but tonight was different."

"Sabine then told me how handsome I looked in a tuxedo. I was very flattered. Once more, through the power illusion, we ordered lobster for our meal. On this night, money was not a problem. Afterwards, Sabine was swaying to the music she believed she heard as she sat in her chair. So, I asked her to dance."

"I just couldn't help but stare at Sabine's body, as she swayed to the music. I was really embarrassed, as I hoped she would not notice my uncontrollable manhood. We danced a couple of times, and once more there was an interruption of Nazi guards, so we took our leave, secretly slipping away."

"We made our way back to my cabin where I knew we would again be safe. Sabine was giddy from the champagne or perhaps just the low percentage of alcohol of the beer. That didn't matter. What mattered was how she behaved. After I closed the door, she grabbed me, giggling all the while, as she still wanted to dance. I tried to make her stop, but she continued."

"Then without a word, Sabine cupped my face within her hands and kissed me.

I finally succumbed to my feelings of passion. I picked her up, carried her to my small bed where we made love most of the night. We finally collapsed into an exhausted sleep."

"The next morning we awoke to the sun shining through the small porthole. The first thing I tried to do was to apologize for my behavior the night before. Sabine would not hear of this as she greeted me the next morning with a kiss. She just said we must hurry because soon we would dock at Portsmouth."

"When the ship docked we made our way to the train station where from there we would go to London. Just after we docked you could see the signature of war, everywhere you turned. There were solders everywhere and many of the buildings had been reduced to rubble. We were fortunate that the train station and the tracks has somehow managed to survive to this point."

"After we were on the train I tried once more to apologize, but Sabine told me she was as drawn to me as I was to her. She said what had happened was fate. She was, of course, glad it had happened. I, in turn, was glad I came into her life. She told me she loved me, and she knew I loved her too. She could see it in my eyes. Even our age difference did not seem to matter to her. She loved the man I was no matter what my age was."

"Well, this made me so happy. I replied to Sabine, with a kiss, from that moment on, we were two instead of one. The war was drawing to a close. But never the less, when we got to London, it was not the London, that I remembered. There was debris of the once beautiful city everywhere."

"I had fallen in love, something I hadn't expected. I had to make sure Sabine would be safe before I went on to Germany. I told her I had some business to attend to in another part of England. Then I added that I would personally deliver her to the resistance where I knew she would be safe. I would be back for her in about a month."

"I had a hard time leaving her, but I had to keep telling myself that it was for her own good. I went back to Portsmouth to find passage to the Netherlands. From there I took a train to Germany."

"I finally reached Berlin. While most of the rails were devastated by Allied bombing runs, there were still a few that were usuable. Once I arrived, I began a search for the head quarters of the Third Reich and Hitler. I just could not believe the ruins and debris here left from total madness and lunacy. People on the streets moved as if they were in a trance. I surmised it was from the horrors of everything that was going on around them."

It was time for another lunch break. Damien and Jacques changed the subject and relaxed as they had a quick lunch. Then, they headed back to the terrace, so Jacques could continue.

"I finally found the headquarters or what was left of it. I could see how well guarded it was. So, I used my powers to bend the light about myself. This effectively made me invisible."

"I walked into an elaborately decorated hall. I overheard two men speaking in German. I moved slightly closer. One was heavyset, tall, and wore the uniform of the Luftwaffe, the German Air Force. The other man was much shorter and wore a more simple tunic with much less decoration. I also noted that the shorter man's arm was hanging limply as if he had suffered a war injury. Then I saw who that second person actually was. It turned out to be none other than Hitler. His arm had indeed been severely injured during an attempt on his life a few years back. This man was the main cause for all the insanity in the world at that time!"

"It was really hard to believe that this one man I now studied caused so much upset in the world. Hitler was speaking to what appeared to be a General, discussing battle strategies even though the man of the Luftwaffe seemed to be protesting. Hitler would have none of it as he raised his voice. From what I could hear, I hated to admit this to myself, but from what I understood, he was brilliant. In a very small way regarding military tactics, he reminded me of myself in Atlantis in another time."

"Suddenly, and this is so difficult to explain, I found that I could not carry out my plan! I just saw TOO much of myself in him. So in shame, I turned and walked away. I felt so guilty! I simply could not bring myself to rid the world of this German plague. What I did not know at that particular moment was that through circumstances of the war's progress, Hitler would commit suicide later that same month."

"I quickly retraced my steps and soon emerged into the ruins of Berlin once more where I dropped the facade of invisibility. I tried very hard to gain my composure through my feelings of guilt."

"I figured there was only one thing left to do and that was to go back to England for Sabine. I took solace in the idea that no one but I would know of the inadequacies that I displayed here."

"So, I began my journey back to England."

Finale — Part One

"I returned to England, wallowing in my shame. But I would have to put on a happy face for the sake of Sabine!"

"I eventually arrived at the flat in London that was provided by the resistance for her and still everywhere I looked I could see mass devastation and death."

"When I reached the flat, Sabine was outside talking with some of her neighbors. It was a privilege, just to watch her, the sun shining on her hair. She was beautiful. Then she saw me and came running up to me with open arms."

"She hugged and kissed me. Then she exclaimed, with a big smile on her face, have you heard? The Germans have surrendered and Hitler is dead by his own hand. Now we can be free! No more having to hide in the shadows. God, I love you and have missed you so much."

"It really touched me to see how happy she was. I told her I hadn't heard the news, but now that this atrocity was behind us we can love freely. Then I asked her if she would she do me the honor of becoming my wife?"

"This made her incredibly happy. She looked up at me with tears in her big blue eyes and accepted my proposal. Then she told me she had more news. As a result of our love making, she was going to have my child."

"Well this was like the cherry on top of the whip cream. Not only did I know the end of the war but also I had Sabine, and a baby on the way, to a world without the lunacy of Hitler. I was so happy."

"I was still hugging Sabine and so I dailed to notice the man that was standing behind us. Suddenly I heard someone utter the name of Archimedes. It was then that I turned around and saw him."

"It appeared to be the same Luftwaffe General in civilian clothes that I had seen talking to Hitler only a few weeks before. Now he was standing before me and the woman I loved, with gun in his hand."

"I tried my best to shield Sabine but it was far too late. The shot rang out. I stood, frozen, as I held her in my arms. This horrible man had just shot the woman I loved. As I held Sabine, she looked up at me. She smiled, took her last breath, and then she died."

"All I could do was hug her so tightly then I let out a loud NNNNNNNN NNOOOOOOOOO!!!!!!!! I looked incredulously at this stranger and I cried out WHY? WHY?"

"The Nazi laughed wildly, and replied in an evil tone, "By this you will know me Archimedes. But first let me give you a clue. I did the same thing to Delyse and your twin sons." My mind stood still as I realized I once again faced my arch enemy, Uric, in the form of this Third Reich officer."

"With a lecherous look on his face, he said, it was he, in the form of a Luftwaffe office that was talking to Hitler. He went on to tell me that even though I was using a cloak of invisibility, he felt my presence. He then followed his senses, which led me here."

"Uric also seemed to take great pleasure when he said that he knew he couldn't kill me but he could again kill the one I loved. It would leave another hole in my heart. I heard wild laughing, and then he was gone!"

"I just couldn't believe it! Once again, Uric had won. Yet somehow I knew there would come a time I would triumph. I gently lifted the lifeless form of this lovely woman and took her inside her flat, where I started preparations for her funeral."

"On that day that was supposed to be a joyous celebration, but once again I had lost all I loved! Once again the same crazed maniac had somehow found a way to destroy my happiness. However, this only strengthened my resolve to destroy Uric. One day, I vowed, I would have my revenge."

"The awful thing about it was that even with all my powers, I couldn't help Sabine. I couldn't help Delyse; I couldn't help my twin boys from Atlantis."

"World War II unjustly claimed the lives of millions. Mankind and their petty differences were part of it along with the bickering, the fighting, setting brother against brother. Yes, it was all insanity."

"Even though I had the power to ease the war to some degree, since Atlantis, I had vowed never to interfere in the natural evolution of history and man. The love of my life once again lost to death's oblivion."

"I was getting very tired, I was ready to give up on mankind. Yet, I still didn't have the answers to the questions for which I so desperately sought."

"You see, my friend, I can not die. I would have to self terminate my existence. But my quest for my answers was like a fire burning within my soul. Surely, mankind wasn't put on this earth to destroy themselves."

"The unquenchable thirst for answers; even aware of the fact of knowing that one day I would also get even with Uric, keeps this old heart beating and filled my entire soul with the determination I must have."

"With this fire burning inside of me, I had to live on. I had to find my answers; the same answers which you seek, Damien! One day our thirsts will be quenched and we shall have our answers. But it was not to be on this day."

"Together we will find them. While I am so tired, you, my dear boy, are my strength. I must continue to teach you. One day, when I feel you are ready, you will stand in my shoes, but until then, we shall continue to search."

A world of pain,

Brother against brother,

Fighting, and then nothing is gained,

Wars, rumors of wars, this life, there is no other.

I'm tired, I feel time is running out,

I want to abandon this morbid life,

Hatred, death, all I can do is watch as it mounts,

I want peace, calmness, no more of mankind's petty strife.

Now rested once more, Damien and Jacques arose to another beautiful day. But having told Damien about World War II returned raw stinging feelings to Jacques' inner being that he thought were gone. Jacques forgot how devastating the war had been on him until he began speaking of it to his devoted listener.

Both men, still somewhat sleepy, went into the small kitchen to stimulate their bodies with their daily caffeine fix. They had their coffee then retreated to the compact living room in the small flat. Here Damien begged Jacques to continue his story. Jacques hesitated. Long buried feelings had emerged. Never the less, Jacques wanted Damien to know all. So he continued.

"After the death of Sabine, I more or less became a recluse. I remained in England. She was laid to rest here and I desired to be close to her and my unborn child."

"Once again I was so totally devastated just like in Atlantis. Uric had won yet again. I had such a hard time accepting the fact I could have done something. My entire being was being eaten up by guilt. I intensely felt it was all my fault."

"As I search my inner self and wallowed in my guilt, the British people were doing their best to rebuild their lives after knowing one of the biggest evils the world had ever known."

"Amidst all the death and devastation, these poor souls still managed to hold their heads up. They were proud of their history and their heritage of not showing their anguish, as they tried so hard to put this mass devastation behind them."

"At the time I didn't realize I could have learned a thing or two from them. Yet I did not, because I was just too overcome by my guilt."

"Within my body, I felt a parasite, a sickness, and I knew if I didn't try to heal myself, I would die. However, simply put, at the time I just didn't care. I was ready to pass over fully believing I would see all those I had loved and lost once more."

"I relished in the idea of peace, calmness and sleeping eternally. I was so tired."

"At that time I had decided there was just no hope for mankind. So, I thought that I should merely exit the scene as the best answer."

"There was a park across the street from where I used to live in London. I would often go there to get lost in the calmness of the place. One day, like any other, I was just sitting on the park bench minding my own business, as I wallowed in my sorrows."

"Then to my surprise, a little girl came up to me, holding out a single flower. She sweetly told me that she was supposed to sell these to help get money for her mommy. Then she told me that since I looked so sad, she had to give me one. She knew it worked because I was then smiling."

"Damien, this one act of kindness made me realize there was hope for mankind, if only a tiny hope. This little girl had magically convinced me that I wanted to live. So I began to heal myself."

"This sweet little child had showed me compassion. She convinced me to give mankind another chance."

The two men again realized how late it had become, so they went inside to prepare for a late day meal. Damien unconsciously turns on the television that daily tells of the status of the world.

Jacques paid attention to the announcer as he spoke, "Today, we have to fear those in search of nuclear weapons. We must for those that believe if they have this power also believe they can force mankind to their way of thinking."

"There are those that believe they can conform the western countries to their ideology by either mass genocide, or by using terrorism as a weapon to achieve their ends."

Jacques turned off the television. He shook his head from side to side. He thought to himself, "The world has only gotten worse and I wonder if mankind can change their inevitable fate."

Jacques thought of the things going on in the world today. He heard of atrocities committed against mankind as well as wars of disease, and terrorism. He wept for how man had never learned to protect their mortality. He knew of the day when the world would reap revenge upon its inhabitants.

That once glimmer of hope Jacques felt for mankind, like a flame of a candle, had been extinguished. He really thought that man was on the road to its own demise.

Jacques was brought back to reality as Damien bid him a good night. Jacques was now left alone with his thoughts. He was worn out from the day and so Jacques decided he would also turn in for the evening.

As he headed to his small room off of the kitchen, he was suddenly overcome by feelings of dread. This feeling was all too familiar. It was one he only got when he felt the presence of the madman Uric.

Yet, he tried not to succumb to those feelings. Instead, Jacques tried to get his mind on other things. Then he heard a voice in his head saying, "Archimedes, Archimedes, you know it is me! One more time meet me. You may even get lucky this time. Maybe this time you will win! It will be something a little different, wouldn't you say?"

Jacques tried his best to get some sleep. He tried to ignore the taunting voice and burning desire within himself, but it was just too strong.

He realized it did no good to fight. He tried to concentrate on where the taunting voice might be coming from. He did his best to visualize within his mind's eye to focus in on where his old nemesis might be.

Jacques concentrated with every part of his being. His focus was so hard that it brought forth a sweat. He began to see sand everywhere and in the backdrop. He could make out a pyramid. However, it wasn't just any pyramid. It was the step pyramid, the one right outside of Saqqara. It was the one he designed so long ago as Imhotep. He realized he was seeing the Sahara desert. Now he knew what he must do.

The next morning Jacques rose early. He had to confront Damien. The man knew that Damien would want an explanation. The two men had been together for a couple of months now searching for the meaning of life, together as a team.

But, Jacques knew that he must go on this journey alone. It was a journey he had been ready to take for many centuries.

Jacques heard noise from Damien's bedroom. Jacques called to Damien and told him that they had to discuss something.

Jacques already had coffee waiting as Damien sleepily made his way into the kitchen. As he sat down at the small bar which adjoined the kitchen, Jacques said, "Damien, my boy, I must go to Egypt. There is something I have to do. It's a very pressing matter."

Damien replied, "All right. As soon as I finish my coffee I will make the arrangements for us to go."

Jacques replied, "No, no, I don't think you understand. This is a journey that I must go on alone. It will be very dangerous. I'm afraid if you go with me, it might endanger your life. So you can't go with me. No one can go with me."

"I do promise you that I will be in touch with you after I have eliminated the danger, and then once again, we can continue with your studies. I promise I will contact you. You see, one day I hope for you to fill my shoes."

Reluctantly, Damien agreed. Then Jacques went to the phone, and placed a call to the airport to make reservations on a plane that would take him to Egypt. Jacques prayed that this might be the final conflict.

Aboard the plane, Jacques impatiently sat. In his mind he was taunted and challenged by the notions of a mad man. However, he took solace in knowing, that this face off was what he had been waiting for. And now that it was so close, he was determined he would prevail.

Throughout the entire journey, nothing but anxiety plagued Jacques. Finally the plane set down in Cairo. From the Cairo airport, Jacques rented a jeep and began his drive across the endless sands until he reached Saqqara. From here he knew he would find Uric.

An old feeling found its way into Jacques' soul. He saw familiar surroundings the closer he got to Saqqara. Then, like a looming monster on the desert horizon, he saw his work of genius from so long ago, the Step Pyramid.

That one feat of ancient architecture caused Archimedes, when he was in the indemnity of Imhotep so long ago, to almost possess the status of a God. He came from a society that was so much farther advanced than ancient Egypt. By Archimedes sharing his knowledge here, Imhotep had been regarded as holy as the Pharaoh himself.

As he drove along the ageless, timeless sands, Jacques noticed a tent on the horizon. He dismissed it as likely one that belonged to a Bedowyn. However, as he drew closer, he would learn just how wrong he was.

Now only a few hundred meters from the tent, he could see a camel outside as well as a place that would be used for cooking. Then he saw a sight that he just couldn't believe.

He saw an old man outside the tent, using a crutch. The closer to the tent Jacques got, the more he realized he was staring at the shell of the man that used to be Uric.

As the old man shielded his eyes from the sun, he tried to see who in the world would be way out here in the middle of no where with him. Then Uric realized it was Archimedes.

While it was true that Archimedes wasn't as strong as he once was, it was clear that he was not in the same weakened state as Uric. He stopped the jeep once more and jumped out. The feet of Archimedes hit Egyptian soil, just like they did so long ago.

Uric was never shy. He greeted Archimedes by saying, "Well my old friend, I see my plan worked! I knew if I taunted you enough you would come. Now once more I can have my way with you. You see I am dying. The bloodstones that once fed my power no longer work. I have caused many battles and plagues, so the negative forces could feed my stones. But now, it is to no avail. So, I knew that if I challenged you, and as you are an honorable man, it would give me strength. We could face each other with both of us having the same strength. I knew you couldn't give up the chance for revenge."

Archimedes replied, "My old friend Uric, I see you still have your most pleasant personality. As always you are trying to manipulate and control. However, in this case you are very wrong about something, my old friend. Yes, while I am a fair man, I am anything but fair where you are concerned!"

"You must be daft to think that I would heal you after all the heartache you have caused me! And so I say let the battle begin!"

Archimedes had a sickness within. He had decided not to heal it alone in hopes that his long journey of life would end. But now he had to heal himself in order to achieve victory over a battle he had waited so long to fight and triumph.

All of a sudden, there was a bright beam of light which bathed Archimedes. The light would heal the thing that plagued him.

In the timeless and infinite sands, it was the time that the two men prepared to face each other. The long awaited battle began.

As each faced the other, both men threw lightning bolts at each other. It was evident that Archimedes was the more powerful of the two. He began to really beat down his old nemesis. Then, without a sound or a word, Uric disappeared. He was running like the coward he was.

Archimedes was very much now more powerful than ever. His ability to feel the presence of Uric was evident, regardless of where Uric might try to hide.

He got back in his jeep and began to drive once more. He was following his intuitions which would lead him across the sands, to a location just twenty kilometers outside of Cairo.

Archimedes stopped the jeep as the feeling grew so very strong. He looked upwards from where he had stopped the vehicle and saw, on a rocky ledge, a cave. He now knew that was Uric's hiding place.

Using the utmost care and stealth, Archimedes climbed the extremely rocky ledge. Although he slipped several times along the way, he was determined to reach the cave.

Finally he reached the ledge. As he stood considering his next move, he prayed that Uric was so weak that his presence couldn't be detected. He positioned himself at the entrance of the cave and tried his best to remain in the shadows.

Then, he saw the madman. To prevent any escape again, Archimedes put a force field around Uric which made escape almost impossible. Oh, the sense of satisfaction Archimedes felt, knowing finally he had a very weak Uric cornered.

Archimedes moved very slowly as quietly as was possible under the conditions he faced so as not to disturb any loose rubble. if any noises were made, it would alert Uric to the presence of his approach. Thankfully, though, in his weakened state, Uric had lost the ability to sense the man and Archimedes knew this.

Archimedes tried to sneak up behind the old crazed magician. After experiencing the healing force earlier, he had brought himself back to his full potential. He now appeared as a man of forty.

Uric appeared leaning over, intently looking at something. As Archimedes crept up behind Uric, he saw it was a book. It wasn't just any book. No, instead it looked like the ancient Book of Life, which had been stolen from the temple of Atlantis from so very long ago.

Archimedes then accidentally made a very slight noise. But it was loud enough to alert Uric to his presence. Uric looked up from the book. Then he saw Archimedes and said, "Well, I knew you would find me. I knew your lust for revenge would bring you directly to me. I know that is one driving force within you that you cannot control."

That remark made the blood of Archimedes boil. Without a word, a lightning bolt appeared from no where, which struck Uric with such force that he became incapacitated. The man was pinned to the ground and lying in a pool of blood. He was dying, and Archidmedes knew this.

Uric was unable to move. He knew he had one chance to survive, so he put his plan into effect. Uric looked up at Archimedes and said, "It appears as if you are going to win. But before you strike the final blow, know this. I know how much you want to know of your origins and also all the answers to all the questions of the universe."

"The book lying there is the Book of Life. It contains all your answers. All I ask of you now is that you spare me and make me whole once more. Then the book is yours. Yes, I stole it from the temple in Atlantis long ago, because I also craved the answers. If you choose to not honor my request, I will destroy the book and all its contents. That would be my last thought before you destroyed me. So what say you?"

Archimedes was torn between his hatred and his desire to know of his beginnings, and the answers to all his questions.

Archimedes simply glanced toward the Book of Life and it vanished. Uric looked at the man as he let out a sinister laugh, despite the evident pain he was in and uttered, "Archimedes, my old friend, did you really think I would be daft enough not to have a bargaining chip? I hid the book, the genuine book and not an illusion, here. You heal me, and then the book is yours. You will know fully your origins, answers to all your questions. You will quench that burning desire within your soul. Heal me and you will have it all."

Archimedes knew that trusting Uric seemed to always have a price. But his enormous need for answers had to be satiated, and so he came up with an alternative approach.

He began to concentrate incredibly hard. Then, a light appeared all over Uric, the soft glow totally engulfed the wicked man. Archimedes watched intently as the old, broken man was transformed into a man also about the age of forty.

Uric laughed. He called Archimedes a fool. Then he raised his hand and.... nothing happened! Archimedes told Uric that he had stripped him of his powers and now he was but a mere mortal of around thirty. As Archimedes turned away from Uric, he begged for death. He cried out that he would rather die than live as an ordinary man.

Now it was Archimedes' turn to laugh and laugh he did. He told Uric with a meaure of glee that they were in the middle of the desert without food or water. he believed that Uric would die soon enough. In another instant, Archimedes was gone. The sobbing Uric fell to the floor of cave, motionless.

In the last analysis, Archimedes knew better than to trust the old magician. So instead of playing Uric's game, he changed the rules. He healed the evil man so as to make him mortal. But the book! What about the book? Uric said the book was hidden within the part of the cave they were in. Archimedes simply believed that one day he must return to this place and find the book that contains all the answers he would ever need.

He left the cave and returned to the Jeep. Now it was Jacques that headed toward Cairo, only wanting the comfort of his motel room. Somehow Jacques wasn't expecting that he would leave one of the most anticipated events in his long unending life in such an uneventful manner. But there were things even he could not know.

To his inner surprise, in a way he felt remorse over what just occurred. He was actually feeling sadness. He attributed his feelings of sorrow to the fact he knew Uric, now mortal, would eventually die, even though the madman had tormented him for so long. The last of his kind was ending. Uric, had the same heritage as he did. Uric was also someone that was bred the same as he was, and the last lost soul, besides himself that had survived Atlantis.

In a while Jacques reached his motel room in Cairo. He was happy because of this event's ending. The man was starting to feel of the sickness that dwelled for so long within his body. He felt very weak and tired. This time there was no reason to heal himself. After this final battle, the man was ready for the sweet escape of death.

Archimedes was very tired. All throughout the centuries, mankind had never changed Somehow there was always the thirst for domination and power over each other's brother. The only thing that had changed was mankind's weapons. They were more fierce as time had gone on. The weapons of today so easily caused mass devastation. he felt deep inside that when man's greed eventually destroyed the Earth, he did not wish to see that.

Once inside the sanctuary of his room, Jacques headed straight to his bed so he could rest awhile, while he anticipated his next move. As he lay down, he began to think and plan. He knew his time was limited. He wanted to live his final days in the place, that he was most at peace.

He mused about his villa in Greece where he had lived during World War II. He had maintained his villa and visited from time to time as he also remembered his sweet Sabine. He had hired a local man as caretaker. Archimedes was a wealthy man because of all he had acquired throughout the centuries.

In his final days, he yearned for peace. He just wished that mankind felt the same. So now Archimedes decided to go back to Greece. He also decided he would send for Damien since he knew there was little time.

Damien had been such a good friend and student. Jacques, having no heirs, planned to leave everything he had acquired to his new devoted friend and student. He wanted Damien to fill his shoes. He planned to pass his powers to Damien. He felt that now was the right time since Damien had shown him compassion and true friendship. In a way, Damien had become like a son.

Knowing time was of the essence, Jacques cabled Damien to join him in Greece.

Later on during the day, back in Paris, Damien received the cable from Jacques. In the cable, he pleaded with him to come join him in Greece. Damien got very upset, because his mentor sounded so desperate in the cable. So, Damien booked a flight, packed a few clothes, and was on his way.

Aboard the plane anxiety and fear filled Damien's soul, he didn't know what to expect. He just knew from the cable he received, something was wrong, very wrong.

Jacques had become like a father to the youthful Damien. Damien's parents died in a car crash when he was a very young age. He was raised in an orphanage. as a result of this early childhood, his relationship with Jacques was very special to him.

The plane finally landed in Greece. Damien exited the plane and headed inside the airport as he expected Jacques to meet him there. Instead, he saw a man holding up a poster board with his name on it. Damien walked over to the man and introduced himself. "Where is Jacques? Is he all right?"

The man replied, "Mr. Caron hired me to meet you and drive you to his villa. Mr. Caron is very ill and that is why he sent me!"

This made the anxiety in Damien's soul even worse. Damien explained to the man, "Well let's hurry then! I am so worried about him!"

The two men headed toward the car and were on their way. As Damien gazed out the car window, he was mesmerized by the beauty of the landscape. He could easily understand why Jacques chose this place.

As they arrived at the villa, Damien noted that Jacques was not outside to meet him. There was only the houseboy outside. He instructed Damien, "Master Jacques, is waiting for you. His bedroom is at the top of the stairs on the right!" Damien hurriedly made his way to Jacques' bedroom.

As he hurredly headed toward Jacques' bedroom, Damien grew stronger and stronger. He grew more worried with each moment that passed. He finally reached the bedroom and entered. Damien stood still, frozen in his tracks. His mouth dropped open as he looked at Jacques.

The vibrant man he knew always looked about the age of forty or forty five. However, now he saw a man who appeared to be the age of seventy. Furthermore, the man looked as if he could barely move.

As they embraced each other, Damien was at a loss of words. He stared at the man that he had come to love as a father. Jacques then replied, "This is not quite what you expected, is it? I have a sickness within my body as you can see!

Damien momentarily hesitated. he didn't know how to answer. Finally he said, "Why are you doing this to yourself when you know full well that you have the power to intervene?"

Jacques looked lovingly at Damien and answered, "Yes my son, I could stop this. But it is my wish to step into the unknown of death. I have had a long and painful existence, and now I long for peace. The world has literally been turned upside down by all the evil today. I just want to be released! I hope you can understand my wishes and the logic behind them."

Damien, his head slightly bowed, replied, "I do understand your plight, sir. But I have become very fond of you, and you will sorely be missed! You are like my father!"

Jacques embraced Damien and responded, "My son, everything I have, when I die, will be yours. I want you to fill my shoes! I have kept myself alive for one sole purpose. I met Uric one more time in Egypt and by now he is dead. But in the place I met him, he had hidden The Book of Life. I must to go back there, with you, in hopes of finding the book and reading it, before I die."

Damien answered, "Are you sure you are up to such a trip? Is this the best thing for you?"

This angered Jacques somewhat, yet he tried to keep his composure as he understood Damien's concern. He replied, "My life is in my hands. As long as I hold on to my powers I will be fine! The Book contains my answers I have searched for so very long. The desire for this has kept me going for centuries. I must find the Book!"

After the decision was made to return to Egypt, the two men booked a flight to Cairo while there was still time. This was the reason and the sole purpose why Archimedes had prolonged his life.

At the airport, they rented a Jeep. the 4-wheel drive vehicle made it easier to travel over the enduring sands of the desert. By now Archimedes was very weak, yet his determination to find the Book kept him going.

Soon they were driving across the sands, traveling to a place that had been preserved in time, just as the long life of Archimedes had been.

Jacques soon recognized a rock that appeared to be out of place. He remembered this was the cave location. He instructed Damien to stop.

Damien brought the vehicle to a stop and the two men stepped out of the jeep then looked up. There on top of a rocky ledge, was the entrance to the cave. From there stopping point they began the start of a very hard climb.

Jacques was very weak. Damien had to help the man along the arduous journey. Once in a while, as they stopped to rest, Jacques acted as if he had a bad case of pneumonia. His breathing was short and labored, yet his power and determinaton remained strong.

That still burning desire within his soul would soon be quenched. They were almost at the entrance of the cave.

As they reached the entrance, Jacques simply had to sit and rest for a while even though the man sensed that he was being drawn toward the Book. Never-the-less, he had to rest.

While Jacques remained seated, Damien walked into the cave with no idea of what he was going to find inside. He had no inkling that maybe, just maybe, a very important chapter in their journey was about to close.

Finale — Part Two

Upon entering the cave, Damien was not prepared for what he found. There, in the corner of the cave, he saw an elderly man, bent over something. What he saw was Uric. The vision of a dead old man breathing shook him quite a bit. In turn, Uric was startled by Damien's approach.

The old man stood up. Damien saw he was standing over some sort of leather bound book, whose pages were yellow from the ages of time. Damien realized that this volume must be the book that contained all the answers, The Book of Life.

Damien watched Uric carefully. Uric seemed to be reaching for what looked like a crudely made wooden spear. As he saw this action by the old man, Damien looked around for something he could use as a weapon. All he could find was a rock which he quickly took in hand.

The two men confronted one another. Uric lunged for the youthful Damien. He resembled someone doing some type of dance. Damien, of course, tried his best to avoid the sharp end of the spear. As he quickly darted one way then another, Damien saw an opening. He grasped the rock tightly and swung. His aim was good as the rock hit Uric squarely against the side of his head. Damien also remembered that Uric was mortal. In one movement as if in slow motion, Uric fell to the floor of the cave, dead. Finally, the plague that was upon this earth was no more.

With Uric now definitely out of the way, Damien picked up the priceless Book and placed it upon a nearby rock. Then he looked around. he tried to determine just how Uric survived. Damien then spotted a fresh water pool in another part of the cave. It was evident that Uric sustained his existence by eating whatever he could find and kill. Damien realized there was not much variety here, just scorpions and other desert creatures.

Next, Damien turned his attention again to the Book. He had to get Jacques, because what he held was the very reason the two men came to Egypt. Still,

OF ATLANTIS

Damien was very worried about Jacques. he was convinced that he wouldn't last much longer.

As a warm desert breeze blew, after a short rest, Jacques mustered enough strength and energy to enter the cave. What he saw totally caught him off guard. He was sure that Uric was dead already. But now he saw the evil magician lying on the cave floor, clearly dead. It wasn't a pretty sight either. In fact it was rather grotesque for Uric lay in a spreading pool of blood about around his crushed head.

Jacques looking down at the dead body and remarked, "I honestly thought Uric was dead. Had I known that I was premature, I wouldn't have let you enter the cave on your own. Believe me, I would have never subjected you to that kind of danger and for that I am sorry! Really, I thought he was dead!"

Damien looked at Jacques with loving eyes. He replied, "My dear Jacques, did you forget that Uric was but a mortal man and an old one at that? Clear your conscience my dear friend as I was in no kind of danger." It was very evident to Damien that Jacques had started having memory lapses. He wondered to himself how much longer the man actually had to live.

As Damien was contemplating this thought, Jacques was drawn directly to the Book that was on the rock. Archimedes reached out for the ancient volume and picked it up. Then Damien's attention returned to the Book. He noticed a peculiarity of the binding and said, "Look, Jacques, the leather binding goes all the way around the Book, and there is a lock. It seems to need a key!"

Archimedes told Damien not to worry. From around his neck, he removed a chain that held a small brass key. But even before Archimedes unlocked the Book, he felt that as a decent person, even toward Uric, he commented, "Uric may have been an evil soul, but he still demands the respect of a descent burial, don't you agree?"

Damien had to agree. He wondered, however, how would he bury someone in the earth if there was no ground in which you could dig? Then he saw a rather substantial pile of rocks on the cave floor, that evidentially fell from the ceiling at one time. Damien dragged Uric's lifeless body next to the pile of rocks. Here the men, together, managed with some effort, to cover Uric's body with the available rocks.

Archimedes looked down on the grave and prayed. "You know, I never thought I would feel such remorse over Uric's death, but as I look over his grave, things seem to be so final."

"This man, this evil wicked man, I would guess is the last of my kind. As much as I hate to admit it, I feel sadness and remorse. The only link I had left to Atlantis, is no more."

Damien was very concerned for Jacques' physical well being. But now he had a different worry, the worry of how the death of Uric would take its toll on the already fragile Jacques. Damien was at a loss for meaningful words. All he could do to console the over-wrought man, was to stand beside him and rub Jacques back. He did his best to console this shell of a great man.

As Damien was trying to console him, he heard a strange noise from outside the cave which sounded like a hurricane or tornado. Damien guardedly walked to the entrance. He was amazed and startled by what he saw. The entire desert appeared to be in motion. It was truly beyond belief! He had never observed a major sand storm that looked like all the sand in the desert was twirling.

Damien turned from the entrance of the cave and watched a distraught Jacques. Then, Damien said, "Will you be alright here for a while? It seems that we have no choice but to remain here for the time being as there is a terrible sand storm outside, unlike anything I have seen before."

Jacques made his way over to Damien's side and as he looked at Damien he instructed, "Just stand back and watch!" Then Jacques raised his arms in an attempt to control nature, but nothing happened. It was now evident that Jacques was so weak physically, his powers were even failing him.

Jacques looked at Damien in disbelief and sighed, "It seems the end is closer than either of us thought. Even my powers are now failing me! Is there another part of the cave we could go to? I just don't want to stay where I can view Uric's grave."

Damien took Jacques by the arm and helped him as they went deeper within the cave. Both now carried flashlights to light their way. They moved toward the room in which the fresh water spring existed.

As they entered the area, the two men saw several dead scorpions as well as other unkown things stacked against the wall. This area apparently served as Uric's food supply.

Jacques remarked, "You know, even for Uric, what he had to go through at the last is really sad. Not that he didn't deserve his fate, but it still makes me sad."

The two men bent over the pool of water. As they cupped some of the water in their hands and drank, they were both surprised by how cool and good the water was. It tasted like the water one might enjoy from a cool, crisp mountain stream. They easily quenched their thirst from the pool.

Jacques suddenly looked at Damien and exclaimed, "I just realized something! The Book. I left it in the other part of the cave. Would you go back and get it, so we can look over it together?"

Damien replied that he would be glad to return for the Book. But before he left Jacques, he had to check the old man. He had to be sure that the old man would be all right if he was left alone, if only for a minute.

After Damien left, Jacques was indeed alone. The man's mind could now run rampant with all kinds of thoughts, mostly thoughts of the sweet escape of death and thoughts that his long journey was about to come to an end.

While Archimedes was lost in such thoughts, he was thrown back to reality by the shaking of the earth. All of a sudden there were rocks falling everywhere. There was nowhere for him to run or nowhere to take shelter as it seemed the whole ceiling of the cave was coming down.

Suddenly a big rock fell! Although Archimedes tried his best to shield himself, it was to no avail. The huge rock landed on top of his body and pinned him to the floor of the cave.

Archimedes realized that the rock that fell on him likely broke some ribs. He wasn't aware that it also totally shattered his right leg. For the first time in his long life, he felt intense pain. He was too weak to heal himself. Thankfully, he was able to muster enough energy so he could use his powers to lift the rock off himself, and cast it to the side.

Soon Archimedes was aware of Damien's presence. Damien made his way back to the old man, despite the fact he had to make his way over what seemed to be a mountain of fallen debris. Damien knelt down beside Archimedes and asked, "How bad do you think you are hurt? What can I do for you?"

Archimedes looked at Damien with pain in his eyes and replied slowly, "My son, there is nothing that can be done! I am dying! I take solace in the fact that you are by my side. The end will come soon. It is an end I have longed for, for so very long. The Book, Damien, did you rescue the Book?"

Damien had indeed found and rescued the Book. He slowly and somewhat reverently placed it in Archimedes' hands. He noted that his friend didn't even have the strength left to lift the Book, so Damien helped him, and together they unlocked the clasp.

Just before Archimedes opened the Book he said, "All the centuries, I have searched for the Book. In a way it's ironic that I do so as I am dying. But, the Book doesn't hold all the answers. Are you familiar with Mayan legend? I never spoke of this because after we left here, I thought we would have time to go to South America and find the answers ourselves!"

Archimedes continued. "After you leave here my son, you must go to South America. Thank God, you are safe from the rock slide, because now you can go in my stead. While The Book will answer all questions about origin and the universe, for the future, you must refer to the Mayan mythology."

"When Atlantis was destroyed, several of us survived. We all went our separate ways in the ancient world. Just look at all the ancient architecture and you can see. Look at all the pyramids everywhere in the ancient world. That is Atlantean technology. The three sides of the pyramid mean Love, Peace, and Harmony. One of the most advanced societies was that of the Mayan. There were thirteen crystal skulls that were created by the Mayan. This was the ancient equivalent to computers of our time. The legend says that if all thirteen skulls are placed in a circle, their contents will be revealed. I know seven have been found. Now it will be left to you to find the remaining six. According to Mayan legend, the end of the world will come about on December twenty-one, two thousand and twelve. You must find the remaining skulls to prevent this from happening."

"So see my son, you must be the deliverer. It will be your job to find the remaining skulls, so you can thwart the total demise of mankind as we know it! It was my intention to do this with you. But as you can see, that will now be impossible!"

"The only thing I really regret is the pain I know my death will cause you! But, you must be strong so you can continue where I left off!" Then Archimedes cried out in intense pain, something he was very unfamiliar with.

Damien looked down at him with tears in his eyes. Archimedes said, "There is but one thing left I must do!" Mustering what little strength he had left, there came an appearance of a bright light which totally bathed Damien as Archimedes transferred all his powers to Damien. This passage, gave Damien a legacy like no other.

Damien stared down at the dying Archimedes and replied, "You crazy old man, what have you done? Don't you know without your powers, you will die?" Damien tried to keep his composure, but the transfer of powers he sensed were really strange.

As he bent down over the old man, Damien uttered, "Now that I have the power I will use it to try and heal you!" Another bright light appeared from a glowing Damien, as he tried to heal Archimedes. Unfortunately the damage was too severe. There was nothing he could do.

He sat beside the old man and spoke softly, "I am so sorry that I have all this power and yet my hands are tied." Damien took the hand of Archimedes into his, as he knew the inevitable was near.

Archimedes weakly said, "Now my son, I hope I taught you well! The Book and the answers I sought will never be mine. Instead, they will be yours! Use the Book. Find the skulls, and do what you must to save mankind! Now, my journey is complete! As I take my last breath, I give you my blessing, my son!" And then it was that Archimedes passed into oblivion.

Damien now with tears running down his cheeks knew that the old man, after so very long, was finally at peace.

He looked down at the body of Archimedes. Damien thought to himself that he must bury the body. But again, with no earth to dig, the only thing at hand were all the rocks from the rock slide.

As Damien arranged rocks over the body, he wished he could do more for Archimedes, because he was royalty. The thought tht a King should be simply covered with rocks bothered him greatly. This was not a proper tribute. But Damien had no other choice .

After burying the body, Damien saw the book Archimedes so wanted to read. He couldn't help but think how ironic it was that Archimedes had the book within his grasp, but before he could read it, he died.

Archimedes carried a knife from Atlantis. Damien had retrieved the knife from the body of the old man. Then he ceremoniously placed the knife on top of the rocks. It was something of a tribute he felt. It was what he could do.

For a while, Damien stood and paid his devoted respects. Then he remembered Archimedes' words of the Mayan. Then, slowly and deliberately, he picked up the Book, opened it and......

Death's Peaceful Slumber

Seems my search and my lives are almost over now,

For millennia, I have longed for the sweet escape of death.

All the distastefulness, fate within my life has allowed,

The pain from loved ones dying, the pain of knowing immortality, oh how many times have I prayed to take my last breath.

But, I guess I'm like any other man, afraid of the unknown,

Not knowing what lies beyond, in the dark raven of death.

This causes me to embrace immortality because life is all I have ever known.

But now I am tired. I'm ready for the restful, uninterrupted peace of death.

So long ago it seems, I Archimedes, was royalty, King of Atlantis.

My life then was so complete, I had not a worry or care.

I was so happy then, I was completely in the arms of happiness' bliss.

The destruction of a place that was so dear, fate was so unfair.

For so long I have witnessed wars, with brother against brother

Even from the time, when I was King.

But my thirst for answers to my questions, my quest and knowledge being my lover,

Has kept me going; now I think I have found my answers, my heart feels as if it could sing.

The Book of Life from Atlantis, stolen by Uric, my old and only foe

He is now dead, and the book is within my grasp.

So long I have waited for this, no more hardships will I have to hoe.

I can now finally rest, into death's open arms I can now lapse.

OF ATLANTIS

To carry on in my place, searching for millennia, I found just one man,

Damien, my apprentice, my protégé, my friend, will step into my shoes.

When I die, he will take over my life; he will carry on what I had planned.

Now, I can die happy, my journey is finally over; in my life I have overpaid many dues.

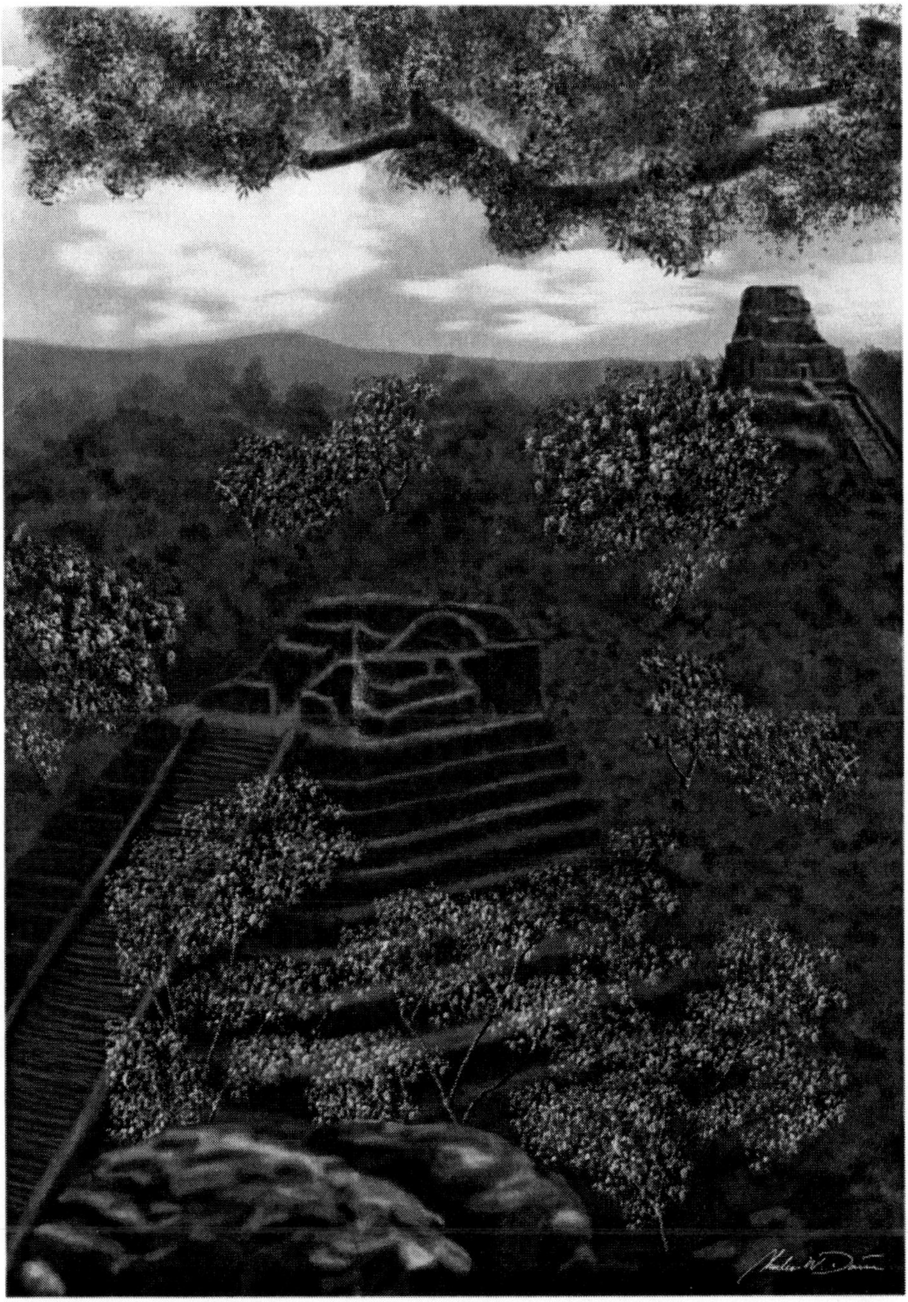